"Before you leave, can I hold Ava?"

Jewel couldn't have looked more startled if he'd demanded full custody. "She, uh, doesn't like strangers."

Strangers. Tanner hated the sound of that.

"Just for a minute," he said.

They squared off in silence, Jewel reluctant and Tanner insistent.

"I've held babies before. Daniel's two kids."

She swallowed. Finally, she scooted closer and lifted Ava, depositing her in Tanner's lap. "She's going to cry."

And when that happened, Jewel was taking her back. She didn't have to say it, her message was crystal clear.

The wiggly weight on Tanner's lap felt odd at first. Remembering his sister-in-law's instructions, he nestled Ava in the crook of his arm, making sure to support her head.

All at once she lifted her head to peer up at him, and Tanner's breath caught.

"Hi there." A huge smile spread across his face.

Ava peered at him owl eyed, and then her small mouth opened into a silly toothless grin.

Dear Reader,

I'm very excited to bring you book three in my Sweetheart Ranch series, *The Cowboy's Christmas Baby*. This wasn't the easiest book for me to write. Jewel and Tanner face some difficult and heart-wrenching problems. While they love each other and want to spend their lives together raising their beautiful daughter, whichever way they turn, someone is going to get hurt. It was a real challenge for me to create a believable way for them to navigate this nearly impossible situation and find their happily-ever-after.

But at a place called Sweetheart Ranch, how is a happy ending *not* possible? I admit, I came up with the idea of a Western-themed wedding ranch a few years ago when I was looking for a venue to host my own wedding. I melded a Victorian wedding house I found with a cowboy ranch I once stayed at, and Sweetheart Ranch was born. I think if my life hadn't taken the path it did, I could see myself owning and managing a place just like this. What could be more fun and rewarding than helping couples celebrate the best day of their lives? Only one thing I can think of, mixing it with the holidays—the best season of the year.

Warmest wishes,

Cathy McDavid

PS: I love connecting with readers. You can find me at:

CathyMcDavid.com

Facebook.com/CathyMcDavidBooks

@CathyMcDavid

HEARTWARMING

The Cowboy's Christmas Baby

New York Times Bestselling Author

Cathy McDavid

HARLEQUIN® HEARTWARMING™

Recycling programs
for this product may
not exist in your area.

ISBN-13: 978-1-335-51089-1

The Cowboy's Christmas Baby

Copyright © 2019 by Cathy McDavid

Printed in U.S.A.

Since 2006, *New York Times* bestselling author **Cathy McDavid** has been happily penning contemporary Westerns for Harlequin. Every day, she gets to write about handsome cowboys riding the range or busting a bronc. It's a tough job, but she's willing to make the sacrifice. Cathy shares her Arizona home with her own real-life sweetheart and a trio of odd pets. Her grown twins have left to embark on lives of their own, and she couldn't be prouder of their accomplishments.

Books by Cathy McDavid

Harlequin Western Romance

Mustang Valley

Cowboy for Keeps
Her Holiday Rancher
Come Home, Cowboy
Having the Rancher's Baby
Rescuing the Cowboy
A Baby for the Deputy
The Cowboy's Twin Surprise
The Bull Rider's Valentine

Harlequin Heartwarming

The Sweetheart Ranch

A Cowboy's Christmas Proposal
The Cowboy's Perfect Match

Visit the Author Profile page
at Harlequin.com for more titles.

To my mother. You are, and always will be,
my sunshine.

CHAPTER ONE

THE HORSE TUCKED in so close to the barrel and at such a severe angle it was a wonder the rider didn't topple off.

Watching the practice run from the arena fence, Jewel Saunders held her breath as the rider spurred her horse into a gallop for the last stretch. She imagined herself in the rider's place, leaning forward over the saddle horn, heart pounding, the wind whipping her face, and all the while silently urging the horse to give every ounce of speed it possessed.

She'd been this rider once and on her way to a potential world championship at the National Finals Rodeo. But that was a year ago, before her life had drastically changed and the worst thing imaginable happened to her—followed by the best thing.

At the same moment the rider galloped across the electronic timer's invisible line, Ava awoke and let out an unhappy wail. Blinking herself back to reality, Jewel leaned over the stroller and lovingly stroked her four-month-old daughter's cheek.

"Shh. It's okay."

Ava wasn't soothed. Jewel took hold of the handle and gently rocked the stroller. That sometimes did the trick, lulling Ava back to sleep. Not today, however, and her crying intensified.

Jewel removed her phone from a side pocket of the diaper bag stowed in the nylon sling beneath the stroller. For convenience's sake, she'd quit carrying a purse and transferred everything into the diaper bag. That was the day she'd realized her entire existence revolved around being a mother.

It was also when she'd started thinking seriously about a career direction, either returning to barrel racing or expanding her paying photography hobby into a full-fledged business. Now it was early December, and she was finally taking steps toward making a decision.

Checking the time on her phone's display, she said, "Let's go, sweetie pie, we don't want to be late," and started off toward the ranch office. With any luck, the stroller's bumpy ride on uneven ground would quiet Ava. That was another of Jewel's tricks.

Stopping at the covered porch in front of the office, she lifted the stroller up and over the two short steps. A carved wooden sign hung from a rope beside the door reading Welcome to Powell Ranch.

Being briefly transported through the air had apparently distracted Ava for she, thankfully, quit crying. Jewel doubted hunger or a diaper emergency were the cause of her daughter's distress. Both needs had been recently attended.

It was probably being in a strange place with unfamiliar sounds and smells. For Jewel, arriving at the horse facility had been like coming home. She'd spent more than half her life, ever since junior high school, in places just like this one.

Refastening the top button on her jacket, she surveyed her surroundings. Ahead was the large arena used for roping, team penning, horse training and, of course, barrel racing. The spacious horse barn behind the office housed at least three dozen enclosed stalls. Beyond those were a row of covered outdoor stalls and acres of open pastures. Also nearby was a round pen, horse walker and washstand. And lastly, to her right, stood a large hay shed and storage building with a tractor parked beside it.

Yes, indeed, just like the other horse facilities. So why was she suddenly overcome by a flood of anxiety?

The answer was easy. Jewel had only ridden a handful of times since discovering she was pregnant. She hadn't barrel raced even once since last December. It had been during the first week of the National Finals Rodeo when she'd learned Tanner, the man she'd been planning to marry in a few days' time, wasn't the person she'd thought he was.

She'd neither seen nor heard from him since. He had no idea he was a father, though it wasn't for lack of trying on Jewel's part. She'd exhausted every avenue available to her attempting to locate him. The fact was, Tanner didn't want to be found. Wherever he'd gone after the cheating scandal broke, he hadn't left a trail. In Jewel's opinion, that spoke volumes about his guilt.

Ava began fussing, a sure indication her crying was about to resume. Sighing, Jewel reached in and, after unclipping the buckles, lifted a fleece-onesie-clad Ava into her arms. Another day, she might have let Ava fuss for a little while. But Jewel's two appointments, the first here at Powell Ranch and the second a quarter mile up the road at Sweetheart Ranch, were too important to her. She'd do whatever was necessary to keep Ava content and quiet.

Just as she was nestling the baby against her chest, the office door opened. Ronnie Hartman, owner and manager of the barrel racing school at Powell Ranch, emerged and immediately spotted Jewel.

"Hello! You're here."

"I am." Jewel returned the other woman's warm smile while bouncing Ava.

"Good to see you again. It's been ages." Ronnie reached out her arms. "And look at your baby! She's beautiful."

They managed a sideways hug because of Ava, who was fascinated by this new person. She usually fussed when being held by strangers, but she did enjoy looking at them and stared transfixed at Ronnie.

"I can't thank you enough for agreeing to take me on," Jewel said.

"Are you kidding? I'm thrilled."

"You have a great place here."

"I wish it was mine. I simply lease the facilities for a certain number of hours a week. Of which, five of those hours Monday through Friday belong to you. We start at seven tomorrow morning, by the way."

Jewel couldn't help grimacing. "You have your work cut out for you. I'm pretty rusty."

"Like riding a bike, my friend."

Jewel was less convinced. Her barrel racing skills would return, she had no doubt. The drive and endurance were another matter. She worried she'd lost those, too, when her life had imploded.

She and Ronnie stood on the porch catching up for several minutes. The pair were old acquaintances and had been rivals back in the day. Both had since retired from the rodeo circuit, though, in Jewel's case, the retirement might be temporary. Much depended on the upcoming month, the length of time which she'd contracted with Ronnie's barrel racing school.

Jewel mentally crossed her fingers that Ronnie wouldn't mention Tanner, his and Jewel's "almost" wedding or the cheating scandal. Thankfully, Ronnie avoided the subjects, and Jewel allowed herself to relax. Even after all this time, she flushed with acute shame whenever her ex-fiancé's name came up.

Common sense told her she had no reason—she wasn't the one caught attempting to bribe a bull riding judge. That had been Tanner. Nonetheless, she felt tainted by association. The sympathetic platitudes some people offered were as bad as the malicious gossip others spread behind her back.

Making a spectacular rodeo comeback might be the perfect way to obliterate the emotional torment she'd been through. She was willing to try.

"Where's your horse?" Ronnie asked.

"In my trailer." Jewel nodded toward her vehicle parked beside the arena fence.

Traveling from Tulsa to Arizona with a baby and hauling her horse had made for a grueling trip. They'd stopped frequently, giving Teddy Bear, Jewel's palomino gelding and beloved barrel racing partner, a chance to stretch his legs and Ava a break from her car seat.

"He'll be fine for a while longer. We'll move him to a stall when we're done." Ronnie placed a hand on Jewel's shoulder. "Come on. I'll give you the tour."

"Can I leave the stroller?" Jewel asked.

Ava was quiet, and Jewel would gladly carry her if that ensured an uninterrupted meeting with Ronnie.

"No problem."

"I've seen the arena already." Jewel arranged Ava in a baby wrap, securing it around her waist. "Very impressive. Are those your students practicing?"

"Two of them. Not all the barrel racers using Powell Ranch belong to my school. The local 4-H group has a large number of members who practice here with their own staff of trainers."

The tour lasted a good twenty minutes. There wasn't anything Jewel didn't like about Powell Ranch or Ronnie's philosophy when it came to barrel racing, and she was certain the two of them were going to get along well. Jewel had her family to thank for this opportunity. If not for their financial support, she couldn't have afforded to hire Ronnie or make the trip.

Only by happy coincidence had she landed a part-time job at Sweetheart Ranch next door. She'd been researching the area for employment and cheap short-term housing when she came upon the wedding ranch's website. Seeing their posting seeking a part-time wedding photographer, she'd mustered her courage and called the owner. To her incredible surprise and delight, they'd agreed to give her a trial run after viewing her online portfolio, compensating her with room and board and a modest stipend.

Jewel couldn't pass up the opportunity. Especially when the wedding ranch owner was willing to work around Jewel's barrel racing lessons and practice schedule. She even had a trustworthy babysitter in mind for Ava.

The fact that everything had fallen so neatly into place must be a sign, Jewel had thought. She was meant to come to Mustang Valley and resolve her career dilemma. If all worked out, she'd choose a direction by the end of her month's stay.

Her one and only hesitation was Tanner's parents. They lived in Queen Creek, fifty miles from Mustang Valley. She'd resisted telling them about Ava all through her pregnancy, wanting Tanner to be the first to hear. But that hadn't happened. After finalizing her plans to come to Sweetheart Ranch, she'd decided to visit them at some point during her month-long stay. Telling them in person would be better than on the phone.

The tour ended in the horse barn. Thankfully, Ava behaved through most of it.

Ronnie stopped in front of an empty stall. "I thought we'd put Teddy Bear here."

Jewel nodded appreciatively at the spacious and tidily kept stall. "Works for me."

Ronnie reviewed the feeding times, horse boarding prices and barn rules. "We can handle the paperwork in the morning if that works better for you," she added when Ava became restless.

"Thanks. One of us is getting bored."

Outside on the porch, Jewel returned Ava to the stroller. They left her near the front of Jewel's truck, well away from the trailer's rear gate. Teddy Bear tended to exit quickly and had been known to inadvertently trample small objects in his path, like a foot or a dog or a piece of equipment.

The horse lived up to his reputation, causing an enormous commotion as he scrambled backward from the trailer. Once on solid ground, he came to a stop and surveyed his new surroundings, head held high and ears pricked forward. Jewel's hand on the halter shook as he whinnied loudly, announcing his presence to the other horses.

Ronnie grinned and gave his head a scratch. "I think even the broodmares in the back pasture heard you."

"Do you mind?" Jewel held out the lead rope. "Come on, big fellow."

Ronnie led the horse to the stall. With Ava re-swaddled in the baby wrap, Jewel followed a few minutes later.

After Teddy Bear had spent several minutes inspecting every inch of his new accommodations, Ronnie returned with a flake of hay, which she dropped in the feed bin. Teddy Bear's head disappeared, only to pop up a moment later, his mouth full of hay.

He'd eaten earlier that morning at the horse-friendly inn where Jewel and Ava had spent the night after arriving in town yesterday. But Jewel allowed the horse a second breakfast, knowing eating would help settle him. Kind of like it did Ava.

"I've got to run," Ronnie said. "I have a wedding cake sampling at Sweetheart Ranch in an hour."

"That's right. Your cousin's getting married. When's the big day?"

"A week from Saturday. I'm the matron of honor. We're hoping you'll take the photographs."

"I'd be thrilled."

The two hugged again, and Ronnie left. Jewel stayed behind. She didn't have to be at Sweetheart Ranch for a while yet, and she much preferred the horse barn over sitting in her stuffy hotel room. She'd feed and change Ava soon and, fingers crossed, the baby would nap through Jewel's appointment.

Hmm. Maybe she'd run into Ronnie again when she got there.

Ava cooed and flailed her arms and legs. She probably wanted out of the wrap.

Jewel patted the baby's bottom. "Not much longer, my sweet little girl."

Hearing a noise, she glanced over to see a man half hidden by the shadows and pushing a wheelbarrow into the horse barn from the opposite end of the aisle. She didn't pay much attention, not until he drew closer.

She sensed more than saw him come to a stop, and she slowly turned to face him. The hairs on the back of her neck inexplicably rose.

Whatever words she'd been about to utter lodged in her throat as the man emerged from the shadows and his features took shape beneath the weathered cowboy hat he wore. A wild rush of shock and then alarm coursed through Jewel, and she involuntarily tightened her grip on Ava.

She couldn't have been more stunned if she'd seen a ghost. Then again, she supposed she had, for Tanner Bridwell stood before her.

He looked different. The beard was gone, but she'd have known him and those arresting steel-gray eyes anywhere. How could she not, when she'd spent endless hours gazing into them and countless nights dreaming about them?

"What are you doing here?" she blurted out.

His stare hardened, and he replied with a question of his own. "Is the baby mine?"

JEWEL'S FACE HAD always been easy to read, the subtle nuances clearly telegraphing her every emotion. There was hardly a time Tanner had been unaware of her thoughts, especially when it came to her feelings for him.

Today was no different. Except trepidation had replaced the love he'd once seen.

He'd reconciled himself to Jewel no longer being a part of his life. Spotting her standing at the end of the barn aisle, a baby in her arms, he'd sworn his imagination was playing tricks on him. As he'd approached, he'd realized it wasn't his imagination, and the wall enclosing his heart had split wide open to release a flood of emotions. Surprise. Shock. Confusion. Joy. Hurt. Even anger. How dare she have a baby, *their* baby, and not tell him! Regardless of what had passed between them, he deserved to know. He had a *right* to know.

He was no expert at judging children's ages, so doing the math was pointless. His gut, however, insisted he was the father of this one. The tiny cleft in her chin bolstered his conviction. Until he'd shaved his beard, few people had known he, too, sported a similar cleft.

"Tanner..." Jewel stood utterly still, her gaze taking him in.

"Is the baby mine?" he repeated, even though he was certain of the answer. He needed to hear her say yes. Or, more accurately, he needed to see if she'd try and deny it.

"She is."

He let the information sink in before responding. "We need to talk."

"I'm meeting the owner of Sweetheart Ranch in forty minutes."

Surprise nearly knocked him sideways. "You're getting married?"

Sweetheart Ranch was a destination wedding venue and bed-and-breakfast that had opened last fall. Their selling point was providing couples with the full cowboy experience for their ceremony and honeymoon.

"Ah, no," she stammered. "I'm starting work there. As a part-time photographer."

Tanner shouldn't have been relieved. He had no claim on Jewel. Not after what happened between them. But he was vastly relieved, nonetheless. He told himself he'd rather she was commitment free until they sorted out their situation, but that was only half true.

Then again, just because she wasn't getting married didn't automatically make her single. She could have a boyfriend. A woman as attractive as Jewel, with hair the color of honey and the most expressive brown eyes he'd ever seen, would catch the attention of any man. She'd filled out some, he noticed, and on her, the curves looked good.

"The job's temporary," she said. "I'm returning to Oklahoma after the holidays."

The baby waved her arms in the air as if to get Tanner's attention. She was a cute little thing, with her big blue eyes and button nose peeking out from beneath her pink hood.

"More reason for us to talk now." He hitched his chin toward the large open entryway. "My bunkhouse is over there. We can have some privacy."

"I'd rather go somewhere else."

Was she worried about being alone with him? The possibility bothered Tanner, but he let it slide. "There's an old bench around the corner."

"I don't have long."

"Are you making excuses, Jewel?"

"No, Tanner. I'm not." A hint of irritation tinged her voice. "I just don't want to be late."

"Fifteen minutes. You owe me that much." Before she could issue a comeback about him failing her, he said, "I'm the father of our child."

"Fine," she answered tightly, her arm circling the baby. "Fifteen minutes."

"This way."

He walked beside her, the air between them thick with tension. Both remained stubbornly mute.

At the bench, Tanner waited while Jewel sat and unbundled the baby. When she was done and the baby was positioned securely on her lap, Tanner dropped down beside her. There wasn't a lot of room, and they had to sit close. She shifted away from him when their knees bumped.

How different from before, when they would have nestled together, fingers linked and sharing kisses. They might now have been happily wed and raising their daughter together had Tanner made a different decision last December. But he hadn't and, as a result, he'd lost almost everything important to him. Jewel, his home, his career, his friends. Also, it now seemed, a daughter he might have gone his entire life without knowing if not for a twist of fate.

What was the old saying? No good deed goes unpunished? Tanner was living proof. And he couldn't tell Jewel the truth—that he hadn't cheated—without breaking his promise to his dad and older brother.

The price that had once seemed minor had turned out to be significant, and Tanner was weary of paying.

"You're a wrangler?" she asked.

"Technically, I'm assistant barn manager. Small difference."

Watching her expression, he guessed at what she was thinking. Tanner, a wrangler and living in a bunkhouse? He'd been raised with money and had wanted for nothing. His dad's commercial real estate firm was the fourth largest in the Phoenix metropolitan area.

Tanner and his brother had one day planned to join their dad's firm when they retired from bull riding. One more thing he'd lost. Having a confessed cheater on the company's board of directors, his dad had explained, even when that person was innocent, was bad for business. They'd figure something else out. Eventually.

For now, Tanner's brother came first. He understood, yes?

There were days he wished he didn't and came *this close* to telling his dad off. Then, he'd remember his brother, Daniel, his lifelong best friend and staunch supporter, and how their roles had reversed on the day Daniel received his terrible diagnosis.

Tanner set the unhappy memories momentarily aside and concentrated on Jewel. "What are you doing at Powell Ranch?"

"Taking barrel riding lessons from Ronnie. What are *you* doing here?" Jewel countered. "And where have you been the last year?"

He tolerated her animosity without responding. After all, she believed him guilty of attempting to bribe that bull riding judge and blamed him for ruining their wedding, not to mention their relationship.

"Ethan Powell gave me a job."

Tanner had been a teenager and competing on the junior rodeo circuit when he first met Ethan. Though nine years his senior, the former bronc busting champion had taken an interest in both Tanner and his brother and mentored them. They'd stayed in touch all these years.

"I'm surprised no one's recognized you," Jewel said. "There's a lot of rodeo people coming and going in Mustang Valley."

"I keep to myself." Tanner ran a hand over his clean-shaven jaw. "And getting rid of the beard helped. I always wear a hat and sunglasses whenever anyone who might recognize me comes to the ranch. Like Ronnie. Ethan runs interference for me, too."

"I see," Jewel commented dryly.

"I needed a place to stay for a couple of months, away from all the negative attention after...everything." Tanner didn't bother elaborating. Reminiscing wouldn't benefit either of them. "Ethan offered both."

"Why didn't you tell me?"

"You made it clear you didn't care where I went or what I did."

"Point taken," she bit out.

"I don't want to argue, Jewel."

After a moment, she softened marginally around the edges. "It's been a year. Why are you still here?"

"Dad's idea." Tanner's gut clenched as it did every time he talked about their agreement. "He's convinced I can be sued by the arena owners or that his company can be sued because I'm listed as a minority stockholder."

As was Tanner's brother, Daniel, which increased the risk to Bridwell and Associates even more if the truth were to ever come out. Daniel shouldn't have been allowed to compete in his condition. He'd put himself and others in jeopardy. By Tanner confessing, he took the heat rather than Daniel.

"Sue you for what?" Jewel asked.

"Breach of contract. Damages due to loss of income and tarnished reputation. You remember those calf ropers who were caught cheating a few years ago? They were sued by the arena owners and settled for an undisclosed amount. Anyway, Dad thinks it's in our best interests if I continue to lie low for another year. According to the company attorney, the arena owners have a two-year window to file a lawsuit."

Twelve more long grueling months that, with the unexpected appearance of Jewel and their baby, felt even longer and more grueling to Tanner.

"Don't you think if the arena owners were going to come after you, they'd have done so by now?" she asked.

"Yeah, I do. But not Dad and not his attorney. According to them, we should err on the side of caution."

Suddenly, the baby started fussing. Reaching into her jacket pocket, Jewel extracted a neon purple toy shaped like a dumbbell, which she waved in front of the baby's face.

"What's her name?" Tanner asked.

"Ava."

"After your grandmother."

"You remember."

"She always liked me."

"She still does." Jewel's lips compressed into a thin line. "She insists there must have been a mistake. That you would never cheat."

"Huh. You don't say?"

Tanner mentally chewed on that. Jewel's grandmother believed him innocent but not Jewel. She'd immediately assumed the worst and issued him his walking papers. Not that he could have explained in that moment. Still, she might have trusted him a little. He had asked her to give him time, promising he'd reveal the whole story eventually. It still rankled him that she hadn't—made worse by him learning she'd hidden his daughter from him.

"I really wish you'd told me about Ava," he said.

"I tried my best. I contacted everyone I could think of, including your parents and the Powells, and asked if they knew where you were. I even hired a private investigator for a week, but he was expensive, and I couldn't afford him. Right after that, I had several scary moments with my pregnancy."

"What kind of scary moments?" Tanner's knowledge was limited, but he had an idea.

"Cramping. Bleeding. I nearly miscarried and

was on doctor's orders to rest and avoid stress. Since searching for you was stressful, I quit. I had to put the baby first."

"If Mom and Dad knew about Ava, they'd have gotten word to me."

Jewel's spine straightened. "Are you blaming their refusal to reveal your whereabouts on me?"

"A baby is big news."

"I explicitly said I had something important to tell you."

"They're protective." And were employing damage control, especially where Bridwell and Associates was concerned. "Dad thought that you might have been in cahoots with the arena owners and trying to trick him into revealing my location."

"I don't lie."

Implying that Tanner did.

She was right, sadly. He did lie. He'd confessed to a wrong he hadn't committed. His father had conceived the idea, his seriously ill brother had begged him, and Tanner had gone along with them.

"Don't be mad at my folks. I had a rough time after what happened, and they were looking out for me."

"*You* had a rough time?" Jewel nearly erupted off the bench and might have if not for the baby.

"I was the one questioned by the PRCA and the arena officials. The one hounded for interviews. The one whose picture appeared in newspapers and magazines and all over the internet."

Technically, Tanner's picture had appeared, too. He'd also been questioned extensively by the Professional Rodeo Cowboys Association and the arena owners. He didn't correct her, however.

"The one bombarded with questions by literally everyone and forced to endure slurs and accusations and dirty looks. Oh, and pitying looks. Those were the worst." She drew in a ragged breath. "I was the one who had to explain to my family and our friends that the wedding was off, then suffer the humiliation of returning the gifts and canceling the honeymoon trip. All you did was disappear into thin air."

Tanner let her vent. He and his family had put her through a lot. When she finally lost steam, he spoke.

"I'm sorry. I really wish things could have been different."

She shook her head with exasperation, only to swallow a sob. "You cheated, Tanner. How could you?"

God, he wanted to tell her the truth. Holding back was pure torture.

"It's not what it seems." He paused. Maybe if he gave her a little of the story she'd put two and two together. "My brother was already struggling with the side effects of his brain tumor before finals. Dizziness. Memory issues. Loss of coordination. Not that anyone could tell. He got quite good at disguising his symptoms."

She looked chagrined, as if she'd forgotten other people in the world had problems worse than theirs. "I heard about his surgery. How's he doing?"

Tanner shrugged. "As well as possible, I suppose, for someone whose right leg functions at thirty percent and who can't remember much from one minute to the next. At least he can walk and communicate. That was up in the air at first."

Sympathy filled her eyes. "What about his wife and children? How are they doing?"

"Coping as best they can. Rosalyn's been standing by him. So far. But they've had their struggles. He's not the person he used to be."

That only scratched the surface, thought Tanner, his heart heavy with grief and guilt. His brother had gone from being a high-earning champion bull rider, devoted husband and active, doting father of two young children to someone who—until just a couple of months ago—hadn't been able to dress or feed himself.

"The cancer's in remission, and his prognosis is cautiously good," Tanner said. "That's something to be grateful for, though he's on disability and may never work again."

If not for Tanner's parents helping out, Daniel and Rosalyn would have lost their house. Yet another reason for Tanner to cover for Daniel and protect the company. A lawsuit could financially ruin more than the business. His brother and family could be left homeless.

Jewel shifted Ava to her other knee. The baby had shoved the neon purple toy into her mouth and was gnawing on it. "Please give him and Rosalyn my best when you talk to them."

"I will."

"Are you planning on staying in Mustang Valley indefinitely?"

"That's complicated. I'd like to talk about it more when you aren't rushed."

"I do need to get going."

"Wait. Before you leave…" He hesitated. He was still getting used to these new feelings of his. "Can I hold Ava?"

Jewel couldn't have looked more startled if he'd demanded full custody. "She, ah, doesn't like strangers."

Strangers. Tanner hated the sound of that.

"Just for a minute," he said.

They squared off in silence, Jewel reluctant and Tanner insistent.

"I've held babies before—Daniel's two kids."

She swallowed. Finally, she scooted closer and lifted Ava, depositing her in Tanner's lap. "She's going to cry."

And when that happened, Jewel was taking her back. She didn't have to say it; her message was crystal clear.

The wiggly weight on Tanner's lap felt odd at first. Remembering his sister-in-law's instructions, he nestled Ava in the crook of his arm, making sure to support her head.

All at once, she lifted her head to peer up at him, and Tanner's breath caught.

"Hi there." A huge smile spread across his face.

Ava peered at him, owl-eyed, and then her small mouth opened into a silly toothless grin.

Tanner felt like he'd been kicked in the gut by a mule. This baby was his daughter. *His daughter.* He was a dad.

"Aren't you gorgeous?" He pulled Ava closer, and she pressed her small head against his chest.

"I need to go." Jewel promptly stood up and swooped Ava away from Tanner, winding her up in the wrap thing.

Tanner also stood; the remarkable elation that had filled him while he held Ava continued coursing through him. "Are you free after your meeting at Sweetheart Ranch?"

"I'm busy." She started walking.

Tanner kept pace, refusing to give up. "Tomorrow?"

"I... I have a lesson with Ronnie at seven."

"After that?"

She stopped and evaluated him, obviously weighing the pros and cons of stalling him indefinitely. "All right. I should be done by nine."

"See you then."

Tanner didn't accompany her to her truck and trailer. He figured her hackles were already raised enough. Best to give her some space.

On his way to the horse barn where he'd left the wheelbarrow, he retrieved his phone from his pocket and placed a call to the one person who had always been in his corner.

"Mom, hi. I have incredible news. Are you sitting down?"

CHAPTER TWO

TANNER WAS IN Mustang Valley! Jewel couldn't believe it.

What was she going to do? Forget her plans entirely and leave? Stay and attempt to avoid him? Not avoid him and hopefully navigate the inevitable turmoil? None of the choices appealed to her.

Everything she'd planned to say when she finally found him completely abandoned her the instant she'd seen him. The anger pulsing through her had come as a surprise. She thought she'd moved past that but evidently not.

She was justified, of course. No one would fault her. He'd attempted to cheat, lied to her, and then left her with a huge mess to clean up. Okay, technically she'd yelled at him to get out and never come back. But, deep down, she hadn't believed he would. When he did leave, he took the last of her faith in him with him.

Honestly, she'd nearly choked when Ava had smiled up at him. Was it possible for a baby to instinctively recognize their father and form an immediate bond? No, it wasn't. Stuff like that only happened in movies.

Even so, Jewel couldn't shake the conviction that Ava and Tanner had connected on some level. Perhaps she'd just been responding to him. He had looked besotted. If Jewel wasn't battling a slew of conflicting emotions, she might have found the sight of them endearing instead of...

She hated admitting it, but she was scared. Regardless of what Tanner had done, he was Ava's father and had rights. Unless he voluntarily chose to walk away and leave them alone, he was going to be a part of her and Ava's life to some degree.

"Jewel, it's nice to finally meet you."

She whirled at the sound of a friendly voice behind her. Apparently, she'd been standing at the parlor window for some time—long enough to momentarily forget she was at Sweetheart Ranch and meeting with the owner.

Mustering what she hoped was a warm smile, she returned the greeting. "Same here."

Emily O'Malley-Foxworthy had to be in her late seventies, though she was clearly active and still a handsome woman. She'd mentioned during their phone conversations that she herself was a newlywed, having gotten married last fall. Jewel thought it was wonderful that love could blossom at any age.

She shifted Ava to her left arm in order to shake Emily's hand. "I really appreciate the opportunity and won't disappoint you."

"We're just glad to have you on board. We've been needing a staff photographer for months. This will be a good test run for both of us. Hopefully, things will work out and the arrangement will become permanent."

"Yes." Jewel wouldn't say more than that until she decided on a career. And with Tanner unexpectedly in the picture, she was less sure than ever which direction to take.

"My, my." Emily's gaze landed on Ava, and her wrinkled face radiated pleasure. "Aren't you just adorable?"

Ava stared, wide-eyed.

Emily extended a hand and gently squeezed Ava's pudgy fingers. Instantly, Ava squealed and pried her fingers loose.

"It's okay," Emily said soothingly. "We'll become friends soon enough, I'm sure."

Jewel marveled at how Ava had accepted Tanner, a rugged looking and deep-voiced man, right off the bat and wanted nothing to do with this sweet grandmotherly woman.

The absence of a beard had made him appear more approachable, she supposed. Jewel had always liked his neatly trimmed facial hair. She had to concede, however, he was far more handsome clean-shaven and looked younger than his twenty-eight years. That, or the beard had made him appear older.

On the other hand, the cleft in his chin had surprised her. Sure, he'd told her about it and his father sported the same attractive cleft. But actually seeing how closely Tanner's resembled Ava's had been disconcerting.

His shaved face also emphasized his well-defined cheekbones and strong jawline. Add to that his shoulder-length brown hair—a huge change from his previous close-cropped cut—and he could have passed for a country singer or celebrity soccer player. She understood why no one had recognized him, especially when he wore sunglasses.

"How about we start with a tour?" Emily suggested.

It would be Jewel and Ava's second tour of the day. "Sounds lovely. Give me just a minute." She rearranged Ava in the baby wrap just in case she needed her hands free.

Emily swept her arm to encompass the charmingly appointed room with its many antiques. "This, of course, is the parlor. Besides wedding receptions, we host social club luncheons, family reunions, corporate events, you name it. My granddaughter Molly is head of guest services and helps me with coordinating weddings. My other granddaughter, Bridget, is our resident chef. Her fiancé, Ryan, is in charge of the carriage, hay wagon and trail rides. The other employees, like you, are part-time or seasonal. Winter holidays are our busiest time of year next to Valentine's Day, which is why I requested you stay on past New Year's Day for your trial run."

Jewel swallowed, silently wondering if she was in over her head.

"Bridget was hoping you'd have some time to take pictures of the cake she's preparing for tomorrow's wedding. It's decorated to look like a staircase with a gold banister and miniature bride and groom at the top. I'm not kidding."

"I'll make time. Absolutely."

They continued the tour, which included the kitchen, library—soon to be converted into a small wedding boutique—the separate bride and groom dressing rooms and, lastly, the chapel.

"It's lovely," Jewel gushed as they entered.

"I like to think we have the nicest wedding chapel in the state." The older woman winked. "I may be prejudiced."

"How many people does it hold?"

"Around forty-five. We can seat over a hundred on the lawn for outdoor weddings."

Bright sunlight streamed in the large picture window and bathed the twin rows of pews and aisle leading to the altar in a golden glow. At the moment, the chapel was empty of decorations and flowers, but Jewel could easily imagine how beautiful it would look during a wedding.

A wave of nostalgia washed over her. She and Tanner had planned to marry in a chapel, though not one as nice as this, right after the National Finals Rodeo. They'd hoped at least one of them would also have won a championship, giving them double the reasons to celebrate.

A quickie Vegas wedding had made sense, though Jewel had sometimes dreamed of more traditional nuptials. Most of their friends were in the rodeo world and already in town for the finals, and both sets of parents and siblings had come to watch Jewel and Tanner compete.

It'd had all the components for a happy ending. Only that hadn't happened. Instead, she'd heard from fellow competitors right after her event that Tanner had been caught attempting to bribe one of the bull riding judges. When she'd confronted him, he hadn't denied it. And, just like that, Jewel's world had fallen apart.

Pain squeezed her throat. Ava must have

sensed the shift in Jewel's mood, for she suddenly whimpered.

"Shh, it's okay." She swayed back and forth, rocking Ava.

"Let's head outside," Emily suggested, obviously aware of Ava's distress but unaware of Jewel's. "I'll show you the quarters above the carriage house. A change of scenery might quiet the baby."

"She does love being outside."

Jewel gave Ava a pacifier before they ventured outdoors. Emily chatted about Jewel's portfolio as they leisurely strolled to the stables and carriage house on the other side of the clubhouse and fenced swimming pool. She mentioned particularly liking Jewel's action shots.

"You have a good eye for capturing your subjects at just the right moment," she said. "That'll come in handy while photographing weddings and receptions."

"Thank you." Jewel returned the compliment. "This place is just incredible. Straight out of a picture book."

"The main house was built in the 1880s. My late first husband and I bought it more than fifty years ago, when we first came to the Valley. The cabins are new as of last summer." Emily pointed to the row of six cabins that had been designed to resemble the ranch house. "I'll show you one tomorrow after the guests check out."

"I'd like that."

"The clubhouse was a former storage building. We expanded it and built the pool."

"You could never tell."

They reached the small stables and carriage house next to it. "We have two draft horses for pulling the carriage and hay wagon and three trail horses for rides. If we need more horses for larger groups, we lease them from Powell Ranch."

Emily led Jewel into the carriage house, which contained a white fairytale-style carriage and the hay wagon. She explained about the ranch's signature amenity, a carriage ride through town for the newlyweds the day after their wedding, and the monthly hayrides and square dances.

"Our next hayride and dance are this coming weekend. A Christmas theme, as you'd expect, since that's the weekend before the annual Holly Daze Festival. We'd love for you to take some shots of the ride and the dance and also our booth at the festival. Our web page is in desperate need of updating."

Jewel's head spun. "You mentioned a babysitter."

"Tracee. She's the granddaughter of my best

friend, Nora. Both of them help out at the ranch during busy times. Tracee is a senior in high school and an experienced and reliable babysitter. She can watch Ava while you work and are at barrel racing practice, if you're comfortable with that. She'll be here later this afternoon to meet you and Ava."

"That's great, but what about school? Won't babysitting interfere?" Jewel was thinking of her early morning barrel racing lessons.

"She's taking most of her classes online so that she can work and save money for college. Her schedule's flexible."

"Okay."

Jewel followed Emily up the dusty wooden staircase. At the top of the landing, Emily opened a plain painted door with squeaky hinges.

Jewel wasn't sure what to expect when she stepped inside. It certainly wasn't the lovely sight that greeted them.

"Oh, wow." She paused and let her gaze wander. "This is nice."

"We did add a few extra touches for you." Emily placed a key on the tiny two-person dining table, next to a vase with fresh flowers. "The curtains and bedspread are new."

"I love it."

A wrought iron bed occupied one corner of

the spacious room. Beside it stood an antique chest of drawers and on top of that sat an old-fashioned lamp with a pull-string switch. Other than the cedar chest at the foot of the bed, the only other piece of furniture was a cozy recliner in the corner. Lovely reproduction landscapes and still lifes adorned the walls, and a braided area rug covered the floor.

Most interesting to Jewel was the compact kitchen unit installed in the corner opposite the bed. She'd never seen one like it. The unit consisted of a camper-sized sink, two-burner stove, small overhead cabinet and an under-the-counter refrigerator. A microwave sat atop a cart next to the kitchen unit.

She thought she'd put Ava's travel crib alongside the bed at night when they slept and move it out of the way during the day to make more room.

"The bathroom's a recent addition," Emily said. "Bridget's fiancé Ryan built it when he lived here for a short while." She slid open an accordion partition to reveal a tiny bathroom with just the bare necessities: a sink, a toilet and a shower the size of a broom closet. "The water pressure's not the best. I recommend showering at night when there's less demand."

"It's adorable," Jewel insisted and meant every word.

"As I mentioned before, we serve a continental breakfast in the parlor from 7:00 to 9:00 a.m. for guests and employees. There are generally leftovers after the receptions or other events, and you're welcome to fix yourself a plate. For anything else, there's the market in town or you can drive to Scottsdale or Rio Verde if you'd rather shop at a proper grocery store."

They discussed the details of Jewel's duties not previously covered. While there was a wedding tomorrow evening, that couple had hired their own photographer. Emily requested Jewel attend simply to observe and get a feel for the kind of services provided at Sweetheart Ranch. The two Saturday weddings would be her first paying gigs, and Jewel was getting nervous. Having to deal with Tanner only increased her anxiety.

"Are you okay?" Emily asked.

Jewel gave a start and felt her cheeks grow warm. Again, she'd let her attention drift. "Sorry. I was just wondering how I'm going to get all my stuff up here." It wasn't exactly a lie—she had wondered that while they were climbing the stairs. "Guess I'll wait until Tracee arrives."

"Nonsense. I'll have Tanner help you. He'll be here shortly."

Jewel's legs nearly went out from under her,

and she placed a hand on the dinette table to steady herself before she dropped Ava. "Tanner?" she mumbled weakly.

Emily obviously misunderstood her response. "He's a wrangler at Powell Ranch. We need a few extra horses for today's trail rides. I can usually wheedle a favor or two out of him in exchange for some of Bridget's homemade pastries."

Tanner was a frequent visitor to Sweetheart Ranch? Good grief, what were the odds?

"You'll like him," Emily continued. "He's a polite young man. Very quiet."

Jewel absently rocked Ava, her mind racing. If she rejected Emily's offer of Tanner's assistance, she'd have to explain why, and Jewel wasn't ready for that. Her story was too personal and too private to share with someone she'd known less than an hour. On the other hand, she couldn't possibly carry up all her things without help.

Drawing in a fortifying breath, she told Emily, "That'll be just fine."

TANNER SHUT THE rear gate on the horse trailer and slid the latch into place, securing it with a metal snap. The three horses inside shuffled for space, their combined weight causing the trailer's floorboards to creak and groan.

The lone mare apparently didn't like the gelding behind her getting a little too personal, and she gave him a swift mind-your-own-business kick that grazed his shoulder. He squealed and jerked back, colliding with the horse behind him who nipped him on the rump in retaliation.

"Play nice, you three," Tanner hollered, though by then the horses had accepted the inevitable and were quieting down.

They were veteran trail mounts, used to being trailered to various locations and carrying riders of all experience levels. They would do well for the group at Sweetheart Ranch.

This was hardly Tanner's first trip taking horses next door. Powell Ranch and Sweetheart Ranch enjoyed an amicable agreement that benefitted both. They regularly referred customers to each other, and, like today, Powell Ranch leased Sweetheart Ranch the extra horses they needed for special trail rides, weddings on horseback or corporate events.

It was, however, the first time Tanner had taken horses next door with a knot of anxiety the size and density of a cannonball residing in his stomach.

Would he see Jewel again? He imagined her and the baby sitting on the veranda's porch swing. They'd make an appealing sight. He liked the idea of himself seated beside her, but that probably wasn't going to happen. Not without an enormous amount of animosity—hers, misplaced because she didn't know the truth, and his, justified because she'd kept an important secret from him by not telling his parents when she had the chance.

Seeing his boss and friend Ethan Powell approach, Tanner tested the latch one last time. "Just about ready."

"When will you be back? We have team penning practice at five thirty."

"Long before then."

Ethan rested a hand on the trailer's rear gate. Tanner had noticed the other man's limp was especially pronounced today and wondered if the brisk winter weather was affecting his prosthesis. Ethan had lost his leg just below the knee many years ago when he'd served overseas in the Middle East. He hadn't let the missing limb stop him from doing what he loved, namely breaking and training green horses.

"I have a request," Tanner continued. "Any chance you can do without me for a couple hours tomorrow morning? After feeding, sometime about nine."

Ethan gave Tanner a once-over. "Everything okay? You seem a little distracted today."

"Guess that depends on your definition of okay."

"Want to talk about it?"

Tanner debated only a moment. He could use an ear to bend. "Jewel is at Sweetheart Ranch. She's their new photographer."

"No fooling!"

"I ran into her this morning in the horse barn. She's boarding Teddy Bear here and taking barrel racing lessons from Ronnie Hartman."

Ethan knuckled his cowboy hat back and scratched his forehead. "What are the chances?"

"And get this. She has a baby. *Our* baby." Tanner hoped Ethan didn't notice the husky quality to his voice.

"You have a kid?"

"She said she'd wanted to tell me and looked for me." He told Ethan about the private investigator.

"Shoot, buddy. If I'd have known she was pregnant when she called me—"

"Not your fault. Don't worry about it." Tanner was still greatly bothered that Jewel hadn't mentioned her pregnancy when she was searching for him, especially to his parents. She'd been having his child. Hadn't he deserved to know? It made him wonder if she had just been going through the motions and hadn't searched as hard as she'd claimed.

Ethan propped a shoulder against the horse

trailer, taking the weight off his prosthesis. "This mean you're coming out of hiding?"

"I'd like to."

"Your dad still opposed?"

"He's convinced the arena owners will file a suit against me and Daniel if I crack under the pressure and admit he was the one who approached that judge. With Daniel and I being minority shareholders, the arena owners could also come after Bridwell and Associates."

The thing was, Tanner's dad wasn't far off the truth. Tanner had spent every day this past year torn between helping Daniel by living the lie and convincing him to fess up. And that was before Tanner learned he was a father. Only his loyalty to Daniel had kept him quiet.

"Would that be so bad?" Ethan asked. "The truth coming out?"

"Daniel thinks so. He's lost so much already."

"You, too. The whole reason you took the blame in the first place was because Daniel wanted one last chance to compete and possibly win a championship in case he didn't survive the surgery. Well, he did survive. Your reason doesn't apply anymore."

"Yeah, he survived. But he's physically and mentally impaired and entirely dependent on his wife. While I hold down a job and lead a normal life." Guilt ate at Tanner. "He's improving with therapy, it's true. But he won't ever fully recover."

"That's not your fault, buddy."

"It isn't. But I can guarantee he's remembered as a world champion bull rider and not as someone who attempted to bribe his way to that championship."

The irony that Daniel had won the championship without having to buy the judge's cooperation wasn't lost on Tanner. It ate at him day and night.

"At what cost to you?" Ethan asked. "Much as I like having you work here, I know you're miserable. You should be competing at the NFR or sitting in a corner office at Bridwell and Associates, earning a boatload of money and using your championship status as a way to lure new customers."

Tanner swallowed. Admitting his boss was right was more than he could deal with at the moment. "Mom's promised to talk to Dad again. See if he'll change his stand. I'm not expecting much."

"He has a new granddaughter to consider."

"I doubt that'll make a difference."

Not that Tanner needed his dad's consent to come out of hiding and reenter the world. Except if he, and worse, his dad's company, did wind up being sued, it could potentially rip his family apart and destroy what was left of Daniel's marriage. Rosalyn wouldn't appreciate having been kept in the dark. If she took the kids away, Daniel would be devastated. So would their mother—she adored her grandchildren.

"I bet your mom's happy about the baby," Ethan said.

"She'd be here right now if I'd let her. I convinced her to wait a couple of days."

"Jewel won't deny your mom the chance to visit, will she?"

"I doubt it. We just need to talk before my family descends on us. Mom's already making plans for spending Ava's first Christmas together. Not sure about Dad." Tanner had thought his father would call him after hearing about Ava and congratulate Tanner. He'd thought wrong, obviously.

"Do you think the arena owners really care that you breached your contract?" Ethan asked. "I can't see where it'd be worth their while to come after you or even his company."

Tanner shrugged. "According to Dad's attorney, they say the scandal negatively impacted the arena's future rodeo sales and their reputation and could claim damages. Apparently, there's the precedent to set. If they let me get away with cheating, who's to say others won't try?"

Ethan made a sound of disgust. "That's a reach."

"Dad insists I wait another year."

"I suppose if you're okay with that…"

"I was more okay with it before finding out I have a daughter." What Tanner was and wasn't willing to do had changed.

"Much as I hate admitting it," Ethan said, "your dad has a point. His company could lose a lot if the arena owners sued and prevailed."

"They were just my sponsor. They didn't know a thing about the cheating or have any part of it."

"Neither did you," Ethan reminded Tanner.

"They're the ones with the deep pockets."

"Does the company have insurance?"

"The attorney isn't sure it would pay out under these circumstances. And even if it did, the company might never recover from the loss of its reputation. Another reason he wants me out of sight and out of mind and not on the company payroll."

Ethan placed a hand on Tanner's shoulder. "You need anything, anything at all, you let me know."

His friend and former mentor had already been a tremendous help. Tanner hated asking for more.

"Just the time off tomorrow morning. Jewel

and I are getting together after her lesson. Hopefully, we'll iron out a few details."

"Take as long as you need, buddy."

Ten minutes later, Tanner parked his truck and trailer in front of the stables at Sweetheart Ranch. He looked over to his right to see Jewel's truck in front of the carriage house. The bed appeared to be loaded with items waiting to be carried upstairs to the guest quarters.

Emily O'Malley-Foxworthy came strolling up the winding drive to meet him. She carried what looked like a plastic food container. Normally, Tanner would have been delighted—her daughter Bridget was a great chef. But he wasn't hungry. His thoughts were completely occupied by Jewel and Ava.

"Hi, Tanner. I've been waiting for you." Emily walked toward him in her usual unhurried manner, cheeks flushed from the cool breeze. "Don't suppose you could lend me a hand when you're done with the horses?"

"Sure. What do you need?"

Being preoccupied wouldn't stop him from helping Emily. He liked her, and she'd been decent to him. Granted, she didn't know about him and Jewel and the cheating scandal. Unless she did. Jewel might have mentioned him.

"We hired a photographer. For a month. If things work out, she'll stay on permanently."

Emily followed him, chatting as he unloaded the horses. "She needs someone strong to carry her belongings upstairs to the efficiency apartment. I'm not sure, at my age and with my bad hip, that I can manage."

"Does she know you've recruited me?"

"Yes." The older woman gave him a puzzled look. "Why?"

"No reason." No reason that he would divulge, leastwise. "Let me finish here."

"I'll just put these blueberry turnovers in your truck." She held up the plastic container. "They're fresh from the oven."

"If you weren't already married, I'd propose."

Emily waved him away with a laugh and then headed for his truck.

He'd saddled and bridled the horses before leaving Powell Ranch, so they were ready for the ride. Sweetheart Ranch's three horses were also ready and stood at the hitching post, their eyes half closed and tails swishing. No self-respecting horse missed the opportunity to doze in the sunshine, even on a chilly December day.

Ryan DeMeres emerged from inside the stables and meandered over to say hello. Like Emily, the wrangler wasn't involved in the rodeo world and had no idea about Tanner's past. That had allowed them to become casual acquaintances, though not exactly pals. Tanner kept his distance from Ryan as he did with everyone.

Not because of his dad or any potential lawsuit. It was just easier that way. Tanner wasn't convinced he deserved friends, his health, good times or happiness. Not when his brother had lost those very things and might never have them again.

The people arrived in one big group for their trail ride. An entire wedding party had rented the cabins at the ranch and several of them had signed up for the ride.

"I'll fetch Jewel," Emily told Tanner once the riders had mounted and were trotting off with Ryan in the lead.

That proved unnecessary. She must have been watching from a window, for she emerged from the carriage house, Ava in her arms, at the same moment the last rider awkardly loped his horse to catch up to Ryan and the others.

"There you are," Emily said in a singsong voice. "This is Tanner. The young man I told you about."

He watched Jewel, gaging her response. Until this moment, he hadn't realized how much he wanted her to acknowledge their former relationship and him as Ava's father.

"Thanks for agreeing to help."

Nothing. Her answer was a big fat nothing.

"What first?" he asked.

She started off, Ava still in her arms. The wrap thing she'd used earlier had been left behind. At her truck, she struggled to lower the tailgate one-handed.

"I'll get that."

Tanner took over for her. Once the tailgate was down, they exchanged glances. Their first since she'd come out of the carriage house. He silently asked her how long she intended to carry on the ruse with Emily. She silently answered that she wasn't ready to disclose their history. Not yet.

"If you don't need me," Emily said, "I'll mosey along."

"We're fine," Jewel answered tightly.

Tanner, in the meantime, had grabbed an old suitcase he remembered from when he'd loaded and unloaded Jewel's belongings during their rodeo days. He'd no sooner lifted the suitcase out of the truck bed when the zipper split apart and the side fell open, dumping the contents onto the ground.

At the sight of her underwear, lingerie, socks and pajamas lying in the dirt, Jewel let out a gasp. "What happened?"

"The zipper broke." Setting down the suitcase, he started grabbing bras and panties from the pile.

Emily had returned, her expression worried. "Everything all right?"

"We're f-fine," Jewel stammered.

She didn't normally embarrass this easily, thought Tanner. Then again, neither did she normally have to endure her ex-fiancé picking through her unmentionables in front of her new boss—who had no idea he was the father of Jewel's baby.

"Nothing a little washing won't take care of," Emily noted sympathetically.

Tanner reached for a pair of skimpy panties.

"I'll handle this," Jewel told Tanner, her voice rising. "You get a different box to take upstairs."

This was going overboard, even for her. He ignored her and continued collecting clothes.

"No!" Jewel bent at the waist but immediately straightened, readjusting Ava.

"Here." Emily held out her arms. "I'll take the baby."

Jewel handed Ava over. Almost immediately, the baby began to cry.

"I'll take her," Tanner said and promptly removed Ava from Emily's arms.

Jewel reached for him. "Give her to me."

"She won't cry. She didn't earlier."

"Tanner. Please." She appeared on the verge of tears.

"I don't want to keep playing the I'm-her-father

card, Jewel, but I am her father." He lifted Ava onto his shoulder, patting her back as he'd done with his niece and nephew when they were her age.

"My, my." Emily's glance cut between Tanner and Jewel. "Is there something you haven't told me?"

CHAPTER THREE

TANNER DEPOSITED THE last of Jewel's belongings in the middle of the floor, next to the small mountain of cartons, crates, suitcases, boxes of disposable diapers and photography equipment. The first thing he'd carried upstairs was the travel crib, where she immediately placed Ava for an afternoon nap.

No amount of noise they made had wakened the baby, from Tanner thumping around to Jewel issuing instructions. He wished he slept that soundly. He couldn't remember when he'd last dropped off quickly and remained asleep. Nighttime was when his personal demons liked to come out of their caves and taunt him.

"Don't suppose I could trouble you for some water," he said.

"Emily stocked the fridge." Jewel scurried over to the kitchen unit where she extracted two bottles of water from the under-the-counter refrigerator and brought one to him.

"Thanks." He unscrewed the cap and drained half the bottle's contents in three long swallows.

"Thank Emily."

He remembered the blueberry turnovers in his truck. "She's pretty thoughtful."

"I'm going to like working for her."

This was the most he and Jewel had talked since her suitcase had sprung open and he'd announced he was Ava's father. The tension erupting between them from the moment they'd seen each other in the horse barn had escalated to a suffocating level.

Tanner was ready to put an end to it. "How much are you planning on telling Emily about us?"

"As little as possible."

Emily excused herself shortly after Tanner had taken Ava from her, citing a task requiring her attention. More likely, she was being considerate and giving them privacy.

"I'll say I had no idea you were working at Powell Ranch," Jewel continued. "Which is the truth. And I'll offer to leave if she's not comfortable with the situation."

"Why would she be uncomfortable?"

"She might feel deceived. That I wasn't entirely honest when I applied for the job."

"I doubt that."

Jewel looked unconvinced. Perhaps it wasn't Emily who had her worried.

"Are you?" he asked. "Uncomfortable?"

"I'm not scared away, if that's what you're asking."

She crossed the room to the dinette set and sank into one of the chairs. Strain had drained the color from her cheeks along with her energy.

"If she does want you to leave," Tanner said, "promise me you'll stay a few days at least so that we can talk."

She nodded numbly.

"I told my mom about Ava." He pulled out the other dinette chair and sat.

"How'd she react?"

"She's thrilled. She can't wait to meet her."

To Tanner's relief, Jewel was agreeable. "Let me chat with Emily first. Get an idea of my schedule and when I'll be free. And make sure she still wants to employ me."

"She will."

"I think so, too. They've already booked a dozen photography jobs for me. If I were to leave, they'd be in a jam." Jewel sighed. "I'm not being intentionally difficult, but my days are full. I have barrel racing lessons every morning starting at seven, and Ronnie insists I enter the practice competitions if I'm not working."

"Maybe late morning one day next week," Tanner suggested. He thought he could stall his mom that long.

"I'll let you know by tomorrow."

"Which reminds me." He retrieved his jacket from the doorknob where he'd hung it and fished his phone from the pocket. "I promised Mom a picture of Ava. Mind if I take one while she's sleeping?"

"No. Go ahead."

He noticed Jewel watching him from her place at the table while he leaned over the travel crib and snapped several pictures with his phone. Ava slept through that, too, her thumb in her mouth and her lips moving noiselessly.

His chest tightened with emotion. She was so tiny, yet absolutely perfect.

"Mom's already talking about Christmas." He returned to the table. "I realize we haven't even decided on a first visit, much less the holidays—"

"My parents are flying in from Oklahoma," Jewel said, cutting him off. "They don't want to miss Ava's first Christmas."

"That shouldn't be a problem. Our folks always got along."

"They used to."

Meaning before everyone believed Tanner had cheated.

He held back the response he desperately wanted to give in favor of another. "We're all adults. We can behave for a few hours."

"Does Emily know that you cheated?"

"No." Tanner shook his head. "We're not that close, and she isn't a rodeo fan as far as I can tell. Plus, it's none of her business."

"People are cruel." Sorrow clouded Jewel's features. "I've endured a lot of insults."

"Emily's not that way. She's really nice."

"But her clients and guests might not be. I've had people I've never met before confront me on the street and accuse me of helping you cheat or covering for you. I'd hate for Emily to fire me because I'm damaging the reputation of Sweetheart Ranch."

Tanner would have felt Jewel was overreacting if not for his dad saying almost the exact same thing about Tanner coming to work for him.

"Worse," she continued, "I don't want anyone treating Ava poorly because she's your daughter."

He felt as if he'd been pushed off a steep cliff. Every muscle in his body clenched in readiness for impact. Yet another reason to resent his circumstances.

It wasn't entirely his father's fault. Daniel bore his share. He'd had his reasons for approaching that judge, which, while skewed, were understandable. He'd been handed a devastating diagnosis and wasn't thinking clearly. But Jewel was also partially responsible for Tanner's current state. She sent him packing without first giving him a chance to sort through the mess. Had she waited even a week before breaking up with him, shown the slightest trust in him, it might have made all the difference in the world. Instead, she'd jumped to conclusions. Part of the reason he'd left and not insisted on sticking around was because of the deep hurt her actions inflicted.

"I get it," he said. "You're embarrassed of me."

She didn't deny his accusation. "It's been hard. You have no idea."

"I do, actually. I read the social media posts and online articles. Listened to the PRCA broadcasts." Until he couldn't take another second and stopped.

"Not the same."

Her hand lay on the small table between them and, for one completely insane moment, Tanner considered reaching for her. They'd once been there for each other through thick and thin. Then he remembered her refusal to give him a chance and quickly came to his senses.

"I didn't imagine for one second the repercussions would be what they were."

A slap on the wrist from the PRCA, a couple of months staying under the radar and the cheating scandal would fade away, replaced by something new. That had been his dad's prediction.

But Huck Bridwell had been wrong. Very wrong. It hadn't taken long for Tanner to realize his dad had pushed his own personal agenda and Daniel's. Tanner's rodeo career, Jewel—his entire life had been expendable.

"Easy to say now," Jewel muttered, her tone dry.

"Trust me, it wasn't an easy decision."

She frowned as if he were one of those rude people who'd confronted her, not the man she'd once loved to distraction. "When is cheating ever an easy decision?"

"The circumstances were extenuating."

Tanner still marveled at how he'd gotten away with taking the blame for Daniel. According to his brother, the bar where he'd approached the bull riding judge had been dark, the man four bourbons into a good drunk and Daniel hadn't provided his first name. When Tanner had stepped forward and confessed, the judge had confirmed it was him. Tanner and Daniel looked enough alike that they were occasionally mistaken for each other.

"There's no reason to cheat." Jewel stiffened. "Short of life or death."

Life or death. Memories of the night Daniel had revealed his grim prognosis a few weeks before the NFR flooded Tanner, along with feelings of helplessness and despair. Tanner had vowed in that moment to do anything for his brother. And then, he'd been asked. Forgiving himself if he hadn't stepped up when Daniel most needed him would have been impossible. What if Daniel hadn't survived the surgery? So Tanner had made the only choice he could with the information he had.

"Tanner?" Jewel stared at him intently.

Before he could respond, a loud knock sounded at the door. This disruption did wake Ava, and she began crying.

"That must be the babysitter." Jewel popped out of her chair. "I'll get Ava. You mind answering the door?"

Tanner did as she asked. A teenaged girl stood on the landing.

"Hi, I'm Tracee. Is Jewel here?"

He'd seen the girl before. She came with her friends to Powell Ranch for gymkhanas and horse shows.

"Perfect timing." Jewel appeared beside Tanner. "Come on in."

Tanner retreated a step so Tracee could enter. "Nice to meet you." He shook her hand. "I'm Ava's dad."

A flicker of surprise lit Tracee's eyes, only to

promptly disappear when she smiled broadly. "Emily didn't tell me you'd be here."

"She didn't know."

Tracee was a friendly, talkative kid, and Tanner liked her immediately. Ava was fascinated with her and stared fixedly when Tracee held her and made funny faces to match her silly voice.

Before long, Jewel and Tracee came to an agreement about how often and when Tracee's services would be required. Jewel appeared satisfied with Tracee as a babysitter, and Tanner had to agree. Tracee had even brought along a list of references for Jewel to contact.

At the door, Jewel gave Tracee several phone numbers in case of an emergency, including her mother's. Tracee was about to leave when Tanner stopped her.

"Don't forget my number."

"Oh, yeah." Tracee entered the number he recited into her phone.

Tanner ignored the stern look Jewel sent him. He was Ava's father and should be one of the contacts. Second on the list after Jewel.

Once the door was closed behind Tracee, Jewel returned Ava to the travel crib and activated a mobile attached to the side. Five butterflies of various colors rotated in a slow circle, accompanied by a tinkling version of "Rock-A-Bye Baby."

Tanner came up behind her. "You're angry at me."

"Nope."

"I don't want to fight with you, Jewel, but I refuse to be excluded."

She spun to face him, her arms folded over her middle. "What about when my job here is over and I go back to Oklahoma?"

"Emily mentioned the job could be permanent."

"It could. Or I might start rodeoing again. I haven't decided."

"In other words, I shouldn't get too attached to Ava because she may not be around for long."

"Maybe."

A challenge? Possibly. They were both competitive people. But Tanner could dig in his heels as well as the next person, especially when the stakes were high.

"What if I traveled with you?" he suggested. "Took care of Ava while you're competing?"

Jewel drew back is if doused with cold water. "Are you crazy?"

"Or, I could have custody of her while you're on the road."

"That. Isn't. Happening."

Tanner retrieved his cowboy hat from the table and shoved it onto his head. The riders would be returning soon. He needed to get downstairs to meet them.

"Guess we have a lot to discuss," he said before heading toward the door.

THANK GOODNESS TEDDY BEAR knew what he was doing, thought Jewel as she and the gelding sailed through the arena gate. That made one of them. If that practice run she'd just completed was any indication, having a professional rodeo comeback was highly unlikely, if not impossible.

Slowing Teddy Bear to a walk and heading back the way they'd come, she released a long, dismal breath. Her first lesson and practice session with Ronnie Hartman was officially a flop.

The problem could be explained in a single sentence: Jewel's mind wasn't on the task. Instead, it remained fixated on the uninteresting-to-most-people scene playing out thirty yards away at the arena fence.

Tracee watched Ava, who was enjoying being the center of the teenager's attention. She'd bundled Ava snugly in the stroller and was constantly entertaining her with toys and squeaky-voiced games of peekaboo and short little trips back and forth along the fence line. That was good. Great. Precisely what Jewel wanted in a babysitter. She'd been reassured every time she'd glanced in their direction.

And then about twenty minutes ago, Tanner had wandered over from the horse barn. He'd yet to leave. Every few minutes he'd dipped his head and interacted with Ava, a broad smile on his face. Tracee had welcomed him like an old friend, and the two of them chattered away nonstop.

What was so darn riveting? Jewel couldn't hear from this distance. She stared at them, biting down hard until her jaw ached.

"Jewel!" Ronnie called from where she stood inside the arena right behind the finish line. "You're up again. And this time, try not to tighten your grip. You're pulling back on the bit and confusing the horse. Not to mention losing precious time."

Jewel *had* been gripping the reins too tight, the result of hearing Tanner and Tracee break into uproarious laughter.

She waited while Ronnie's other student finished her run. The young woman, somewhere in her early twenties, was a good rider. Jewel remembered her as a rookie on the circuit last year and noted how much the woman had improved since then. Today, she was kicking Jewel's butt.

Teddy Bear needed no prodding. The instant the rider sped past them, he took his place in the lane outside the gate, ready to fly when Jewel gave the signal.

She studied the barrels, forcing her attention away from Tanner and Ava and Tracee. Normally, Jewel executed a right-handed pattern. Teddy Bear tended to cut tighter corners on his left side, and that allowed Jewel to make adjustments if they started out slow.

Another burst of laughter reached her ears. A quick glimpse revealed Tanner's boss, Ethan, had joined the little gathering. Tanner had removed Ava from the stroller and was showing her to Ethan, who patted Ava on her stocking-capped head.

Jewel tensed, expecting Ava to cry. She didn't. Big, ruggedly handsome men obviously appealed to her. Like mother like daughter, Jewel supposed.

"Hey, Jewel!" Ronnie called. "You working on your Christmas shopping list or what?"

"Just getting into the zone," she called back and attempted to do precisely that.

More laughter from the arena fence. Did these grown men have nothing better to do than dote on a baby?

Jewel resumed studying the barrels. Yes. She was definitely trying a left-handed pattern.

Closing her eyes, she visualized herself running the barrels, silently counted how many strides at a full gallop were required to reach the first one, and determined at what point she'd swing Teddy Bear around and head him home. Beneath her, the gelding tensed.

"Go!" Jewel shouted and dug her heels into his sides.

He was off in a flash, his hooves digging into the soft ground and sending dirt flying. They neared the first barrel in what Jewel knew was their best time today. Adrenaline surged in her veins. Her wildly beating heart drilled into her rib cage. A roar filled her ears. She and Teddy Bear rounded the first barrel, slipping into the pocket clean and neat and emerging like a Formula One race car firing on all pistons.

And then, abruptly, total chaos. Teddy Bear veered right. Of course he did—he was used to a right-handed pattern. Jewel cued him to left. He obeyed, but only after a moment's confusing hesitation. With their rhythm completely obliterated, they cut too close on the last barrel and Jewel clipped it hard with the side of her stirrup. She didn't need to look over her shoulder to confirm the barrel had fallen over.

Still, she pushed Teddy Bear hard to the finish line and through the gate. Her mistakes shouldn't take away from his training.

"What the heck just happened?" Ronnie hollered, marching across the arena.

Jewel turned Teddy Bear and walked the

gelding toward her instructor, making sure to give his neck a pat. "My bad. For a change I thought I'd try a left-handed pattern. Teddy Bear didn't get the memo."

"You think?"

"I'll do better tomorrow."

Ronnie shook her head. "You can't do much worse."

The criticism was harsh. It was also deserved. Ronnie's job wasn't to coddle Jewel but rather to demand she reach her full potential.

"I did say you had your work cut out for you."

Ronnie studied her critically. "Are you just rusty or is there some other problem?"

Yes, in fact, there is. Twenty-four hours ago, I had no idea where the father of my baby was or if I'd ever see him again. Then, he suddenly appeared out of nowhere, has formed an instant and intense bond with our daughter and is talking about sharing custody. He lied to me and cheated, and I don't trust him as far as I can throw him. So, yeah, you could say I have a problem.

"Everything's fine," Jewel said. "My head'll be in the game tomorrow."

Teddy Bear blew out a lusty breath, almost as if mocking her. Fabricating an excuse, she turned the horse and left.

By now, Ethan was nowhere in sight, having

presumably returned to work. Not Tanner. He remained with Ava and Tracee. As if sensing her gaze on him, he offered Jewel a friendly wave. She didn't respond and aimed Teddy Bear in the opposite direction. They'd walk in circles behind the horse barn to cool him off.

"You're being childish," she scolded herself once she was out of sight.

Tanner had done nothing wrong. Today, she amended. They'd agreed to meet after her barrel racing lesson, and he'd arrived a few minutes early. His boss stopping by to see Ava wasn't all that unusual. Men did show off their children to their friends and coworkers. Jewel's brother had, taking his newborn daughter and wife to the office and introducing them around.

Jewel's brother had been enormously proud. Was Tanner? He'd learned only yesterday he was a father. How long did it take for pride to develop?

Thirty minutes later, she returned Teddy Bear to his stall, properly cooled off, unsaddled and well brushed. No, she hadn't been able to resist checking on Tanner. Multiple times. He was still with Ava and Tracee, though all three had relocated to the covered porch outside the ranch office. Tracee sat in one of the wooden chairs while Tanner stood with his back propped against the railing, one boot crossed over the other and his hat tugged low on his brow.

He looked good. Masculine and sexy and confident. Those were the qualities that had caused Jewel to notice him in the first place. His easygoing nature and sense of humor had ultimately won her over, even though she'd insisted she wasn't ready for a committed relationship.

The memory gave her pause. Other than when he was with Ava, Tanner had been serious and somber since their meeting yesterday in the horse barn. Quite a change from his previous self.

A result of the cheating? His brother's brain tumor? Both? Something else?

"Thanks for watching Ava," Jewel said to Tracee as she neared. "How was she?"

"Super good. I hardly did anything except rock the stroller."

And talk up a storm with Tanner. "Glad to hear it. I see you had help." Jewel forced a smile, which Tanner returned.

"I finished the morning feeding early," he said. "Hope you don't mind."

"Not at all."

Jewel did mind. Very much. She had no good reason to, and certainly no right, but she minded nonetheless. Until yesterday, she had been the one in complete charge of Ava and with final authority. Now, she had to tolerate an interloper into her close-knit mother-daughter relationship and would likely be required to make concessions and compromises.

All right. Not an interloper. Tanner was Ava's father. But he was obviously adapting more quickly than Jewel to his new role in their lives.

"Well, I'd better get going." Tracee extracted her car keys from her backpack. She'd met Jewel here rather than at Sweetheart Ranch and had driven her own car. "I have a ton of studying. Finals are next week, and then I'm off until January for Christmas break."

"See you tomorrow morning," Jewel said.

"Bye-bye, little Ava." Tracee reached into the stroller and tweaked Ava's sock-covered foot, which had somehow escaped the blanket.

Ava offered Tracee a big gummy grin.

Jewel watched as Tracee hurried toward the nearly empty parking area and her older-model compact car. Powell Ranch had been bustling with activity when Jewel had first arrived at seven o'clock, with horse owners squeezing in prework rides much like fitness enthusiasts squeezed in prework runs. Two hours later, the ranch was practically deserted.

The lull would likely continue until the afternoon, when school let out and the students arrived. Weekends were probably a different story, with activities from sunup to sundown. She'd heard from Emily that tourists arrived in Mustang Valley by the hundreds during the holidays, what with the Holly Daze Festival and other local events like Sweetheart Ranch's holiday hayride and square dance. She'd be spending a fair amount of time this weekend photographing the events per Emily's request.

The goings-on were also one of the many reasons her parents were looking forward to their visit—besides celebrating Christmas with their grandchild. Jewel's parents were considering becoming "snowbirds" and wintering in Arizona when her dad retired this coming spring. Their plans included getting the lay of the land while they were here.

Jewel's mom had assured her yesterday when she'd called with the news about Tanner that nothing would change and advised her not to worry. The pep talk had done no good, and Jewel couldn't shake the constant anxiety plaguing her.

As if in response to her thoughts, the cause of her anxiety pushed off the fence and came to stand perilously close to her. Jewel caught a hint of spice-scented aftershave. That was different. Apparently, something he'd started using since he'd begun shaving regularly.

"You have a chance to talk to Emily about your schedule?" he asked.

"I did." The wedding ranch owner had thoughtfully not inquired about Tanner when Jewel had gone to the main house yesterday after the suitcase malfunction. "How about if your folks visit late Monday morning, say elevenish?"

"I'll let Mom know. She just needs to rearrange Dad's appointments."

His mother obviously still worked as his dad's administrative assistant. It had always been Tanner's dream to become part of the family business. Unlike his brother, he'd gone to school for years in between rodeoing, eventually earning a marketing degree.

And now he worked as a wrangler. He must be disappointed.

"Where shall we meet?" She leaned into the stroller to pull the blanket over Ava's exposed foot.

"My bunkhouse? I'll make lunch."

Jewel straightened. She remembered him as being utterly inept in the kitchen. "When did you learn to cook?"

"One of my recently acquired skills since living alone."

"Really?"

"People change, Jewel. Discover things about themselves."

A twinkle lit his eyes. The same kind that used to cause a fluttering in Jewel's stomach. Judging by her reaction, it still did.

"I have to get back to work," she said.

"I'll talk to you tomorrow. Confirm our plans for Monday." Tanner reached a hand into the stroller and cupped Ava's rosy cheek. She cooed and flailed her arms in response. "See you later, kiddo."

Touching. There was no other way to describe Tanner's interaction with Ava. Well, there was. Endearing. Whatever he'd done in the past, he adored their daughter.

One mistake, her mind whispered. That, technically, was thwarted before he carried it through to completion.

But a big mistake, she silently answered back. *With enormous repercussions.* And not one easily forgotten.

She watched him walk away, spine straight, shoulders squared, and a slight spring to his step. That was not the posture and gait of a guilty or beaten man. Did Tanner not regret what he'd done or feel bad about it? No, he'd been affected. She'd heard it in his voice and seen his expression change when they'd talked yesterday in her quarters.

"Jewel! Got a sec?"

She glanced up at the sound of her name to see Ronnie strolling toward her. "Hi. What's up?"

"You know that guy?" Ronnie hitched her chin toward the horse barn, though Tanner had already disappeared inside.

"Yeah, I do."

She wasn't sure how much to say. Ronnie would remember Tanner and the scandal, certainly, being actively involved in the rodeo world. Jewel could hear the comments and see the shocked reaction.

"Okay. I was concerned some strange man hanging around your daughter is what had you distracted during practice."

"He's not some strange man." Jewel swallowed. Did she have a right to out Tanner's identity when he'd been clear that was his prerogative? "He works here. Plus," she admitted reluctantly, "we've met."

Ronnie gave her a funny look. "Are you sure?"

"I am." Jewel swallowed and spoke more firmly. "Really."

"All right, then. Just make sure to leave whatever's bothering you at home on Monday when you show up for your lesson."

"I will. I promise."

"Because if you can't focus during practice, there's no way you can make any kind of a barrel racing comeback." With that, Ronnie returned to the arena where her next student waited.

Monday. The day Jewel had just arranged with Tanner for his parents to meet Ava. What had she been thinking?

CHAPTER FOUR

"ARE'NT YOU JUST the sweetest thing in the whole wide world? I'm in love with you. I am, I am."

Jewel watched as Molly, head of guest relations and one of Emily's two granddaughters, cooed to Ava and rocked her gently back and forth. Ava stared up at Molly as if mesmerized, perfectly content to be held by unfamiliar arms.

Her daughter had been meeting all sorts of new people these last few days, Jewel mused. Perhaps she was becoming less wary and more comfortable. The thought that her little baby was changing and growing and gaining confidence triggered a pang of sadness that Jewel tried to push aside.

Just this morning, Ava's purple overalls had no longer fit. Jewel had instead dressed her in a Christmas sweatshirt and matching green corduroy pants that her mother had bought and insisted would be simply precious. She'd been right. Ava could easily be on the December page of a baby calendar, posing beside a dog wearing reindeer antlers. Which reminded Jewel, she should take some pictures of Ava. She'd been doing that two or three times each week without fail, her intention being to make a photo journal of her daughter's first year.

"These are gorgeous," Emily said, scrolling through the wedding pictures on Jewel's tablet and pausing on each one. The three women stood in the foyer at Sweetheart Ranch beside the antique desk that served as a registration counter.

"Glad you think so."

Jewel had been a little nervous during her first professional paying gig on Saturday evening. Correction, a lot nervous. If she failed right at the start of her new job, she could forget staying the remainder of the month. Her parents were generous, but they couldn't afford to pay her entire living expenses, as well as her barrel racing lessons and horse boarding.

In addition to the Saturday weddings, Jewel had risen at four thirty yesterday morning in order to photograph a small, intimate sunrise ceremony on the veranda. Tracee had arrived at five thirty to watch Ava and, since the baby was still asleep, crashed in the recliner to doze. Jewel had then spent her entire Sunday afternoon transferring the photographs she'd taken during the morning wedding and the other one from Saturday onto her tablet and organizing them. She'd next transferred the photos onto thumb drives for the two sets of newlyweds who happened to both be honeymooning at Sweetheart Ranch. Lastly, she'd uploaded a few of the very best ones to her online portfolio, as her contract with the brides and grooms permitted.

"We have the use of three images from each wedding," Emily said and tilted the tablet for Molly and Jewel to see. "Which ones should I pick? Here are the Ochoas."

Molly twisted, moving Ava in order to view the tablet. "I love the one of them kissing in front of the window."

"That is nice," Emily mused. "I like the one where they're exchanging rings. She's glowing and he looks like he just won the lottery."

"Well, in a way he did," Molly said, her expression dreamy. She was entitled, thought Jewel. She was getting married in just over two weeks, on Christmas Eve, after a yearlong engagement to her fiancé, who'd proposed the previous Christmas Eve.

Jewel had been like that once, brimming with happiness and seeing love everywhere she looked. She'd been secretly fretting that photographing weddings would prove difficult for her, what with too many sad reminders of her almost marriage to Tanner. There'd been some sad reminders, for sure. But she'd steeled herself, doing what needed to be done in order to perform her job. With each wedding and reception, the ache inside her had diminished.

"Look at the cake," Emily exclaimed and then sighed. "It's gorgeous. Bridget outdid herself."

Personally, Jewel had preferred the one from Friday's wedding, with its elaborate staircase and miniature bride and groom standing at the top.

Eventually, Emily and Molly made their photo selections. Jewel took back the tablet and emailed the pictures to Emily. When she was done, Emily raised the subject of Christmas decorations.

"I hired a company this year since we're going all out. The crew's arriving Thursday morning at nine to start on the outside and should be done with everything inside and out by Friday at noon, including the parlor and the tree in the foyer. They'd better be done," she added. "We have a wedding Friday evening."

"I think we can manage the inside ourselves," Molly said. "We did last year, and it looked great."

Emily shook her head. "We have more weddings scheduled than last year, one of them being yours. I think we have enough on our plate. And I'm still of the opinion you should take the week before Christmas off from work."

"I'm taking the week *after* Christmas off for the honeymoon. And, frankly, I don't know how you're going to survive without me."

Molly had told Jewel earlier about her and her fiancé's plans to stay at a quaint inn in Sedona, and Jewel very much approved. She and Tanner had driven through the scenic Arizona town a few years ago, and she'd fallen in love with the place.

"We'll figure out a way," Emily said. "Nora can step in again. She did a great job last year helping out when Homer and I eloped and went on our honeymoon trip."

Molly continued rocking Ava, though the baby had long since fallen asleep. "I'll spend the entire honeymoon worrying about how you and Bridget are faring without me."

"Good grief. You'd better not be thinking about us and instead be having the time of your life," Emily replied.

Besides Molly's nuptials, two other weddings were also scheduled for Christmas Eve and two more on Christmas Day. A Canadian couple were having their nuptials on Boxing Day, and seven ceremonies were taking place between New Year's Eve and New Year's Day. That wasn't counting the other weddings between now and then. Sweetheart Ranch was indeed a busy place for the holidays.

The phone on the registration desk rang. Molly pouted and handed off Ava to Jewel. "I hate giving her back, but duty calls."

"For me, too."

"You off to meet Tanner's parents?" Emily asked as she and Jewel headed toward the parlor.

"We are."

Jewel had told Emily as few details as she could get away with about her history with Tanner. The older woman had been sympathetic and understanding and not at all angry, much to Jewel's relief. Like Jewel's grandmother, Emily had expressed doubt that Tanner could have cheated. She believed him to be a genuinely nice person. Jewel didn't dispute her. Emily only knew the Tanner who did favors for her whenever she asked.

"Come to the kitchen first." Emily put an arm around Jewel's shoulders and guided her and Ava along. "I have something for you to take to the lunch. Bridget tried a new recipe this morning."

"You don't have to—"

"Nonsense. The leftovers will just go to waste."

In the kitchen, Emily removed a container from the refrigerator and presented it to Jewel. "Baked butternut squash. It's delicious."

"I'm sure everyone will love it." Jewel moved Ava to her shoulder in order to take the container.

"If you don't mind me saying, you look nervous."

"I am. Practically shaking."

"Do you like Tanner's parents?"

"Very much. His mom's a doll." His dad could be brusque and demanding, though never unkind. Jewel didn't mention that.

Bidding her employer goodbye, she returned to her quarters briefly for the diaper bag and a thumb drive she'd made for Tanner's mom that held several dozen choice pictures of Ava from birth through to last week. She hoped it would serve as an icebreaker, if nothing else. Tensions were bound to be high.

Tanner's parents were already at Powell Ranch when she arrived. She parked her truck next to their luxury sedan outside of Tanner's bunkhouse. She'd hardly set her feet on the ground when the door to the bunkhouse burst open and Tanner's mom, Shirley, emerged, her face bright with excitement.

"Jewel! Oh, honey. It's so wonderful to see you."

She hurried over and enveloped Jewel in a warm hug. Okay, tensions weren't going to be high, after all.

"Hi, Shirley. Good to see you, too." Jewel returned the hug.

"How are you?" Shirley asked. "You look fantastic. Pretty as always."

"I admit, as ragged as I'm run most days, I don't feel very pretty." She brushed at a lock of hair falling in her face and wished she'd remembered to put on lipstick.

"Nonsense. Motherhood suits you."

"Thank you. I love being a mother. Is Huck inside?"

"Yes." Shirley dismissed her husband with a wave. "You know men. They like to stay out of our way where babies are concerned."

Did they? Jewel's dad wasn't like that. Neither was Tanner.

She opened the rear passenger door. Ava, asleep in her car seat, roused, wriggling her arms and making funny little sounds.

Shirley peered inside the truck and let out a gasp of delight. "Would you look at her. She's an angel." The next instant, she covered her mouth with her hands and held in a sob. "I can't believe it," she said when she was finally able to speak.

"Would you like to hold her?" Jewel surprised herself with the offer. She hadn't been certain how she'd act with Tanner's parents, but Shirley's emotional response had strummed her heartstrings.

Shirley's eyes went wide. "Can I?"

"I should warn you, she sometimes cries when unfamiliar people hold her. Though, she is getting better."

Jewel unbuckled Ava and handed her to Shirley, who took the baby as if she'd been entrusted with a precious treasure for safekeeping. The next moment, she burst into tears.

"My beautiful little granddaughter."

Jewel felt her own eyes fill. Shirley had two other grandchildren, Tanner's niece and nephew. Ava wasn't her first. But with the other two, she'd been able to participate in her daughter-in-law's pregnancies and be there at the babies' births, along with seeing them often. She'd only just learned about Ava a few days ago. That probably warranted an emotional first meeting.

Ava whimpered softly, perhaps agitated by Shirley's tears. She didn't start to wail, however, so Jewel decided to see how things progressed before taking her back.

Grabbing the diaper bag, car seat/carrier and the container of butternut squash, she said, "Shall we go inside?"

"She looks just like Tanner did at this age," Shirley commented as they entered the bunkhouse.

Jewel had thought the same thing herself. It

wasn't just the matching chin clefts; Ava also had her father's expression when she smiled.

Drawing on her courage, Jewel entered the bunkhouse behind Shirley. Though small and modestly furnished, it was surprisingly comfortable. A sleeping alcove was separated from the main sitting area and kitchenette by a partial wall. And the once-attractive furniture, while worn, was serviceable.

The bunkhouse was also a far cry from the spacious and affluent home Tanner had been raised in and where his parents still lived. What did they think of their son residing here and of his job as a wrangler? Tanner didn't seem to mind. He moved about with ease, unlike his dad whose furrowed brow telegraphed that he'd rather be anywhere else than here.

Unless it was Jewel making Huck Bridwell uncomfortable. She supposed that was possible.

"Huck," Shirley said as she gingerly lowered herself and Ava onto the old sofa. "Come see your granddaughter. Isn't she beautiful?"

While Tanner relieved Jewel of her load and placed the food container in the refrigerator, his dad sat on the sofa next to his mom and inspected Ava as if she were a new appliance he was considering buying.

"She's cute," he announced, making no attempt to touch or talk to her.

Was he like that with his other two grandchildren? Jewel didn't remember.

Ava produced the unhappy frown she often did before starting to wail.

"She might be hungry," Jewel said. "She did just wake up."

"Are you hungry, little one?" Shirley lowered her face close to Ava's. "Your daddy always wanted to eat when he woke up from a nap."

Jewel glanced around the bunkhouse in search of privacy.

"You need something?" Tanner asked.

"A place to… I need…" This was a little embarrassing. "I have to nurse Ava. She's finicky and doesn't do well when people are nearby."

"There's a chair next to the bed. It's out of view."

"Okay." What a relief.

He nodded at his parents. "Mom is thrilled."

"She's good with Ava."

"She watches Daniel's kids a lot. More since his surgery and rehabilitation."

Ava chose that moment to vocalize her demands at the top of her lungs. Jewel retrieved her from Shirley and disappeared into the sleeping area with the diaper bag. Twenty minutes later, when she was done feeding and changing Ava, she reappeared. During her absence, a stack of gift bags had been left in the middle of the floor.

"We brought a few things for the baby," Shirley pointed and smiled broadly.

A few things? Jewel thought. There had to be six or seven bags.

"Go on," Shirley urged. "Open them."

Tanner pulled a chair over from the table for Jewel to sit in while she opened the gifts. Then he took charge of Ava, who stared at him with the same intense concentration as yesterday.

Self-conscious, but not wanting to hurt Shirley's feelings, Jewel tackled the gift bags one at a time. There were footed Christmas pajamas with Rudolph on the front, a stuffed pony that Shirley swore matched the one Tanner had as a baby, a music box with a dancing ballerina on top and several outfits.

"Shirley, Huck, this is too much. Thank you," Jewel gushed.

"Nonsense. I got everything on sale."

Tanner gave Ava back to Jewel when she was done with the gifts. "I'm going put lunch on the table."

Shirley offered to help.

"Let me," Jewel said and stood. "You spend time with Ava. We have to leave right after lunch for work. I have a photography session."

She gave the baby to Shirley and joined Tanner in the kitchen. He hadn't been lying when he'd said his cooking skills had improved during the last year. While Jewel was setting out the platter of sandwiches, the butternut squash and array of delicious-looking sides, he came to stand beside her.

"Thank you."

"You did all the work," she insisted.

"No, I meant for giving me a daughter."

She stopped and turned toward him, her free hand floating to her heart. If the genuine tone in his voice wasn't enough to convince her of his sincerity, the warmth in his eyes did it. She may not fully trust him. Yet. But no way could she keep lying to him. Not about this.

"You're right. I didn't search for you as hard as I could have. As I *should* have."

"You were angry."

"Yeah, I was. And embarrassed that my fiancé was a cheater."

"I appreciate your honesty. And speaking of which…" He shifted his weight uncomfortably. "There's something I need to tell you. It's about what happened last year."

His troubled expression triggered a prickle of alarm. "What?"

He didn't get the chance to say because at

that moment Huck Bridwell interrupted them. "I'm starving. Let's eat."

"Sure." Tanner produced a smile.

Jewel started for the table, her curiosity piqued. And her worry.

TANNER SAT ON the sofa, Ava propped upright in the crook of his arm. She was far more interested in her new stuffed pony than him. Or not, for she abruptly released her grip and the pony tumbled to the floor, completely ignored for a full minute after that.

He retrieved the toy and set it on the cushion next to him, catching bits and pieces of the two conversations simultaneously occurring. Beside him on the sofa, his dad conferred on his phone with a business associate about an upcoming meeting. In the kitchen, his mom and Jewel chatted amiably while they tidied and put away the leftovers.

His mom had insisted on clearing the table, and Jewel had insisted on washing dishes. Tanner was okay with the arrangement as it gave him time to spend with his daughter.

He still couldn't believe it. How could a big lug like him have fathered such a pretty, delicate little girl? Tanner had always imagined himself a parent to boys, like his own father. Rough-and-tumble rascals whom he'd teach to ride and play sports and, when they were old enough, how to treat a lady right. While he hadn't always seen eye to eye with his dad, he gave the man credit when it came to spending time with his children while they were growing up.

It was only after Tanner and Daniel left home that their dad became absorbed with the business. Was there a connection? Without children at home, was his father filling the void with work? Tanner hadn't considered that possibility until now.

Then again, his perspective had been changing about a lot of things these past five days—all due to Ava. Tanner would move boulders with his bare hands in order to protect her. Sacrifice everything to give her what she needed. Cherish her until his dying day.

He'd also make darn sure she and everyone else knew he was a decent, honorable, moral man. Not the cheater the world believed him to be. How and when he'd accomplish that, he wasn't sure.

"When are your parents arriving?" His mom wiped down the table with a damp cloth while Jewel washed the last of the dishes they'd used during lunch.

"Shortly before Christmas. They're staying until January third."

Tanner listened to them while ignoring his

dad's conversation. Ava listened to no one and instead watched her feet with intense fascination.

"That's a nice, long visit," his mom said.

"Dad's retiring soon. They're seriously considering buying a condo and spending winters here. Mom's arthritis is worsening, and the dry climate's supposed to be beneficial." Jewel talked as she rinsed dishes. "They've been in contact with a real estate agent and are planning to look at some places during their visit, though they're told the holidays aren't a good time to buy."

"How exciting. I can't wait to see them again."

Tanner smiled to himself. He really appreciated his mom's efforts to make the upcoming visit with Jewel's parents go well. He reminded himself to tell her later.

"Have you settled on plans for Christmas Day?" she asked.

"Not really. Any suggestions?"

Jewel was also doing her part to make the impending visit go well. Tanner wished his dad hadn't interrupted him before he'd had a chance to tell her about Daniel being the one who'd cheated. Part of him had wondered if the interruption was intentional and then decided no.

How could his dad have known what Tanner was about to say?

"Fixing a big meal in this tiny kitchen won't be easy." His mom looked around, arms crossed over her middle.

"Same with my quarters at Sweetheart Ranch," Jewel added. "The kitchen there is even smaller."

"What if we all went to a nice restaurant? There's bound to be one open on Christmas Day. I can call around and then get back to you with a couple suggestions."

"That would be great!"

"If I recall," Shirley said, "the Desert Vista Golf Club has a very nice upscale restaurant that offers brunch on the holidays."

"We could celebrate beforehand at my place." Jewel offered. "Exchange gifts and have coffee."

"Sounds lovely." His mom beamed. "I can't wait. I have a friend who crochets these darling baby sweaters. I'll ask her for one in Ava's size."

"You already gave her gifts."

"Nonsense, it's her first Christmas," his mom answered, as if that was explanation enough. "Do you mind if Daniel and his family join us? Afterward, Huck and I can go back to their house for Christmas with the children."

"Of course not. That'd be nice."

"If Daniel's up to it," Tanner's mom said, a

sad note in her voice. "He has good and bad days."

Jewel patted her arm sympathetically. "It must be hard on you, watching your son struggle."

"Watching both my sons struggle. This has been a difficult year for Tanner, too. He didn't deserve—" Tanner's mom cut herself short and squared her shoulders. "He's a good brother to Daniel. I'm very proud of him."

Tanner had tensed during this last exchange, unsure how much his mother would reveal. When she didn't elaborate, he relaxed. This was his story to tell.

His dad ended his call and set down his phone on the side table. Without any preamble, he said, "I spoke to Murry Peterson the other day."

"Yeah." Tanner wasn't interested. Murry Peterson was his father's attorney for the business and the one insisting Tanner stay on the down low for another year.

"He can probably give you the name of a good family attorney."

At least his dad wasn't speaking in his normal booming voice. Tanner glanced over at Jewel and his mom, relieved they were still involved in discussing Christmas plans and not paying attention to him.

"Jewel and I only just started talking about custody," Tanner said.

She hadn't raised a single objection when Tanner had requested daily visits with Ava during her stay in Mustang Valley. He wasn't naive—he knew they'd need a formal agreement, one that should be in the works before she left, *if* she left. But he wanted to discuss any custody arrangement with her before hiring an attorney.

"You shouldn't wait," his dad said. "Better to be the first one to act rather than the one reacting. You can bet your bottom dollar she's already retained an attorney."

"I don't think so, Dad."

"Don't get caught unprepared."

Despite the advice being sensible, Tanner wouldn't take it. He refused to start his new relationship with Jewel, as parents to Ava, on the wrong foot by coming on too strong.

As if reminding him, Ava took hold of Tanner's finger and tugged. She might have been tugging on his heart—the effect was the same.

"I'm going to tell Jewel the truth about what happened with Daniel."

Tanner's dad scowled. "That's a bad idea, son."

"She won't say anything."

"One, you don't know that for a fact, and two, the timing is terrible."

"What better time is there, Dad? Things have changed. I'm a father, and I need to put Ava first." Tanner repeated what Jewel had said to him the other day. "I refuse to let any child of mine suffer needlessly because of my decision."

His dad glanced down at the baby. "She isn't suffering."

"Not yet. But it's a possibility. If Jewel returns to barrel racing, Ava could be teased or taunted for what I'm thought to have done. Jewel was. Relentlessly."

"Ava's a baby."

"She won't always be." Tanner steeled his resolve. "It's important to me that Jewel knows what really happened. I don't like her believing the father of her daughter cheated. I'm not a bad person, Dad."

"Neither is Daniel. He wasn't himself when he approached that bull riding judge. He had a brain tumor and was on medication. His judgment was impaired."

"Which is why I don't think the arena owners would win a lawsuit." Tanner had done a little of his own research. "Daniel can't be held responsible."

"Maybe. Maybe not. There are no guarantees. And frankly, we don't have the money for a long, drawn out court battle. We're barely covering our monthly expenses as it is."

Tanner sat up straighter. "Since when?"

"This past year. Several of our clients left after the scandal broke and moved their business to competing firms. I haven't been able to recruit enough new clients to make up the difference."

Tanner saw by his dad's expression he wasn't exaggerating. "I'm sorry to hear that, Dad."

"Unless something changes, we won't be able to continue helping Daniel with his medication and physical therapy not covered by insurance." To their credit, his parents had spent a considerable amount of their own money on Daniel and his family. "You coming clean will generate fresh interest in the cheating incident. We could lose even more customers."

"I'm not sure what any of this has to do with me telling Jewel the truth. She can be trusted to keep quiet."

"Rosalyn's been threatening again to leave Daniel and take the kids."

"I'm sorry to hear that."

"Learning the truth could tip the scales."

Daniel adored his wife and children. Losing them would shatter him and send him into a deeper, darker place. Could Tanner be the one responsible for that?

"I thought his doctor put him on a new antidepressant," he said.

"Hasn't made any significant difference."

"I hate hearing that. For Rosalyn's sake and the kids', as well as Daniel's."

"If she learns he was the one who cheated and not you," his dad continued, "their marriage will be over. Mark my word."

As much as Tanner wished it were different, he knew what his father said was a real possibility. An emotional person to begin with, Rosalyn's current state was fragile—the result of dealing with her husband's brain cancer, his postsurgery disabilities and raising two children virtually on her own. Learning he'd attempted to win a championship by cheating might be the last straw.

In addition to Tanner's parents, Rosalyn's family also did what they could to help. Unfortunately, Daniel wasn't making things easy on her. The aftereffects of the surgery, along with his medication and various limitations, had caused him to suffer bouts of severe depression and mood swings. As a result, he often lashed out at Rosalyn and, on occasion, his children.

No one blamed him, and everyone tried their best to understand. Daniel always regretted his actions and apologized afterward. But there was a limit to how much a gentle and sensitive woman like Rosalyn could stand before walking.

"I'm not asking you to keep silent for me,"

Tanner's dad said. "Do it for your brother. He needs his family. He can't survive without them, and he's lost so much already."

Tanner hesitated before relenting. "All right. For now. But no promises."

He could wait a few more weeks. But regardless, he was telling Jewel after the first of the year, whether she left or stayed.

Lifting Ava into his arms, he stood. "We should get you back to your mom."

His dad also stood and, taking Tanner by surprise, kissed Ava gently on her head. "Bye, honey bun."

When he straightened, he wore a smile. It didn't last, but for a brief moment, Tanner was reminded of the dad from his own childhood—and the dad that Daniel had been before brain cancer struck. The one his children wouldn't get to know if Rosalyn took them away.

CHAPTER FIVE

JEWEL WALKED TEDDY BEAR around the horse barn for his cool down, her spirits soaring. She'd had a good lesson this morning, followed by three successful practice runs.

As if in agreement, Teddy Bear pestered her nonstop, nuzzling her hair and nibbling the end of her ponytail.

"Quit it, you goofball," she said, a laugh in her voice. Rather than push him away, she reached up with one hand and scratched his neck.

He responded with a snort and a shake of his big head.

On her third circuit, she came upon Tanner in one of the outdoor stalls. He crouched in front of the automatic waterer, tinkering with a pair of pliers.

She stopped in front of the stall. Teddy Bear immediately began a sniffing introduction with the stall's occupant, a dappled gray Arabian who'd stuck his head out over the top bar.

"Waterer not working?" Jewel asked.

Tanner glanced up, his elation at seeing her reflected in his broad grin. "I think the mechanism is plugged."

A common problem. Horses often drank with their mouths full, and food fell into the waterer, eventually creating a blockage.

"Okay. Well, I won't bother you." She'd see him later for his daily visit with Ava.

"I watched your practice runs this morning." He stuck the pliers up into the waterer's underside and twisted, his brow knitted in concentration. "You did good."

"Yeah. I think Teddy and I are finally getting our groove back."

"You'll be competing again in no time."

She marveled at how comfortable she and Tanner had become in the past eight days. Nowhere close to where they'd been before, but better. Jewel wasn't fooling herself. They still had a lot of problems to resolve.

They'd yet to broach the subject of custody after her stay at Sweetheart Ranch came to an end. Not since that first day when he'd mentioned seeking shared custody should she return to professional rodeoing.

Of course, until she chose a career direction, they really couldn't make a decision regarding custody. Jewel taking a permanent job at Sweetheart Ranch, if one was even offered, might be the easiest solution. She'd be close to Tanner and his parents. Her parents, too, for five months of the year, if they became winter visitors.

After today, however, she could see herself returning to the rodeo circuit. But what would she do with Ava? The thought put a damper on her previously soaring spirits. Before Tanner reappeared in her life, the answer had been obvious. She'd have taken Ava with her on the road. Other barrel racing mothers did it. Yes, they had help, often in the form of husbands. There were, however, alternative solutions.

But going on the road without Ava wasn't one of them. Jewel couldn't do it. For a single weekend, perhaps. If she had no choice. Not *every* weekend or even every other weekend. She'd just as soon part with her right arm.

Tanner accompanying them wasn't her first choice. Depending on how their custody talks went, though, it might be a compromise she had to make.

"Okay if I come by about two?" he asked, still fiddling with the waterer.

"That should be fine."

"I didn't see Tracee this morning while you were practicing."

"She's watching Ava in my quarters. Finals are next week, and she's hitting the books hard."

Teddy Bear gave a sudden high-pitched squeal

and jerked his head, nearly tugging the lead rope from Jewel's grip. He and the Arabian had decided they weren't friends. Sending Teddy Bear a clear message, the Arabian whirled and kicked and retreated to the rear of the stall.

"Stop it, you two." Tanner pocketed the pliers and grabbed the stall's top rung. Hauling himself to his feet, he tested the waterer, pressing on the activator and nodding with satisfaction when the water flowed freely. He then made his way to the stall door. "Did you have a chance to talk to your parents about Christmas Day?"

"I did," Jewel answered. "They're excited. And your mom called me this morning. She made reservations for brunch at that golf resort."

"She told me." He exited the stall, closed the door and faced her. "How do your folks feel about...me?"

"They haven't really said."

He sent her a dubious look. "Why don't I believe you?"

"They haven't," Jewel repeated.

"You ask them?"

Chagrined, she shook her head.

"Don't want to know? Or don't want to answer their questions?"

"A little of both?"

Jewel's mom had been considerate every time

they'd talked, not putting Jewel on the spot. She'd also kept Jewel's father from horning in on their calls. He'd be less considerate than her mother and push Jewel for answers she wasn't ready to give. Not while her feelings for Tanner remained all over the place. Getting comfortable with each other was one thing, confident she could trust him again, quite another.

Raising her gaze, she was startled to see a shadow of regret darken Tanner's eyes. He'd mentioned losing his friends after the cheating incident. She hadn't thought about him losing the affection and respect of her family until now.

She straightened, reminding herself not to feel too sorry for him. He should have thought of the repercussions before he cheated. His current predicament, hers, too, was a direct result of the terrible decision he'd made.

"I need to hurry," she said. "See you this afternoon."

"You have a wedding tonight?" He moved in closer, resting an arm on the top stall rung and looking like he didn't want her to go.

"Yes. And Emily asked me to photograph the Christmas decorations."

"I drove by the ranch yesterday evening. Very impressive."

He was right. The display, while elaborate, was tasteful instead of tacky. Multicolored lights adorned the house and had been strung along the fence bordering the front yard. Battery-operated candles lit every window. An antique horse-drawn sled, complete with runners, had been set up in the front yard. A pair of lighted life-size reindeer were tethered to the sleigh, which was filled with gaily wrapped fake presents. A huge wreath sporting a big red bow hung on the front door. Smaller matching wreaths adorned the front gate. The twenty-foot saguaro cactus at the end of the driveway had been transformed into a comical Santa Claus, complete with long white beard trailing to the ground.

And that was only the beginning. The decorating company had even more plans for the inside. Jewel couldn't wait to see what they'd done.

"You should bring your parents by," she said.

"Mom would like that." The corners of his mouth tilted up in that attractive way she'd always found impossible to resist. She would have turned away if not for the invisible pull.

No. Not happening. He wasn't going to distract her. Tanner Bridwell wasn't the same man she'd once known, and his moral compass no longer pointed true north.

"I'll see you at two." She ducked past him and escaped before he had a chance to reply. Teddy Bear was forced to trot in order to keep up with her on their way back to his stall inside the horse barn.

The hours dragged by after that. Jewel busied herself with never-ending laundry, updating her online portfolio and touching base with some of her old barrel racing friends who were thrilled with her recent progress. She also gave herself a very lengthy talk about the dangers of avoiding any intimacies with Tanner. When he arrived at her quarters five minutes early, her defenses were firmly in place.

She had just finished putting a bottle of pumped breast milk in the refrigerator when she heard his knock. The skip her heart made in response was irritating. Apparently, she hadn't been listening to the talk she'd given herself earlier.

"Come in." She opened the door wide.

"You okay?" he asked, removing his cowboy hat.

"Yeah. Why?"

He pointed. "You have that funny crease in your forehead you get when you're mad."

"I do?" She ran her fingertips across her forehead and schooled her features into a semblance of calm. "It's nothing."

Tanner's attention was already elsewhere. "Hey, look at you!" He covered the small room in three long strides to where Ava sat in a foam baby seat in the middle of the floor. He dropped to his knees in front of her. "You're sitting up. Like a big kid."

Ava broke into the wide toothless grin she reserved just for Tanner and flailed her arms.

"I just started using it today." Jewel came over to stand beside them.

He reached out his hand, and Ava grabbed the closest finger as she'd done before. "She seems to like it."

"Makes feeding her rice cereal easier. That's also something new we started this week. I was about to give her some when you knocked on the door." She went over to the kitchen unit where the warmed bowl of cereal sat. "I wasn't sure she'd like solid food, but she's taking to the cereal pretty well. It'll help Tracee keep her content when I'm gone for more than a couple hours."

"Or help me when I'm taking care of her," Tanner added.

Jewel's breath caught. Was it possible? Would Tanner be taking care of Ava without her around?

More than possible. It was likely. Inevitable.

Realistically, there was no connection between Tanner attempting to cheat and his ability to care for Ava. Even so, she couldn't stop herself from trying to make one.

She started forward. By the time she reached him, he was galloping the stuffed pony in front of Ava, whose lopsided grin widened. The cuteness overload wasn't enough to diminish Jewel's anxiety.

"Can I try feeding her?" he asked.

"Ah…" She had no valid reason to refuse him. If she did say no, she'd come off as being difficult. Better to save digging in her heels for a bigger battle with higher stakes. She handed him the bowl and spoon. "Small bites."

Tanner took to feeding Ava rice cereal as quickly as she'd taken to eating it. Without being told, he blew on the cereal before offering it to Ava. She tracked the spoon as it neared her mouth, opened wide and wiggled her feet while mouthing the cereal.

"That's my girl," Tanner crooned as if she'd accomplished a huge feat.

His girl?

Jewel continued watching. He was good with Ava, no denying that. Whatever else he'd done, he appeared to take parenting seriously.

All right. Maybe his compass wasn't quite as far off true north as she'd first assumed.

"I think she's done," Tanner announced a few minutes later.

Jewel had been able to tear herself away and pack her camera equipment for the two scheduled shoots, the Christmas decorations and the wedding this evening.

"Here, I'll wash up the bowl and spoon."

She bent and reached down at the same moment Tanner unexpectedly stood. Unprepared, they bumped heads.

"You okay?" he asked, reaching for her.

The touch of his hand on her skin released a tingling sensation that traveled the length of her arm. It was, Jewel realized, their first physical contact since over a year ago, other than passing Ava back and forth.

"I'm fine." She didn't pull away, and he didn't remove his hand.

"You sure?"

Truthfully, she wasn't sure of anything. And not all of her disconcertment was the result of finding Tanner after thinking he was gone from her life forever. A lot of it had to do with her lingering attraction to him.

Darn it! She was supposed to be over him. She *was* over him. "You should go. Now."

His voice deepened. "Is that what you want?"

"Yes."

Why did his grip have be so strong and self-assured? Why did her cheeks burn and her head feel light?

"All right." He let his hand drop, and Jewel's

strength evaporated. "See you, kiddo." He stroked Ava's downy head. "Have fun with Tracee."

Jewel walked him to the door, grateful when it shut behind him. In the very next instant, she scolded herself.

She needed to forget any notion of a lingering romance between them. They couldn't work in close proximity and co-parent Ava with Jewel harboring unrequited…what?

Don't say it, she warned herself. *Don't even think it.*

Except, she did.

To some, December twelfth might seem too early for a Christmas-themed wedding. Not to Jewel. Upon entering the chapel for a few practice shots and to determine the best lighting, she released a soft gasp of delight.

Green and red ribbons with long tails stretching to the floor adorned the ends of each pew. Silver and gold bells hung from the ceiling. Christmas lilies with lovely slender leaves and blossoms resembling white trumpets had been placed throughout. A glittering red carpet adorned the center aisle, and twin miniature pine trees with tiny doves perching on their branches flanked the altar.

Lifting her camera, Jewel began taking pictures. She'd just moved to a discreet spot near the altar, where she'd have a nice view of the bride and groom, when Emily breezed in. She carried a pair of white unity candles with red ribbons fastened around their bases.

"There you are." She made her way to the table behind the altar, where she placed the candles for use later during the service.

"Just checking on the lighting." Jewel impulsively snapped a few quick shots of Emily inspecting her handiwork.

The older woman raised a hand in protest. "Stop that. Don't you be taking pictures of me when a beautiful young bride is due any second."

Jewel joined her at the table and, holding the camera at an angle, showed Emily the photos on the small screen. "See. You look great."

"Ha!" Emily scoffed, but she did linger, studying the images.

"How about I take a portrait of you and your husband? No charge, of course."

"A portrait?"

"Better yet, one of the entire family. You can post it on your website with a holiday wish from Sweetheart Ranch. Or make an ecard and send it to your clients."

Emily chuckled, only to immediately sober. "Let me think about it."

Jewel figured they'd be arranging a photography session once the idea had a chance to sink in.

A noise from the foyer alerted them to the bride's arrival, along with her bridesmaids and parents. The groom was due later, after the bride was sequestered in the private dressing room. Jewel was planning on photographing both bride and groom in their respective dressing rooms getting ready for their big day.

"It's showtime," Emily said gaily and headed for the foyer.

Jewel followed more slowly, waiting for an introduction. Afterward, she wound her way through the house to the kitchen and the pantry where she'd stowed her purse. Emily had a strict rule—no phone interruptions while on duty. Jewel understood and willingly complied. She was being paid to focus on the couple and their guests, not be on her phone.

Besides, she wasn't too worried. Ava was in capable hands and a short walk away. If something were to happen, Tracee could be here in a flash or call the house on the landline.

Finishing, Jewel headed for the bride's dressing room and knocked softly on the door. The bride and her bridesmaids were delighted to pose for their getting-ready photos and requested a few shots of the bride and her mother. Jewel suggested the bride sit on the velvet-cushioned bench next to an antique oval mirror. She then positioned the mother behind her daughter, instructing her to fasten a string of pearls around her daughter's neck.

By the time Jewel was done, the groom and his party had arrived and were in his dressing room. Jewel took a series of similar photos with them. She particularly liked a candid shot of the groom and his father, their heads dipped together and the father's hand on his son's shoulder.

Soon, it was time for the wedding to start. Jewel waited anxiously in the entryway outside the chapel with the bride and her father. The wedding dress, a gorgeous gold-and-silver creation with red and gold beading along the hem and neckline, almost perfectly matched the decorations in the chapel. The effect was enhanced by the bouquet of lilies the bride held and the sprigs of holly clipped to her upswept hair.

The groom's tuxedo, as well as those of his groomsmen, was a soft gray with dark green stripes down the pant legs and on the jacket cuffs. They wore boutonnieres made of the same holly that was in the bride's hair.

The effect should have been corny but was instead stunning. The only thing missing was snow.

Jewel began snapping pictures and didn't stop. She couldn't help thinking that if not for the cheating scandal, she and Tanner would have had a Christmas wedding—though nothing this elegant. Not in Las Vegas, certainly. Still, she might have carried a bouquet of lilies and pinned a sprig of holly to Tanner's shirt collar.

A moment later, she chided herself. She and Tanner were a thing of the past. No purpose was served by thinking about what hadn't happened and never would.

Why, then, did her mind insist on revisiting that moment from earlier today, when her defenses had been momentarily lowered? It had been right after he'd fed Ava her cereal—which, of course, explained it. Jewel was always at her most vulnerable where her daughter was concerned. She quickly steeled her defenses.

Slipping quietly to another part of the chapel, she continued photographing the wedding. It was being officiated by Emily's husband, Homer, a retired minister from one of the local churches. He had a quaint, down-home manner of speaking that, from what Jewel had seen, resonated with the couples and guests.

Something he'd said had her paying closer attention. He was talking about problems appearing less daunting and storms being easier to weather with a loving and trusted partner.

The words circled inside Jewel's head. She'd once trusted Tanner with every fiber of her being and believed them capable of weathering any storm. Then, he'd betrayed that trust, and the storm had hit with a vengeance. She had yet to fully recover.

Could the change in him have anything to do with his brother? After she and Tanner had split, she'd learned from mutual friends that Daniel had been diagnosed much earlier than people were originally told. According to Tanner, Daniel had hidden his condition, wanting to finish out the year competing before having his surgery.

Receiving the news that his brother had a brain tumor, might not survive the surgery and would be disabled to some degree if he did survive must have devastated Tanner. He loved his older brother and had always looked up to him. He'd wanted Daniel to win the championship almost as much as he'd wanted to win it himself.

So why cheat? Jewel couldn't make any sense of it. Unless she hadn't known Tanner nearly as well as she thought she had.

Once the standard postwedding group shots were done, Jewel snuck off for a five-minute break, heading to the kitchen pantry to check her phone. There were no messages or texts. Even so, she called Tracee, who assured her Ava was sleeping soundly.

The reception was well underway when Jewel

reached the parlor. She accommodated numerous requests from guests who wanted photos with an old friend or relatives they rarely saw. The toasts were touching and funny and sentimental. Many a person dabbed at their moist eyes with a tissue.

Shortly after the cake cutting, Jewel was excused. She congratulated the newlyweds before leaving, letting them know when and how to expect the photographs from her. They thanked her profusely. Emily squeezed her arm and told her what a great job she'd done.

Jewel was walking three feet off the ground when she returned to the kitchen pantry at a little after 9:00 p.m. It was moments like these when she started to believe she really could make a successful career as a photographer.

Grabbing her purse, she fished in the side pocket for her phone. The tiny green light flashed, signaling a missed call.

Three missed calls, to be precise, and two text messages. All from Tracee!

Pulse racing, Jewel read the first message, the words exploding off the screen like tiny firecrackers.

Sorry, Jewel, I had to leave. My brother fell and broke his wrist. Taking him to the ER. Called Tanner to watch Ava.

Jewel was instantly on the move, wrenching open the kitchen door. Only when cold air struck her bare arms did she realize she'd forgotten her jacket. Her camera, still hanging from the strap around her neck, bounced with every frantic step.

Surely Ava was all right. She'd been asleep when Jewel last spoke to Tracee and usually didn't wake until one or two in the morning for a feeding and changing. If anyone deserved her worry, it was Tracee's brother.

Still, Jewel increased her pace, nearly running now. All the while, she berated herself for not checking her phone more frequently. Ava was just shy of five months old. Tiny and helpless. What kind of mother was Jewel to leave her alone, even in capable hands?

Except Ava was now with Tanner, who'd had no experience with babies until recently. He would have fetched Jewel at the main house if something were wrong with Ava, yes?

She was breathing hard when she reached the carriage house. That didn't stop her from charging up the stairs, her feet pounding on the wooden steps. At the landing, she threw open the door to her quarters—only to come to a grinding halt just inside.

Tanner sat in the recliner, a sleeping Ava cradled on his lap. He greeted Jewel with a happy smile and an index finger pressed to his lips, warning her to be quiet.

All that worrying for nothing. Her baby was perfectly fine.

Jewel, not so much. As she stared at Tanner, she recognized the light shining in his eyes and knew with struck-from-nowhere clarity that those unrequited feelings she didn't want to admit having weren't unrequited at all. And with so many unanswered questions and unresolved issues, the timing couldn't have been worse.

CHAPTER SIX

Tanner pushed up from the recliner, careful not to disturb Ava, and carried her to the travel crib. Though her eyes remained closed, her arm jerked reflexively, and she mewed softly.

Jewel tiptoed over to them and watched with an eagle eye as he lowered Ava into the crib.

"Lay her on her left side," she whispered. "That's how she likes to sleep."

Tanner did as Jewel instructed. When he was done, she arranged a yellow blanket over Ava and tucked in the corners, then stood unmoving while staring down at the baby.

"You okay?" he asked softly.

She motioned for him to follow and started toward the table. "I practically ran all the way here." Taking the camera from around her neck, she set it and her phone on the table. "I think I may have overreacted a little when I read Tracee's text message."

"She didn't mean to upset you."

"I'm sure she didn't. She was upset herself."

"Ava slept the entire time—she didn't even wake up when I knocked on the door."

Jewel pushed at her disheveled hair. "I'm still pretty new at this parenting stuff and easily panic."

He lowered himself into the chair across from her, observing that the creases marring her lovely brow when she'd first arrived were fading. "You're doing an incredible job."

"You are, too."

Her praise pleased him. "You think?"

"Yeah, I do." Her tone contained a hint of surprise.

He wasn't offended. He was newer at this parenting stuff than she and constantly surprising himself.

"Tracee tried to call you," he said.

"I didn't have my phone during the wedding and reception."

They continued their conversation in hushed voices, though Ava didn't stir.

"How's her brother?" Jewel asked.

"Not sure. He and a pal were skateboarding at the park, and he took a bad fall. Guess he toughed it out in front of his pal, but when he got home and saw his swollen wrist, fear took over. Their parents are at a Christmas concert tonight. They probably had their phones shut off, too. When her brother couldn't reach them, he called Tracee. She felt terrible about leaving Ava."

"She didn't have a choice. Fifteen or not, he's still her baby brother, and she loves him."

Jewel's phone vibrated, and Tracee's name appeared on the display. She grabbed the phone and put it to her ear. "She must have heard us talking about her."

Their call didn't last long. From Jewel's end of the conversation, Tanner deduced that Tracee's brother had sustained a bad sprain and not a break as was initially feared. They'd finally reached their parents who'd met Tracee and her brother at the emergency room. Tracee was profoundly sorry and promised it wouldn't happen again.

"You did the right thing," Jewel assured her. After that, they confirmed what time tomorrow evening Tracee would be there and said goodbye.

Jewel expelled a long breath and sank into the chair.

Tanner asked the question on his mind all during the phone call. "Did she? Do the right thing by calling me?"

"Yes. Of course." Jewel sat up. "Ava wasn't hurt or sick."

Her response didn't exactly reassure Tanner.

"Are you saying that if Ava had been hurt or sick, calling me *wouldn't* be the right thing?"

"No. Not at all. I'd hope, in those circumstances, Tracee would have come to the house and found me."

"All right." That was reasonable, he supposed. "And then you would have called me?"

She hesitated a bit too long. "Sure. Absolutely."

It was getting late, almost nine thirty according to the clock on the microwave. Tanner should leave. Except Jewel's hesitation had bothered him. So instead, he raised the subject that he'd told his dad a few days ago he wasn't ready to discuss with her.

"Have you decided whether you're staying in Mustang Valley or returning to Oklahoma?"

"Not yet. Emily hasn't offered me a permanent job, though things seem to be going well. I imagine she'll wait until my month-long trial is up. I would if I were her."

"And if she does offer you a job, will you take it?"

"Honestly, I'm not sure. The barrel racing's improving. I'm feeling more and more like my old self every day, and Ronnie's optimism is rubbing off on me."

He'd watched enough of her lessons and practice runs to know that was a fact. A year's break from the sport hadn't diminished her talent or her determination.

"Have you hired an attorney? For Ava's custody," he clarified, though the sudden flicker in her eyes gave a clear indication she'd understood him.

"Do I need to?" she asked.

"We have to decide soon. Before you return home." Which was three short weeks away.

"Decide as in who obtains full custody?"

"How we *share* custody."

"All right." She spoke crisply. "I guess I'll be making some calls tomorrow."

What had she been thinking? That he'd go along with whatever she decided and not exert his rights?

"My earlier offer still holds," he said. "I'll go on the road with you if you return to rodeoing."

"In your own vehicle?"

"I can do that." He and his brother had often traveled with a truck and camper from rodeo to rodeo. As far as Tanner knew, the camper was still stored at Daniel's house.

"If people see us together," Jewel said, "and they will, there's bound to be some nasty remarks made. I'm not ready for that again. I realize I can't escape free and clear, but if we're with each other, the remarks are bound to be worse, and my concentration will be shot."

"I'll keep a low profile." He understood her concerns. She might have won a championship title last year if not for him, and he refused to take that from her again should she return to the circuit. But understanding didn't stop him from wishing things were different. "I hope to have the situation resolved soon."

She narrowed her gaze at him. "What does that mean?"

"I'm working on a solution. I promise."

"What kind of solution?"

Not leveling with her was getting harder and harder by the minute. If he hadn't just spoken to Daniel earlier today, Tanner had no doubt he'd be confessing everything to Jewel right now.

But he held back. His brother had been a wreck when they'd talked and had begged Tanner not to say anything. Much of what he'd conveyed to Tanner echoed what their father had said, and Tanner suspected their dad of instigating the call.

Or maybe not. Daniel had also said Rosalyn had taken the kids and stayed at her sister's house the previous night, though she was home now. They'd had a particularly ugly argument, which Daniel admitted he'd started. He'd lost his temper. The exam with his doctor that morning hadn't been encouraging. Daniel's leg would likely not improve, despite continued physical therapy, and may even worsen.

He hadn't taken the news well. How could he possibly provide for his wife and children, get off disability and hold down a decent job if he couldn't drive? Rosalyn, unfortunately, had suffered the brunt of his anger, which he regretted. Daniel was convinced if she found out he'd tried to bribe that judge, she'd divorce him for sure.

"Tanner? What kind of solution?" Jewel repeated.

Shoving thoughts of his brother aside, he said, "I'm not sure yet. Give me time."

"How much? Until our respective attorneys start talking? Until the end of my month here?"

"I'm trying my best. We both are."

She nodded stiffly.

"I can't tell you how much I wish things were different."

"Me, too."

Different how? Did she, like him, often imagine the life they might have had together and long for it? Or did she regret his reappearance in her life and wish him gone? He almost asked but stopped himself at the last second, afraid he might not like the answer. And if he didn't, then what?

"I'd better go." He grabbed his cowboy hat from where it hung on the chair back. "I have an early morning. The ranch is hosting a 4-H holiday event."

She walked him to the door. When he reached for the knob, she stayed him with a hand on his arm.

"Tanner, wait."

He turned.

She took a moment to gather her thoughts. "It isn't always easy for me, relinquishing control where Ava's concerned. Please don't take this as me being difficult or contrary..."

"What?"

"I worry. Constantly. I don't know what lies ahead. For me, career-wise, and for us as Ava's parents."

The slight tremor in her voice pulled at him and, without thinking, he moved toward her. "I can say exactly the same thing about myself."

"I see that you're trying with Ava and with me. I know the good and moral and wonderful man I fell in love with is still in you. Which just confuses me all the more. What happened last year? Were you getting cold feet about our wedding?"

"No way. I couldn't wait to marry you."

"Then what?" Her sorrowful expression tore at him. "Did it have to do with Daniel? Because I know he was sick at the time and hiding it. That had to be terrible for him and you and your entire family."

"It was terrible. And it did affect my thinking." In more ways than she realized.

When he said no more, her shoulders sagged with disappointment. "Guess I'll see you tomorrow at ten."

Jewel didn't have barrel racing lessons on the weekends, and her only wedding was at seven that evening, leaving her free for most of the day. Tanner, too, was free, after the morning feeding.

"Okay to meet at the bunkhouse?" he asked. "I can make coffee. Pick up some breakfast sandwiches from the market."

She started to refuse him; he could see her mouth forming the word *no*. But then she changed her mind. "That would be nice, actually."

A small positive step in the right direction. What if he took another bigger one?

Tanner raised his hand and cupped Jewel's cheek as he'd done a hundred, a thousand times in the past. His thumb stroked the smooth skin that warmed beneath his touch and then grew hot as he lowered his head another fraction.

That wasn't her only response to him. Her breath became shallow and rapid. Her eyes widened with interest, he was pleased to see, and not alarm. Her lips parted. She tilted her head to the side—which Tanner interpreted as an invitation and increased the pressure of his caress.

Kissing her was simply a matter of leaning in and claiming her lips. One small move on his part, and she'd be his again. The timing probably stank, but Tanner wasn't going to think about that now. He couldn't. His mind was too occupied with memories of Jewel and him. Together. In love. Wanting and needing each other. Happy.

He reached for her with his other hand, his arm ready to capture her waist and draw her flush against him. At the same time, she retreated a step, and his hand merely brushed her side and fell. The cool air that rushed in to occupy the suddenly vacant space between them might have been an arctic blast—the effect on Tanner was the same.

"We can't," she uttered, her gaze avoiding his.

"I get that things are complicated." He wasn't ready to give up. "But who's to say kissing might not *un*complicate it?"

"It won't. I… You broke my heart when you put yourself first at the rodeo finals. Winning a championship, by any means necessary, was more important to you than we were. Than I was."

"That's not true." He'd put Daniel ahead, only she didn't know that.

"I'm not sure I'll ever get over it."

Her conviction caused him to take a step back. "*Ever* is a strong word."

"I'm sorry, Tanner. But a man who cheats isn't the kind of man I want for a romantic partner."

Fury at the situation rose up in Tanner and hardened his heart. "And not the kind of man you want for your child's father."

"I didn't say that."

"You didn't have to. I figured that out when you didn't tell my parents or Ethan you were pregnant. You didn't want to find me. Not really."

"Can you blame me?"

Up till recently, he had. To a degree. Tanner acknowledged he was mostly responsible for what had happened. He had agreed to take the blame for his brother. But while Jewel had lost faith in him, he'd lost faith in her, too. If she'd given the slightest indication that she thought him incapable of cheating or would stand by him regardless, he'd have ignored the consequences and his promise to his dad and told her the entire story.

More arguing would get them nowhere, however. Not right now. "I'll see you tomorrow, Jewel."

This time when he reached for the doorknob, she didn't stop him. Not that he would have stayed.

"THAT'S MY SWEET BABY," Jewel crooned and stroked the velvety-smooth face. "You know how much I love you." She slipped her free hand inside her jacket pocket. "I brought you something. A special treat. Because you've been such a good darling."

Teddy Bear snorted and pressed his nose into her hair, sniffing curiously.

"Stop that, you silly boy." She produced a carrot from her pocket and held it out. "Here."

The horse, his head hanging over the stall door, lipped the treat and then grabbed it with his teeth, swiftly sucking the entire carrot into his mouth. Four crunches later, he was done and searching for another handout.

She gave him one. "I should have named you Mr. Piggy."

Ava wriggled inside the baby wrap and made a gurgling sound.

"No carrots for you." Jewel kissed the top of her head. "Not quite yet. And those will be strained."

She finished giving Teddy Bear the remainder of his snack. The two of them were taking the day off from barrel racing practice. The horse loved the sport and would have gladly done whatever Jewel asked of him. But she was without a babysitter until later this evening when Jewel had a wedding to photograph. Ronnie's cousin was getting married, and she was the matron of honor. Since Jewel didn't have lessons on the weekend, and her trainer was occupied, she'd decided a day off was in order.

Hearing voices from another part of the horse barn, she gave a start, her mind returning to the day she had unexpectedly encountered Tanner in this same spot. He didn't appear. No one did, and she silently scolded herself for overreacting.

She wasn't ready to face him. Not yet. Another twenty minutes remained before their meeting at his bunkhouse, and she'd need every one of them to compose herself.

What had she been thinking last night? He'd almost kissed her. *She'd* almost kissed *him*.

For one crazy, irrational moment, she'd been the old Jewel and he the old Tanner. Their mutual attraction, always off the charts, had ignited anew. Perhaps because of the many emotions their conversation had stirred and—she almost hated admitting this—the intimacy created by them sharing a child. She'd been *this close* to reaching for him and losing herself in the passion he so easily evoked. Thank goodness she'd come to her senses before doing something she'd have regretted.

She *would* have regretted it, right? Yes. Of course. Too much unpleasant history lay between them.

Even so, a small part of her kept imagining his lips taking possession of hers and demanding a response as they once had. The thought caused her tummy to flutter with—

"Enough!" she bit out.

"Enough of what?"

Jewel whirled. She'd been so absorbed with thoughts of Tanner, the two of them locked in a heated embrace, she'd failed to notice Ronnie's approach.

"Oops. You caught me talking to myself." She tried to hide her embarrassment with a half chuckle. "Must be from lack of sleep."

"Ava keep you up last night?"

"We were wide-awake at two and far more interested in eating and playing than sleeping."

Jewel wasn't about to admit the real reason for her disconcertment—or why she'd had no appetite this morning and made an excuse when Emily had asked her if she was feeling all right.

"I didn't expect to see you until tonight," Jewel said. "I figured you'd be getting ready for the wedding."

"I'm leaving soon. My cousin's been texting me every ten minutes with something new I need to pick up on my way to the house. We have a stylist coming this afternoon to do our hair and makeup." Ronnie tugged on the tail of her messy braid. "I'm going to need a lot of help."

"You'll be gorgeous. I can't wait to photograph the results."

"I'd leave now, but I promised three of my other students I'd help them get ready for the barrel racing event at the Poco Dinero. I usually go, but seeing as I have another commitment, I can't," she added with the grin of a delighted maid of honor.

The local saloon hosted recreational bull riding on Friday and Saturday evenings and barrel racing on Saturday afternoons. The popular events were well attended, with people coming from all over the state to both participate and watch. Many a former or hopeful rodeo professional competed, along with a few brave amateurs. The events were a great proving ground, providing participants with an experience that resembled the real thing. The prize money wasn't all that bad, either, from what Jewel had gathered.

"That's dedication," Jewel said. "I hope the other students appreciate you."

"I'd feel bad if I didn't help them. Today's

the last rodeo event for the year. There won't be another one until mid-January." Ronnie brightened. "You should sign up."

"I don't know if I'm ready."

"You are, Jewel. More than ready. And besides, you have to get your feet wet sometime. No better place than the Poco Dinero for that. I just wish I could be there."

"Isn't it too late to sign up?"

"You have up until the event starts."

She debated the pros and cons. Ronnie was right about her needing to get her feet wet and the Poco Dinero providing a good opportunity. It might also take her mind off Tanner. At the very least, Jewel would be able to gauge how well she performed with thoughts of him constantly plaguing her. And since the situation was unlikely to change, better to see how she coped sooner rather than later.

"I'd need a babysitter," she mused aloud. "My regular one isn't available. Not sure I can arrange that."

"Well, if you can find someone, you really should sign up."

"I'll try."

Tracee's grandmother had been recommended as a backup babysitter. Jewel might give the woman a call.

A memory of Tanner sitting in the recliner

and rocking Ava popped into her head, but she immediately dismissed him as a potential candidate. He'd probably be working, anyway, and not available.

That was the reason she gave herself, and the one she was determined to stick with.

Ronnie offered Jewel some last-minute advice, as if her competing at the Poco Dinero was a done deal. When Tanner suddenly entered the barn and strode toward them, Jewel was again startled, clear to the tips of her toes.

"Morning, ladies." He nodded as he neared.

What was he doing here! He'd told her that he avoided Ronnie—or anyone else who might remember him—whenever she was at the ranch.

"H-hello," she stammered and snuck a peek at her trainer, inwardly cringing at the mild alarm on the woman's face, followed by recognition. "Ronnie, this is Tanner."

"Good morning." Ronnie offered a curious smile. "It's Tanner Bridwell, right? I hardly recognized you without the beard. I think we met once or twice on the circuit."

"We did." He nodded politely. "Nice to see you again."

"I didn't realize you worked here."

"I tend to keep a low profile. Easier that way."

"I get it. You took a lot of heat last year."

Jewel held her breath, worried where the conversation would go next and if it would become awkward.

Tanner steered it away from him. Cupping Ava's cheek with his large hand, he said, "I just wanted to let you know I'll be done in about ten minutes."

Ava cooed, liking his touch as much as Jewel always had.

"Okay," she murmured, still recovering.

With a nod and a friendly smile, he continued down the barn aisle, the tune he whistled floating in the air behind him.

Ronnie spun to face Jewel, her hands on her hips. "Why didn't you tell me that was Tanner?"

She swallowed. "He asked me not to say anything."

"My God, all these months, I had no idea he worked for the Powells. Did you?"

"Not until my first day. He…surprised me. Right here, in fact."

Ronnie's jaw dropped. "That must have been a shock!"

"You can say that again."

"It's none of my business, and you don't have to tell me if you'd rather not, but I'm assuming he's Ava's father."

Jewel sighed. "He is."

"Did he know?"

She was at a point in the conversation where

she either cut Ronnie off, saying she didn't want to talk about Tanner, or she revealed the entire story. The idea of confiding in someone who knew about her and Tanner without Jewel having to repeat all the painful details was appealing.

"No. I tried to locate him after I found out I was pregnant, but he'd come to Mustang Valley by then and was lying low. He and Ethan Powell are good friends."

"Why lie low?"

Jewel explained about the potential lawsuits from the arena owners and his brother Daniel's cancer battle, ending with, "Tanner and his brother own stock in the family business. His dad's concerned if the arena owners were to come after Tanner, the family business could be named in the suit."

"Suing seems excessive. Would the arena owners really do that?"

"I think it's excessive, too. Not the company attorney, however. He's convinced the potential is very real."

Real enough that Tanner had sacrificed a great deal to protect his family. Jewel was torn. Part of her admired him for putting them first. Another part of her was angry he hadn't put her first. Her feelings weren't necessarily logical, but that didn't change them.

"What are you two doing about Ava?" Ronnie asked.

"We're still deciding. I'll be hiring an attorney soon."

"I feel sorry for him. For his whole family. They've had some pretty hard knocks. His brother, especially." Ronnie shook her head. "I wouldn't wish brain cancer on my worst enemy."

"Me, neither."

"I never really understood Tanner cheating. Not that I knew him well." Ronnie scrunched her mouth in thought. "I mean, he was favored to win. He and his brother. Unless something went terribly wrong, either one of them was likely to walk away with a championship."

"I guess sometimes people become desperate." Even as she said it, Jewel doubted her statement. Tanner had never been the desperate type. He'd had no reason, not with his enormous talent. She was less sure about Daniel.

"Did you know about the cheating? Gosh, I'm sorry." Ronnie looked chagrined. "That's none of my business."

Jewel waved away her concern. "It's okay and, honestly, I had no clue."

Ronnie's phone pinged again, alerting her to a text. "That's probably my cousin. I'd better hurry." She impulsively hugged Jewel. "You going to be all right?"

"I'll be fine."

"If you ever need a willing ear to bend, I'm available."

"Thanks." Jewel felt a lump rise in her throat. "That means a lot."

"And I was serious about you entering the barrel racing this afternoon." Ronnie wagged a finger at Jewel as she walked away.

"I'll try."

Giving Teddy Bear a last pat, Jewel adjusted Ava in the baby wrap before heading toward the bunkhouse and her visit with Tanner. At the door, she knocked. When he didn't answer, she figured she was early and, pulling out her phone, sent Tracee a text asking for her grandmother's number. Tracee responded immediately and Jewel placed the call. A voice mail greeting kicked in, and she left a message after identifying herself.

She was just finishing when Tanner appeared from around the corner of the bunkhouse.

"Did I hear correctly? You need a babysitter this afternoon?" he asked.

Shoot. Now what? "Possibly. I haven't de-cided."

"What's going on?"

She couldn't easily hide her plans. He'd see

her loading Teddy Bear in her horse trailer and leaving.

"I'm thinking about entering the barrel racing event at the Poco Dinero."

"That's a great idea. You should." He opened the door and gestured for her to precede him.

"I'm still considering."

"I'll babysit Ava."

If she refused him, they'd get into an argument. He'd insist he was Ava's father and should be allowed. And he'd be right. The other option was that she didn't enter the competition.

"I probably won't." Inside the bunkhouse, she unwound Ava from the baby wrap. "I need more practice."

"The competition is practice." He took Ava from her and settled the baby against his chest. "You scared?"

"No way!" Jewel immediately realized he'd goaded her and could have kicked herself.

"Then what's holding you back?"

"Nothing."

"Let me guess. You don't want to leave Ava with me."

"Tanner…"

"I'm not going to kidnap her."

Her face heated with embarrassment. "Of course not."

"Then you must think I'm inept at solo parenting. You know, Tracee's not a parent, and you trust Ava with her."

"Tracee has a lot of babysitting experience," Jewel countered. "And she's on the grounds when she's watching Ava, here or at Sweetheart Ranch. Not several miles away."

"Well, I'm going to have to learn eventually." He would, when he had shared custody.

"I'm sorry," she admitted. "I'm really not trying to be difficult."

"What if *we* took her to the Poco Dinero, and I watched her there while you're competing?"

"I thought you avoided places like that." There was always the chance they'd run into people familiar with the scandal and suffer some of the same negative attention as last year. In her opinion, that was another reason for her to enter. She'd need to develop a thick skin if she returned to the rodeo circuit.

"I can handle any flack," Tanner said. "Can you?"

"Yes." She hoped she could. Would it be worse now that she had Ava? Being a mother had changed her. Made her more sensitive and emotional at times.

"Good." He sat with the baby on the couch and began gently bouncing her. "Hey, kiddo, looks like you and me are going with your mom to watch her barrel race."

Indeed. It looked like they were. Jewel gritted her teeth.

CHAPTER SEVEN

TANNER ADJUSTED THE girth on Jewel's saddle. Old habits were hard to break, he supposed. He used to help her get ready for every competition back when they were together. She hadn't objected when he'd begun checking snaps and refastening buckles, so perhaps the same held true for her, too.

Teddy Bear was tied to Jewel's horse trailer—they'd parked behind the Poco Dinero Saloon in a large dirt lot reserved for competitors. The barrel racing had been underway for over an hour and a half and was nearing an end. As the last person to sign up, Jewel would be the last competitor to go. The position offered one advantage—she got to watch everyone who went before her and adjust her strategy accordingly. It was also nerve-racking, having to wait and seeing the others doing well.

She stood at a vantage point not far away that allowed her to observe the runs and hear the results. All the while, she absently rocked Ava in the stroller. The baby was behaving well, considering the level of noise and activity.

The recreational rodeo arena and stands had been decorated for the holidays, along with the inside and outside of the saloon. Posters advertising a holiday dance, taking place tonight right after the bull riding, hung on walls and doors. Patrons sipped from holiday beverage cups.

Tanner didn't consider asking Jewel to the dance, much as he might have liked that. He was maintaining his low profile. Here, at least. At the ranch this morning, he'd desperately wanted Ronnie—wanted *anyone* not part of his or Jewel's family—to know he was Ava's father. The same didn't hold true at the Poco Dinero. To hide his identity, he wore his baseball cap with its rounded brim pulled down over his brow, a pair of dark sunglasses and the collar of his jacket turned up. Ava had cried when she'd first seen him in his getup, until he'd removed the sunglasses and spoken to her.

Though the crowd appeared to be mostly non-rodeo people, there was still the possibility he'd be recognized and insulting remarks would be directed at Jewel. To prevent that, Tanner was sticking near the truck and trailer rather than joining the spectators in the stands. A year wasn't that long, and some observant individual might put two and two together.

Jewel deserved this opportunity to test her abilities and determine if she still had what was needed to successfully compete. Going on the road with her wasn't his first choice. He'd hate leaving his boss in a jam. Ethan had treated Tanner well. Tanner also preferred to stay close to his brother, who needed his support. But he'd go to the North Pole and back rather than be parted from Ava.

And Jewel. He'd be lying if he said he didn't want to spend more time with her, and not just as the mother of his child. Tensions between them ran high as often as they didn't. But wasn't passion a close cousin to tension?

His glance cut to where she'd been standing, only she'd moved and was now taking pictures of the competitors, the crowd, the judge and the riders waiting on deck for their turn.

Looking away was hard, so Tanner didn't. He enjoyed seeing her at work, her lovely features knit in concentration or brightening when something interesting caught her eye.

The next moment, she was approached by one of the earlier competitors. Tanner was certain he recognized the woman from their days on the rodeo circuit, and a ball of anxiety lodged in his stomach. If she was any good at judging babies' ages, she'd correctly deduce Tanner was

Ava's father and possibly say something unkind to Jewel.

Fortunately, no one pointed in his direction or acknowledged him in the least. Jewel's exchange with the woman appeared friendly and relaxed. That didn't stop him from wishing Jewel would turn and beckon him to join her.

The woman fawned over Ava, lowering her head to the baby's level and making funny faces. A third person Tanner didn't know was recruited to take a picture of the woman and Jewel with the woman's phone. When she finally left, Jewel turned and headed back toward Tanner and the parking area, pushing the stroller. As she neared, he noticed her strained expression and that she gnawed her lower lip.

"Nervous?" he asked, hoping her upcoming run was the cause and not her encounter with the former acquaintance.

"A little." She mustered a wan smile. "Okay, more than a little. It's been a year since I competed."

"How soon until they call you?"

"Very soon."

She parked the stroller out of the way and then conducted her own equipment check on the saddle and bridle while Tanner returned the caddy of grooming supplies to the trailer's front storage compartment.

"How's the competition look?" he asked when he was done.

Jewel shrugged and retied one of the ribbons that had come loose in Teddy Bear's braided mane. "There was a time I'd be confident of my ability to leave them in the dust. Not so sure anymore. They're doing well for mostly amateurs."

A minute later, Jewel's number was called to appear on deck. Tanner held the reins with his free hand while she drew in a big breath and mounted Teddy Bear.

"Good luck." Tanner patted her leg as he'd done a couple hundred times in situations just like this before catching himself.

If she noticed the familiar gesture, she didn't let on. "Thanks."

As she trotted toward the arena, he studied the crowd. No way was he staying behind, not if he could help it. Releasing the brake on the stroller, he started toward the stands, his destination a partially hidden spot at the east side where he'd hopefully have a decent view. He thought he noticed someone pointing at him but when he checked again, he decided he'd been wrong.

"There's your mom," he announced to Ava when they arrived at the spot.

Soon enough, Jewel's turn came. A single

exuberant shout erupted to Tanner's left, and he spotted the woman she'd been conversing with earlier through a gap in the crowd.

The next second, Jewel and Teddy Bear blasted into the arena. They bore down on the first barrel, taking the hairpin turn with impressive skill. Teddy Bear stretched his head out as he charged the second barrel. Jewel seemed to mimic him, the upper half of her body leaning forward over his neck in an effort to coax more speed from him.

"Come on," Tanner murmured between gritted teeth. He snuck a look at her time on the overhead electronic scoreboard, his excitement growing. "Yes!" He gripped the stroller handle, inadvertently shaking it. "Your mom's doing great."

Jewel and Teddy Bear barely slowed as they rounded the third barrel. The crowd collectively gasped when the barrel wobbled unsteadily. Tanner's jaw ached from being clenched to the point of bones snapping. Jewel didn't glance back at the barrel and kept going. She knew better than to waste precious tenths of seconds.

Two more wobbles and the barrel righted at the same instant Jewel sailed past the electric timer and out the arena gate. There would be no penalty.

The crowd broke into applause and cheers.

Tanner checked the scoreboard again and whooped when her time appeared. With a clean run and being the last competitor, she'd earned herself a guaranteed second-place spot.

Ava must have been startled by the noise for she began wailing. Tanner eased the stroller from their tight spot. "Your mom won, honey!"

Midway to the trailer, she quieted. A few minutes later, Jewel met up with them, leading Teddy Bear. Her entire face radiated joy. Tanner's heart went still and then began beating again with a force he hadn't felt in a long time. A year, to be exact.

"Congratulations."

She laughed. "At least I didn't embarrass myself."

"Are you kidding?" He lifted Ava from the stroller. "You won second place. I'd say that's darn good."

She opened her arms. Tanner figured she wanted to take Ava from him. He had other ideas, however, and pulled her into a hug, compressing the baby between them. Ava didn't seem to mind, but Jewel attempted to extract herself.

Tanner held on, enjoying the sensation of her in his arms too much to let go. Her resistance faded, and she returned the hug. For five seconds. Then, she broke free, taking Ava with her.

"Mommy took second place," she crooned. "How about that?"

"I'm proud of you." Tanner's gaze lingered on her. "No question, you're ready to hit the circuit come the first of the year."

"I'm not sure. This wasn't a real rodeo."

Tanner could tell her dismissive remark was purely for show. She was thrilled about placing second, even in an amateur event. As she should be.

Jewel's name, along with the first- and third-place winners, was called over the PA system. Barely audible above the rumble of trucks and trailers leaving, the announcer requested their presence at the event booth, probably to collect their winnings. Jewel took Ava with her while Tanner unsaddled Teddy Bear. The crowd of spectators had vacated the stands, many of them heading into the saloon for festivities and celebrating before the bull riding started. A few of the nearby barrel racers tossed curious glances at Tanner, and he continued to keep his head low.

Hearing the unmistakable clatter of a livestock transport truck, he stopped and watched it roll slowly into the nearly empty parking area, brakes squealing and hooves scrambling. Bucking stock was being delivered for tonight's bull riding event. The familiar scents and sounds triggered a flood of memories, and Tanner was instantly transported back in time to his last competition, the one at the NFR when he'd qualified for the final round. Before Daniel had decided to bribe the judge.

If only he'd been aware of his brother's plans, he might have been able to change the entire course of his and Jewel's lives. Of Daniel's life, too, and their parents'.

"Do you miss competing?"

Hearing Jewel's voice, he pivoted. She and Ava had returned while he'd been watching the transport truck.

"Yeah, I do. I wasn't ready to quit."

The answer was out before he could stop himself.

"Then why cheat?"

Of course, she'd asked that question. What had he expected?

"It's complicated," he replied.

By now, the transport truck was backing to a stop beside the livestock pens, its warning alarm beep-beep-beeping loudly. A trio of wranglers piled out of the cab and jogged to the rear of the truck. There, they opened the double gate, allowing the trailer to maneuver into place. Tanner had seen this operation performed countless times at countless rodeos.

He met Jewel's stare. "Not a day goes by that I don't regret my decision," he continued.

She said nothing and promptly put several feet between them. It might as well have been a mile.

He supposed he'd better get accustomed to this kind of reaction from her. As long as she believed he'd attempted to bribe his way to a championship, she was going to treat him coldly. And as long as she continued to believe the worst of him, they didn't stand a chance. Jewel wasn't the only one with a broken heart.

They'd agreed earlier that they'd leave for home right after the barrel racing. With Teddy Bear loaded, Tanner was surprised when Jewel didn't carry Ava over to the truck cab and put her in the car seat. He was more surprised at her next remark, considering the time and place.

"We need to talk about custody, Tanner. Have you retained an attorney yet?"

"No."

She nodded. "Me, neither. But I'm going to. Soon. Probably this coming week. Definitely before the holidays."

And before she left Mustang Valley.

"My dad has the name of a family lawyer for me."

She nodded again but stiffly. What bothered her more? That Tanner already had the name of a lawyer or that the name had come from his father?

"I intend to pay fair child support," he said. "I'm no slacker."

"I know you're not."

What constituted fair child support? Tanner wasn't earning much as a wrangler, though he did have assets in the family business. Assets at risk if the arena owners filed a lawsuit. Would that be factored into his child support payments? It was a good question for his attorney.

Potentially, also a good reason to look for another job, one that paid more. Until he went to work for his dad, leastwise. Or, a second job. He could always train horses on the side or give bull riding lessons. Ava shouldn't be deprived because her father merely scraped by.

"Jewel." There was so much he wanted to tell her.

She started for the truck cab. "Maybe we should leave any further discussion of child support up to the attorneys."

"Right."

Tanner secured the latch on the horse trailer. By the time he climbed into the truck, Jewel had already placed Ava in her car seat and was sitting behind the wheel. They drove to Powell Ranch in silence.

Evening had long fallen when they passed

Sweetheart Ranch. In the dark, the Christmas decorations twinkled merrily. Tanner barely noticed. Neither, it appeared, did Jewel.

TANNER'S HORSE SAW the rattlesnake before anyone else. A split second after the horse jerked sideways, huffing and puffing with fright, Tanner heard the distinctive rattling to his left.

"Whoa, boy."

Pulling back on the reins, he looked down in the direction of the sound. The snake, coiled into a tight circle at the base of a rock, its tail vibrating, raised its head as if preparing to strike.

"Watch it!" he hollered over his shoulders to the five riders behind him and pointed. "There's a rattler by that boulder. Get off the trail now."

He swung his horse to the right. Four of the five riders followed him off the trail and down the slight incline. The last one stopped his horse to take a picture with his phone. The mare he rode wisely refused to get close and resisted all prodding on his part.

"Hey, buddy." Tanner reined to a stop and spoke firmly. "I strongly advise against that."

The man snapped a picture anyway before the mare took matters into her own hands, or hooves, in this case, and hurried away to join the others.

"I thought rattlesnakes went into hibernation

during the winter," the man said, his face flush with excitement.

"They do generally stick to their dens. But we've had a warm spell this week."

Tanner was annoyed with the man and strove to keep his voice level. The danger from the snake hadn't been too great. More likely, the mare would have spooked and bolted and the man toppled off—potentially injuring himself or the horse or his fellow riders. The fact he'd signed a waiver before the trail ride didn't mean Tanner would let him do anything foolhardy.

Leading trail rides wasn't his normal job. And Sundays were supposed to be his day off. But Sawyer had called in sick. The young wrangler had tried his hand at the recreational bull riding last night and taken a pretty bad spill. One of the other wranglers had shown Tanner the video he'd taken with his phone, having himself a good laugh at Sawyer's expense.

Tanner had grimaced. He knew from experience the poor kid was fortunate to have walked away with a few sprains and bruises. That bull had meant business.

He'd have handled the ride differently. Put more of his weight into the lower half of his body. And raised his hand higher for better balance. But Sawyer wasn't a professional bull rider. Merely a twenty-year-old adrenaline junkie without a lick of sense. Or maybe he'd been showing off for some girl. Either way, he was out of commission for the next couple of days and Tanner would be covering for him. He had another trail ride scheduled for later this afternoon.

It could be worse, he supposed. The McDowell Mountain Preserve offered some pretty spectacular views of the valley and the distant cites of Scottsdale and Phoenix.

The rides also afforded him plenty of opportunity to think. Today, his mind was on his conversation with Jewel after yesterday's barrel racing. He wished the subject of Ava's custody didn't always circle back to the cheating scandal. He also wished he'd been competing. Seeing the bulls being unloaded had stirred a lot of memories. Tanner missed his former life with a longing he hadn't thought possible. The bull riding and Jewel.

Would he trade that for his brother's happiness and health? No. Probably not. Darn, the question had been easier to answer before Jewel had reappeared in his life and he'd learned he was a father.

Twenty minutes later, he led the group of riders onto Powell Ranch. At the hitching rail outside the horse barn, they dismounted, thanked Tanner and meandered off toward their various vehicles. He could hear one couple making plans to continue their visit to "the cowboy town" with a beer at the Poco Dinero.

He was brushing down the last horse when Ethan approached. Tanner couldn't help noticing the man's limp was especially pronounced today.

"Appreciate you taking the customers out today," he said upon reaching Tanner. Wincing, he stretched out his bum leg and leaned an elbow on the hitching rail. "I know trail rides aren't your favorite."

"I don't mind."

"That's the thing. You do whatever's asked of you. No complaints. I like that."

"You gave me a job and a place to stay when I needed them. I'm grateful."

Ethan leaned forward and rubbed his knee where the prosthetic joined his leg. "Looks like I'll be having surgery soon. After the holidays."

"Nothing serious, I hope."

"I have some worsening nerve damage. It happens sometimes with amputated limbs. I've been having injections and doing physical therapy. They aren't working."

Tanner had had no idea Ethan was suffering to such an extent—he didn't talk much about his health issues. But Tanner was a little familiar with nerve damage, having known several bull riders with similar ailments, the result of being tossed or trampled by an angry eighteen-hundred-pound bull.

"Sorry to hear that," Tanner said. "Let me know if you need help with anything."

"Glad you brought that up." Ethan grinned. "Doc tells me I have to step back a bit. Claims I'm putting too many demands on my bum leg." He waited to continue until Tanner had untied the lead rope from the rail and they'd started toward the barn. "I'd like to promote you to head barn manager."

The announcement caused Tanner to stop in his tracks. Though his title was assistant barn manager, there wasn't an official head barn manager. Ethan filled the job, along with his other responsibilities as co-owner of the ranch with his brother.

"You serious?"

"Very. Job comes with a raise." Ethan named an amount that equaled a 20 percent increase. "I'm willing to bump that up a bit more after three months, if things work out."

"Wow." It was a generous offer. "Thanks."

"Is that a yes?"

"Can I think about it?" They reached the outdoor stalls where the trail horses were kept. Tanner returned the gelding to his stall, removing the halter before shutting the door behind him. "Jewel and I haven't decided on Ava's custody yet."

"Take your time. Like I said, I won't be having the surgery until after the holidays."

"It means a lot to me. The promotion and your trust. The thing is…"

"You don't have to explain. You have a daughter now. She comes first." Ethan gave Tanner's shoulder an understanding squeeze. "We'll talk again."

Tanner nodded, a surge of unexpected emotion filling his chest. "You're a good friend. And a good boss."

"You've had some tough breaks, pal. Glad I can help."

Once Ethan left, Tanner returned to the bunkhouse. He was in dire need of a pick-me-up. While the automatic coffee maker brewed, he swept the kitchen floor. Housework was another domestic skill he'd mastered this past year and one he didn't mind. The small bunkhouse required no more than an hour or two to whip into shape.

Besides, the mundane work, like the trail ride earlier, gave him an opportunity to think. While he sipped his coffee and tackled the bathroom, he considered the job offer from Ethan.

There were a lot of pros. The increase in salary would enable him to pay more child support. That went a long way in making him feel like a worthy provider. He also liked his job at Powell Ranch and knew himself capable of handling increased responsibility. Lastly, he didn't want to let Ethan down, not after everything he'd done for Tanner.

Then again, he'd hate to accept the job only to leave Ethan in a pinch if he wound up joining Jewel in Oklahoma or on the rodeo circuit. There was also his potential position at his dad's firm, assuming nothing materialized with the arena owners. On the other hand, should Tanner be sued, he'd be glad for his job at Powell Ranch—though Ethan deserved more than being a plan B.

Tanner was returning the vacuum to the closet—his mind continuing to bounce back and forth—when his phone rang. He hurried to the kitchen table and saw Daniel's photo filling the screen. Speak of the devil.

Unsure of his brother's mood, he answered with an upbeat, "Hey, how's it going?"

"Fair to middling." Daniel sounded chipper. A good sign.

They chatted for a few minutes about Ava and their Christmas Day brunch at the golf resort. Daniel and his family were planning on attending and were looking forward to meeting Ava. Another good sign.

"How are you and Rosalyn doing?"

Obviously the wrong question to ask. Daniel grumbled under his breath before answering.

"Not great. She says she'll stay through the holidays, for the kids' sakes. After that, she's thinking we should take a break. Whatever that means."

"I'm sorry, man."

"Me, too. I hate this disease, hate the meds, hate the side effects of the surgery. They've turned me into someone I don't recognize anymore. I've made Rosalyn and the kids miserable, and I hate that, too."

"None of this is your fault, bro. You're trying your best."

Even as he said it, Tanner was struck with doubts. Not to minimize Daniel's condition, but he sometimes used it as an excuse not to try harder or in a bid for sympathy.

The next instant, Tanner berated himself for being unfair and a poor excuse for a brother. He wasn't battling brain cancer, and he was in no position to judge.

"Listen," Daniel continued, "I'm hoping you'll do me a favor."

"Name it."

"Can you take me Christmas shopping? For Rosalyn."

"When and where?"

Daniel also hated being unable to drive and

relying on others to transport him where he needed to go. But between his slowed reaction time and significant loss of mobility in his right leg, not to mention the dizziness and drowsiness caused by his meds, he wasn't allowed to get behind the wheel. They'd hoped, with enough physical therapy and exercises designed to re-teach his brain, he might one day be able to drive again and ride a horse. That hope had been dashed at his last doctor's appointment. Climbing onto the back of a bucking bull was completely out of the question regardless of the circumstances.

"How about today?" He named an upscale department store not too far from his home. "They're advertising a holiday jewelry sale. Rosalyn loves emeralds. Thought I'd buy her a pair of earrings."

An extravagant gift and one Daniel likely couldn't afford. Tanner gave his brother kudos for trying and hoped Rosalyn would recognize and appreciate the effort.

"See you in an hour," Tanner said before disconnecting.

Maybe he could pick up some presents for Ava while they were out. The store must have a children's department. What did one buy a nearly five-month-old baby? His mom would have an idea. Tanner decided to call her from the store.

Getting Jewel a Christmas gift also occurred to him during the drive to Daniel's. A year ago, he'd have already bought her one. Now, he hesitated.

It was nearly four o'clock when Tanner arrived at Daniel's house. He had only a few minutes to visit with Rosalyn and his niece and nephew, who were all excited about having a new member of the family and insisted on seeing pictures despite Daniel rushing Tanner out the front door.

Tanner didn't linger. Rosalyn was clearly stressed, something her enthusiasm about Christmas Day and meeting Ava failed to hide. Her smile appeared forced, and she'd lost even more weight. When Daniel went to kiss her goodbye, she turned her head and presented her cheek. Tanner pretended not to notice, ruffling his two-year-old nephew's hair and tweaking his four-year-old niece's nose.

"You behave for your mom," he told them. "Santa's watching."

Daniel struggled to get into Tanner's truck, refusing to accept help and using only his cane for support. When his right foot caught in the door, preventing it from closing, he swore under his breath and wrenched his foot free. They rode in silence for a while, until the storm clouds brewing on Daniel's face fully retreated.

Things went a little smoother at the store. Daniel was able to find a pair of earrings Rosalyn was sure to love, and Tanner had to agree they were pretty. With his mom's assistance, Tanner narrowed his gift choices for Ava to a plush doll, a pair of purple-and-pink footed pajamas and an activity toy with farm animals.

At the last minute, he chose a leather wallet for Jewel, satisfied it didn't say, *I still care for you and want to resolve our problems so we can be together*, which was how he felt. Given the choice, he'd be buying her a pair of earrings, only his would match the diamond engagement ring she'd returned to him through his parents and that he'd kept.

Packages in hand, Tanner and Daniel headed for the store exit. Daniel's mood had improved during the shopping excursion, his expectations for the earrings high.

Tanner had lower expectations where the wallet was concerned. Until Jewel learned the truth about Daniel bribing the judge and not Tanner, they wouldn't—couldn't—resolve their problems.

Rather than ask his brother to come clean and start another argument, Tanner tried a different approach.

"Knowing what you know now, would you have acted differently?"

"What do you mean?" Daniel hedged.

"Not tried to bribe that judge. Heck, you won, anyway." While Tanner had been banned from competing.

They left the store behind and entered the crowded mall, walking slowly toward the bank of glass exit doors. Daniel's leg had started to bother him, and he limped painfully.

"That really eats at you, doesn't it?" he grumbled.

"Yeah, it does. I sacrificed a lot for you. And all for nothing."

"I've apologized. Plenty. What more do you want?"

"To tell Jewel the truth."

They both stopped and glowered at each other, mindless of the people forced to navigate around them.

Daniel's features turned dark and threatening, and he wobbled unsteadily. "You'll ruin everything for me."

"*I'll* ruin everything? I'm not the one who set this entire catastrophe in motion. Any consequences are your fault. But somehow I'm the one constantly making sacrifices and constantly paying the price."

"And I'm the one with brain cancer." He

gripped his cane with such force his knuckles paled.

They were both silent for a moment, their respective tempers simmering but not waning.

"This isn't a contest about who's lost the most," Daniel said after a moment.

"But I didn't need to lose *anything*. You shouldn't have approached that judge, and Dad shouldn't have asked me to take the fall for you."

"You volunteered."

"After you pleaded with me and he pressured me."

"I didn't think it would turn into such a big deal."

Neither had Tanner. His mistake. "I lost the woman I loved, Daniel. And I may lose custody of my daughter. Jewel could potentially use the cheating attempt against me." The attorney Tanner had retained, the one recommended by Bridwell and Associate's legal counsel, had given him that piece of less-than-glad tidings the other day.

Daniel fought to maintain his balance. "And I could lose my wife and children."

"Not because of me," Tanner insisted. "And maybe not if you told Rosalyn the truth."

"Poor Tanner. You're just a helpless victim

that everyone takes advantage of." Daniel's razor-sharp tone cut deep.

Tanner's, too. "You made a bad decision last year in Vegas. And you've followed it up with more bad decisions and dragging me down with you. Me. The guy who's always had your back."

"Did it ever occur to you that I wasn't thinking clearly?"

"That's the only reason I agreed to take the fall for you and why I'm convinced Rosalyn will understand. It's also why the arena owners won't win if they come after us."

For a moment, Daniel appeared to soften. The next instant, he shook his head and trudged forward, dragging his right leg.

"Too risky."

Tanner chased after him. "Come on, Daniel. Be reasonable. At least think about it."

Daniel ignored him. Ten feet later, he nearly collided with a trio of shoppers absorbed in conversation and not looking where they were going. In his attempt to avoid them, his bum leg failed him, and he almost fell. He would have if not for Tanner grabbing his arm and holding him steady.

"Leave me alone," Daniel snapped and shook free.

Tanner let go and watched as his brother

vented his frustrations on the double glass exit doors, beating on one with his fist.

He'd have liked to vent some of his anger on the glass door, too, and would have if he wasn't certain someone would call security.

CHAPTER EIGHT

JEWEL TROTTED TEDDY BEAR toward the arena gate where Ronnie stood waiting to confer with her after their lesson. The big gelding breathed heavily, his flanks expanding and contracting with each step. Like before, he'd given his best.

And like before, Jewel had been distracted by Tanner's presence at the arena fence, his gaze on her steady. They hadn't parted on the best of terms Saturday after the barrel racing competition at the Poco Dinero. Talk of Ava's custody and his cheating tended to have that effect on them. As a result, his Sunday and Monday visits with Ava had been brief.

Today would likely be no different, which saddened Jewel. They had to reach a resolution, for Ava's sake if for no other reason. She shouldn't suffer because her parents couldn't resolve their differences.

Jewel had spent much of yesterday, when she wasn't working or caring for Ava, on the phone attempting to retain an attorney. The task, hard to begin with, had been made more difficult by her uncertainty about whether to hire someone from Oklahoma or Arizona.

She still didn't know where she'd wind up after the New Year. Between emails, phone calls and video chats, she supposed face-to-face meetings weren't a necessity. Still, she'd prefer to sit down with her attorney and establish a rapport.

For that reason, and on the advice of her father, she'd ultimately chosen an Arizona-based attorney. They had an appointment later today for an initial consultation and to sign the paperwork. Even if Emily didn't offer Jewel a permanent photography job at Sweetheart Ranch and she wound up returning to rodeoing, she could stick around and help her parents when she wasn't competing. During the last week, their desire to purchase a winter home here had gone from probably to a matter of finding the right house.

And, she reminded herself, she'd need to be here to attend any necessary court hearings. The thought that she'd soon be negotiating with Tanner for custody of Ava made her heart hurt. How had she and Tanner gotten to this point?

During a phone call with Tanner last evening about the gift exchange at the pre-Christmas brunch at Jewel's place, she'd informed him that she was hiring an attorney and had given him the woman's contact information. He, in turn, had given *her* the name and number of *his* attorney, something she hadn't expected.

An invisible band squeezed her middle, cutting off her oxygen. Tanner was really and truly pursuing shared custody. A part of her had secretly wished he wouldn't, that he would let her retain full custody.

At the end of the phone call, he'd surprised her by mentioning a disagreement with his brother during a Sunday shopping trip. When she'd asked what the disagreement was about, he'd been vague.

Not for the first time, Jewel questioned the newly strained relationship between the Bridwell brothers. Her instincts told her something other than Daniel's battle with cancer and Tanner's attempt to bribe the bull riding judge were responsible. Odd, really. She'd have assumed problems like theirs would bring siblings closer, not push them apart. Then again, her and Tanner's problems had driven a wedge between them.

Teddy Bear snorted as he and Jewel drew up beside Ronnie. When she pulled on the reins, he bobbed his head and pawed the ground, not quite ready to quit for the day.

"You started out a little slow," Ronnie observed. She was all business today. A far cry from the glowing, dazzling taffeta-swathed bridesmaid Jewel had photographed this past weekend. "But then you found your rhythm."

"Guess we needed to warm up." Jewel didn't admit that the reason for her slow start was that it took place in Tanner's regular spot at the far end of the arena, his arresting eyes fastened on her.

"I heard good things from the other students about your second place run at the Poco Dinero."

The remark brought a smile to Jewel's face. She'd already added her winnings to her rodeo fund. The sport wasn't inexpensive.

"You've been to the Double Eights Rodeo in Apache Junction, right?" Ronnie asked. "It's in early January."

"A few times."

"Might be a good place to get your feet wet. I'm taking a couple of my students. We could all drive together."

Jewel instantly straightened in the saddle, a mixture of excitement and anxiety coursing through her. Despite being a month away, with lots of practice opportunities between now and then, it felt right around the corner. And what about Ava? She'd either have to find a babysitter or take her along. Then there was the matter of Tanner. He'd probably want to accompany them. Or insist on keeping Ava during Jewel's absence.

"Let me think about it."

"Don't take too long," Ronnie cautioned.

"I won't. I promise."

If she dallied, she might lose her nerve and manufacture excuses not to go. She was about to ride off when Ronnie delayed her.

"I saw the wedding pictures from Saturday."

"Did you like them?"

Jewel had spent much of Sunday organizing the pictures and uploading them to the bride and groom's wedding website.

"You did an incredible job. I had no idea how talented you were."

Jewel's smile widened. "Thanks."

"I mean it. Yours are some of the best wedding photographs I've seen. I don't want to lose a student, but, seriously, you could make a living at photography."

"I don't know about that." Could she?

"My cousin's thrilled. She was sharing pictures from her phone yesterday while they were waiting for their flight to Cancun."

"I do love hearing about happy customers."

The bride and groom had called Jewel yesterday, apparently from the airport, to let her know the pictures had been successfully uploaded and that they loved them. Hearing their praise echoed by someone else made it all the sweeter.

"Do you ever freelance and take nonwedding pictures?" Ronnie asked.

"You mean like events?"

"I was thinking of portraits. My dad and step-mom's anniversary is coming up. I'm stuck for a gift idea. Looking at the wedding pictures gave me one."

"I'd love to. In fact, I'm taking a portrait of Emily's family tonight. The whole O'Malley-Foxworthy clan."

Jewel didn't add that she might be leaving Mustang Valley in the near future. That conversation could come later, once she decided. At the moment, she was leaning toward staying, even if she didn't get the job at Sweetheart Ranch.

Ronnie's next student trotted over, ready for her lesson. Jewel waved goodbye to her and Ronnie before turning Teddy Bear in Tanner's direction. She assumed he wanted to confirm his visit with Ava today. Ava and Tracee hadn't come this morning and were staying indoors. The temperature had dropped drastically during the night, and Jewel didn't want her little baby catching a chill.

She passed several riders on her way to where Tanner waited. Out of habit, she mentally assessed each one, deciding if they were barrel racers, trail riders, beginners or experienced.

The ranch was busier than usual. Jewel had heard from Tracee that schools and colleges were on semester break. The teenager had taken her last final exam the previous Friday.

Jewel was feeling considerably better when she approached Tanner, thanks to her talk with Ronnie and the positive feedback about her photography. Oh, and the possibility of an anniversary portrait.

One look at his expression, however, and her worry returned tenfold. Not because he scowled or glared at her. Just the opposite. He studied her with the same glad-to-see-you delight he had when they'd been together. In response, Jewel experienced the same happy hitch inside she always had, desperately wishing her faith in him could be restored.

Danger, danger, her internal voice warned. Feelings like these were confusing and troublesome and needed to end. More than once recently, she'd caught him reaching for her hand, only to withdraw. Thank goodness he had. She had no clue how she'd have responded if his fingers had linked with hers.

Watching the corners of his very sexy mouth curve into a smile reminded her of their near kiss in her quarters and his suggestion that it might uncomplicate their situation. Jewel didn't think he could be more wrong. Especially with Ava's custody undetermined.

His delight intensified the closer she got. A flush of heat warmed her skin beneath her jacket, countering the effects of the recent cold snap.

Uh-oh. Maybe she *should* return to Oklahoma. It would make the custody issue more difficult but also create a safe distance between them.

Unless he joined her there. Would he leave his family? His job? To be near Ava, she thought he might.

"Good morning," he said when she dismounted.

Jewel kept hold of the reins. "I need to walk Teddy Bear."

"I'll come with you."

Naturally. What else had she expected? Was it possible, despite having spent the last few minutes warning herself to tread carefully where the two of them were concerned, that deep down she'd wanted him to come with her?

Too late now to say no. "All right."

Without any discussion, they began walking Jewel's customary circuit of the horse barn. In this weather, it was vitally important that Teddy Bear be properly cooled down after his grueling workout. Before her lesson this morning, she'd unearthed his blanket from the horse trailer. She didn't want her horse baby catching a chill, either.

Speaking of which... She zipped her own jacket. She, too, was feeling the drop in temperature. That, or she required a barrier between her and her companion. His delighted expression had yet to change.

"What's your schedule for the rest of the day?" Tanner asked. "I have to stick close to the ranch for the next couple of hours. We have some potential clients coming by."

"I'm working from two to four. Then I have an early evening session scheduled with Emily and her family for a holiday portrait. If I don't have to postpone—Tracee may go skating at the ice rink with some friends."

"I'll watch Ava."

"I, um..." Her bad. She should have seen that coming. "I suppose that'd be okay."

Portrait sessions didn't normally last long. Surely Tanner could babysit Ava for an hour or less without any problems, despite his lack of experience. She'd likely be asleep for the night or ready for sleep.

A thought occurred to Jewel. "Will you be off work by then?" The ranch was busy, and Tanner sometimes handled the evening feeding.

"I'll take a short lunch so I can quit early."

He spoke as if the arrangement was a done deal. Jewel told herself not to make a fuss. This was just one of the many concessions with Tanner she'd be making. Still, she resisted. The idea of him taking care of Ava made her think about shared custody and her being separated from Ava by hundreds, if not thousands, of miles.

They were leaving the horse barn after putting Teddy Bear in his stall when they met up with a pair of teenaged girls carrying halters. Jewel recognized them from Saturday's barrel racing event and guessed them to be high school students or recently graduated.

She said hello, and the four of them paused to converse. Okay, she and the girls conversed. Tanner stood off to the side, his back propped against the barn wall, his shoulders hunched. She noticed he tugged the brim of his ball cap low over his eyes.

"Congratulations, by the way," the taller of the girls said, referring to Jewel's second-place win at the Poco Dinero.

"Thanks. I kind of wish that hadn't been the last of the rodeo events until after the holidays. I could use the experience."

"It's not. There's one this coming weekend at the Cave Creek Rough Stock Rental Company," the second girl said, fiddling with her pink-dyed hair.

"Don't they lease livestock to rodeos?"

"Every other month they have semiprofessional calf roping, bull riding, bronc riding and barrel racing contests."

"We're going." The taller girl tugged on Jewel's arm. "You should sign up. Barrel racing's on Saturday."

Funny that Ronnie hadn't said anything. Then again, she'd just been in a big wedding.

"Maybe."

In truth, Jewel doubted she'd go. She was free; her only wedding on that day would finish by midafternoon. But Tracee wasn't available to babysit because of family holiday obligations. Her glance cut to Tanner for a brief moment.

"I heard from Ronnie you're thinking of returning to the circuit in January," the girl with pink hair mentioned.

"Hmm." Jewel shrugged. "That remains to be seen."

"I'd love to compete professionally. Except my parents will freak if I don't go to college. You have to get an education," she said in a low voice and wagged a finger in what Jewel assumed was an imitation of her father.

Her friend, also fresh faced and bubbly, bumped shoulders with her. "Mine, too. But I'm not good enough. To compete professionally, that is."

"You went to the NFR last year, right?" the girl with pink hair asked Jewel. "You were number one in...what state?"

"Oklahoma."

"Right. I saw a video online."

Which video? Jewel mused. The one of her flubbing her qualifying run or the one of her and Tanner being accosted by a group of angry bull riders while leaving the event grounds?

"Why'd you stop competing?"

Like they didn't know.

"I had a baby." Jewel offered her standard response.

It wasn't untrue. Even if she and Tanner hadn't ended their engagement, she'd have taken a break from barrel racing during her pregnancy.

She noticed him shifting uncomfortably whenever the girls happened to glance his way. Did they recognize him? If yes, they gave no indication.

"Oh, wow! That's right," the girl with pink hair exclaimed. "I saw you the other day with a stroller."

To Jewel's vast relief, the taller girl announced that they'd best hurry and goodbyes were exchanged.

"See you around."

"Have a merry Christmas."

Tanner pushed off the barn once the girls had moved on. Their high-pitched voices easily carried through the barn.

"You know who that guy is, don't you?" the taller girl asked her friend. "Tanner Bridwell. He's the bull rider who got caught cheating. He and Jewel were gonna get married."

"You're right. I didn't recognize him at first." The girl with the pink hair gasped loudly. "He must be her baby daddy."

"Ew. Why would she still be with a loser like him?"

"She seems really sweet. I bet she has to put up with him whether she likes it or not."

Jewel caught them sneaking peeks at her and Tanner over their shoulders. Memories from last year assailed her, and she willed herself not to slink away.

The girls continued ahead until whatever else they said couldn't be heard. Angry sparks crackled in the air surrounding Tanner, and his mouth compressed into a hard line.

Yeah, well, Jewel was mad, too. At Tanner for causing this untenable and unbearable situation. At herself for being seen with him when she'd known spending time together was a bad idea. At the two girls for their cruel and careless remarks, and at the arena owners for constantly holding a hammer over Tanner's head.

"Sorry about that," he muttered when they exited the barn.

"When is it going to stop?" She spoke with more venom than she'd intended. "I was a fool to think I could get back into competition."

"People will grow tired of talking about us eventually."

She whirled on him. "When exactly? A year from now? Five years? Ten? Rodeo is a small world. Two high school students who aren't even serious competitors have watched videos of us online, for Pete's sake. And your disguise didn't fool them for one second. They're probably posting on social media right now. Guess you can stop lying low."

"Actually, there's nothing I'd like better."

She hardly heard him. "Can you imagine what it would be like if you came with me on the circuit?"

"I'll stay out of the way."

"And what happens when Ava's older and she hears remarks like those? Or, God forbid, she's teased? Bullied? Do you want to be the one explaining to her that her dad tried to win a bull riding championship by bribing a judge?"

He stared at Jewel, his gaze unyielding, his form seeming to swell in size as his fury visibly rose.

Jewel almost took a step back. Had she gone too far? Said too much?

Big deal. What if she had? She was right on all counts.

"I'd tell her the truth," he said in a low voice like sharpened steel.

"Which is what? Sorry, honey," she said in a singsong voice, "your dad didn't have the guts to win honestly and chose to cheat instead."

Jewel was almost shouting. It was as if she and Tanner were back in that Vegas hotel room, the one that was supposed to have been their honeymoon getaway, and she was insisting he pack his bags and get the heck out.

How dare he ruin their lives? How dare he throw away everything they had and then go into hiding, leaving her to endure the backlash? How dare he…he…leave her and tear her heart clean in half? She'd loved him. And he'd supposedly loved her.

Except he hadn't. He'd proven that.

Tanner said nothing, his jaw silently working.

"Is that what you'd tell her?" Jewel demanded.

She was about to storm off when Tanner brought her to a grinding halt with his next words.

"I'd tell Ava I didn't cheat or try to cheat by bribing a judge."

Jewel snorted a laugh. "You'd lie to her."

"No. I would never lie to her." His expression remained stony. "I would never cheat, either. I'm not that kind of person."

"You confessed. To me and to the officials."

"I didn't try to bribe that judge, Jewel. It wasn't me. I swear."

She stared at him in disbelief. "The judge identified you."

"He was mistaken. I wasn't in the bar that night, remember? I went with Jimmy to try and track down his lucky shirt he'd lost."

The memory, long forgotten, surfaced. Hazy, but there.

Jewel's head swam, and she closed her eyes, fighting a wave of dizziness. "You weren't in the bar," she repeated dumbly.

"No."

This made no sense. "Then who approached the judge? And why confess if you're innocent?"

"It was Daniel. I took the fall for him."

The bones in Jewel's legs turned to sawdust, and she swayed unsteadily. Daniel! He'd cheated. Not Tanner.

"I still don't understand," she murmured.

He took hold of her arm and guided her ahead of him. "Let's go to my bunkhouse and talk."

Talk, indeed. This was a story Jewel desperately needed to hear. One that could potentially change the course of her life. And Ava's.

Tanner and Jewel walked in silence toward his bunkhouse. She'd reclaimed her arm from him halfway there.

He'd often imagined her reaction when he finally told her the truth about what had happened. In his dreams, she threw herself at him and kissed him passionately, wild with relief. Reality was vastly different. Her initial shock had morphed into quiet contemplation, followed by what he thought might be suppressed anger.

He, on the other hand, felt amazing, like he'd emerged from a yearlong exile in a black airless cave. Jewel may not be passionately kissing him, but she now knew he was the same man she'd fallen in love with and planned to marry.

"I've wanted to tell you for a long time," he said in an attempt to break the silence.

"Why didn't you?"

"I gave my word." He opened the door to his bunkhouse and waited while she entered.

"To your brother? No, let me guess. Your dad."

Definitely anger. "It's a long story," he said.

She perched on the couch and crossed her legs, all straight lines and sharp angles. "I'm listening."

"I could use a coffee." He started toward the kitchenette, deciding they each needed a minute. "How about you?"

"If I wasn't nursing Ava, I'd ask for something stronger."

He chuckled. She didn't. That had been a joke, right? He glanced at her stony expression. Okay, not a joke.

"I need to call Tracee." She extracted her phone before removing her coat and laying it on the couch beside her. "She's expecting me."

While the coffee brewed, Tanner texted his boss, saying he and Jewel were having a chat, that he might be late returning to work and he'd make up any missed time tomorrow. Ethan answered not to worry and don't rush. From what Tanner made of Jewel's side of the conversation, she was free to stay a little longer.

Fate appeared to be conspiring in their favor. Or not, depending on how well things went. He definitely had a lot of explaining to do.

Adding creamer to her coffee, he carried the two mugs to the couch. She accepted his "peace offering" and noted the cartoon bride and groom on the side.

"I bought you this mug in Vegas. I'm surprised you kept it."

"I've kept everything you gave me." Including your engagement ring, he wanted to tell her.

With her free hand, she slid her coat closer. Tanner got the message and lowered himself onto the opposite side of the couch.

"Why take the fall for Daniel?" she asked. "Because of his brain cancer? Or maybe a better question is why would he cheat in the first place?"

Tanner sipped his coffee and then set the mug on the side table. "You have to understand, he wasn't himself. The tumor was pressing on a vital area of his brain. That and the meds were impairing his judgment. I don't believe he would have ever attempted to bribe a judge under normal circumstances."

"Probably not."

"Add to that, he was terrified. His chances of surviving the surgery were fifty-fifty at best."

Jewel glanced away. Swallowed. "I wish you'd told me how grave his condition was."

"No one other than immediate family knew. Daniel wanted it that way, and I respected his wishes."

"Why go to such lengths?" Jewel asked.

"There was the very likely possibility if news got out, he'd have been disqualified. He figured if he was going to die, he wanted to be remembered as a world champion and not pitied as a cancer victim forced to quit."

"So, he tried to bribe a judge?"

"Regardless if he survived the surgery or not, he wouldn't be returning to bull riding. Vegas was his last ever shot, and he decided to stack the odds in his favor."

"He shouldn't have competed. He was a danger to himself and others."

"I agree."

"What if he'd been killed?" Her voice rose. "You should have stopped him. Rosalyn or your parents should have stopped him. You had a responsibility."

"It's easy to say what someone should and shouldn't do when you're not the one staring your own mortality in the face. Yeah, Daniel might have died in the arena. He also might have died the next week on the operating table."

Jewel's demeanor softened. "I can't begin to imagine what he went through. What you all went through." She paused. "I wish I'd been there for you."

He didn't remind her that she could have been if she'd given him half a chance, not now when he'd finally breached her defenses. That conversation could come later. "Thankfully, he survived both the bull riding and the surgery."

"Wasn't he worried the judge would refuse the bribe and report him?"

Tanner shrugged. "Like I said, he wasn't thinking clearly. Rumors were the man had recently lost a bundle in the stock market. Daniel offered him a considerable amount of money."

"But he won the championship. Are you saying he accomplished that despite the effects of his cancer and the meds?"

"Pretty incredible when you think about it."

"What's incredible is that the entire awful ordeal we were subjected to this past year was for nothing." The straight lines and sharp angles were back.

"Not nothing." Was that true or just something Tanner constantly told himself?

"You could have refused to take the blame for him."

"Then he'd have been disqualified."

"Don't you think he deserved that? Was his thinking affected to the point he couldn't tell right from wrong?"

"If the situation had been reversed and your brother was the one dying, how far would you go to help him?"

"I wouldn't put him in danger or lie to the person I was about to marry in a few days." Pain filled her eyes. "The father of my child."

"I had no idea you were pregnant. You had no idea. If we had, we both would have acted differently."

She heard his unspoken accusation: *you wouldn't have ended our engagement.*

"If you had told me about Daniel," she countered, "we wouldn't have argued like we did. It would've made all the difference."

Tanner wished he'd told her, too. "Everything happened so fast. Daniel and I were just leaving our hotel room when the rodeo official called about the judge's accusation, me first and then him. Even though we both denied it, the man insisted we immediately come to the office. We went next door to our parents' room and told Dad. That's when Daniel confessed. Believe me, I was shocked."

"Didn't you insist he admit what he'd done?"

"Of course. But Dad convinced me to take the blame instead and not tell anyone. Even you."

"That must have been some convincing he did."

"He said I had an opportunity to do what might be one of the last things I could for my brother. Protect his reputation and guarantee he was able to compete that evening in the final round."

"He guilted you," she bit out.

"I wanted to help Daniel. I didn't think I could forgive myself if I didn't and then he died on the operating table."

"You're a good brother, Tanner. A wonderful, kind, generous brother. To give up so much for

Daniel. I hope he appreciates your sacrifice."
She delivered the last part with a punch.

"In all fairness, none of us anticipated the
speed and extent of the fallout. We assumed I'd
be disqualified, banned from competing for a
while, pay a fine and then the whole incident
would blow over. Someone in the arena office
leaked the story, apparently filming us with
their phone as we were leaving. By that afternoon, every competitor at the arena had heard
and social media was exploding."

"You said an official from the rodeo association called you and Daniel both. Didn't the
judge realize it was him and not you?"

"He'd been drinking. The bar was dark. He
wasn't sure which one of us approached him."

"No one else in the bar saw Daniel?"

"Apparently not. And we look enough alike
people have confused us before."

"Why not speak up after things went crazy?"

"What? Go to the rodeo officials a week
after I'd confessed and say no, it wasn't me,
after all?" Traces of the resentment Tanner
had tried to quash these last twelve months
surfaced anew. He tamped it down. "I'd have
been accused of being jealous of my brother's
championship title. My sick brother who was
undergoing life-and-death surgery. I'd have
given people a whole new reason to hate me."

"All right, I get it. You took the fall for Daniel in order to give him what might have been his dying wish." Her voice cracked with restrained emotion. "But why not tell me? Didn't you think I deserved to know?"

"I did. I was outvoted by Daniel and my dad, and my mom, too. They were adamant that the fewer people in the loop, the better for us."

"And you went along. You didn't give me a single thought. Not even a phone call to warn me. I had to hear from a friend. Fifteen minutes before my event. When I tried calling you, you didn't answer."

"We were in a meeting with the attorney representing the arena owners and had shut off our phones."

Jewel drew herself up, clearly struggling for control. "Did your dad and brother ever consider *us* when they hatched their plan for you to take the blame? Did *you*?"

"No one thought we'd break up. Me included."

"We were together for years, Tanner. Surely you guessed I'd be angry and upset and feel betrayed."

"Honestly, I thought you'd have a little faith in me and not kick me to the curb. You barely let me talk before laying into me."

She instantly stiffened. "I just found out the

man I loved had attempted to bribe a judge. You didn't seem to care and just clammed up."

Tanner was through being nice, and gave free rein to his building temper.

"Look at things from my perspective. One minute I was competing for a world championship, against my possibly dying brother, mind you, and getting married in two days' time. A few hours later, I couldn't walk across the arena grounds without being called a dirty name, and my phone was blowing up with hate email and messages. On top of that, I was being threatened with a lawsuit. Excuse me if I forgot just a little about you for a few minutes."

Silence followed as they both took a much-needed breather. When Jewel spoke next, she was considerably calmer.

"No offense, Tanner, but it's not like you're rolling in dough. Even if the arena could prove they lost money as a result of an attempted cheating scandal, how much could they seriously get?"

"You forget I own a percentage of Dad's company. Daniel, too. My share is an asset the arena owners can go after. And if they win, we stand to lose a lot. Enough to possibly bankrupt the company. The good news is our attorney learned that attendance for this year's NFR isn't down."

"Then there's no grounds for a lawsuit."

"Hopefully. And if they don't file within the next year, their window of opportunity closes."

"Ah. I get it. Your dad's worried if I know what really happened, I'll make a post online or tell some of my friends and the scandal will start trending again. This time, focusing on Daniel."

"Something like that," Tanner admitted.

Jewel closed her eyes and sighed, some of the fight draining from her. "I admit I'm glad to learn it wasn't you. Really glad."

"I've wanted to tell you from the beginning."

"Will Daniel come clean in another year when the threat of a lawsuit has passed?" she asked.

"A lot will depend on the state of his marriage and his health."

"What's his prognosis?"

"Too soon to say. At the moment, he's in remission. Tomorrow, the cancer could be back."

"That must be hard, living with so much uncertainty."

"Not just for Daniel," Tanner said. "Rosalyn and the kids have had an equally rough ride this past year. First, they nearly lost Daniel. Then there was his recovery and months of grueling rehab. He's better, but he's not the same person and nearly impossible to live with. His marriage is circling the drain, and he's afraid if Rosalyn finds out he attempted to cheat, she'll divorce him. She's been talking about needing space and taking the kids to her folks for a while."

"She's never struck me as the kind who'd bail on her husband." Jewel frowned. "I think she'd understand why he did what he did. The pressure he was under."

"The Rosalyn from before Daniel's surgery, yeah. No question. But Daniel's mood swings and depression and anger issues have taken a toll on her."

"I'm sure they've considered therapy."

"They're seeing a marriage counselor and each belong to a support group." Tanner removed his ball cap and ran his fingers through his hair. "There's no easy fix to this situation. Believe me, Jewel, I've thought about this long and hard. More these past weeks. Regardless of what we do, someone will get hurt or hurt worse than they already are."

"I hope for the children's sake that Rosalyn and Daniel stay together."

"Me, too. He loves her." Tanner remembered the emerald earrings his brother had recently purchased for Rosalyn.

"I'd like to tell my parents. They'll be so happy to learn you're innocent. And Christmas Day will undoubtedly go a whole lot better."

"Let's wait." Tanner rubbed a hand along his

thigh. "I need to let my dad know I've told you. He won't like it, and that could make Christmas Day go a whole lot *worse*."

"Fair enough." For the first time since he'd revealed the truth, she smiled. "This changes everything."

"How's that?"

"For starters, I won't fight you anymore for shared custody of Ava."

He smiled back at her. "What else?"

She moved her coat out of the way and scooted closer. His heart started hammering.

"No promises," she said shyly. "Let's just say I'm open to possibilities."

"Tell me more." He went out on a limb and cupped her cheek, running his thumb along her satiny jaw.

She melted a tiny fraction. "I've missed you."

"I've missed you, too." To say he'd been desolate without her was an understatement. He'd been lost. Lonely beyond measure. Empty and hollow inside.

He'd never stopped loving her, either, though common sense told him to keep that admission to himself. For now.

"What now?" She gazed at him, her one question containing a dozen more.

"One day at a time?" he suggested.

"Sounds good." She shifted as if to rise. "I

should head home. Tracee has plans this afternoon."

"Can I drop by after dinner to see Ava?"

"Aren't you coming after lunch to watch her during my photography session?"

"That's right." They stood and Tanner helped her with her coat. Impulsively, he reached up and fastened the top button. "I could still come after dinner. We'll finalize our Christmas plans. Mom called yesterday. She has a few more suggestions."

Jewel impulsively stood on tiptoes and gave him a swift peck on the lips. "Sure. Why not?"

Electricity shot through him. He didn't stop to consider his actions and wrapped his arms around her waist, pulling her into a hug...that lasted and lasted. When Jewel's arm went up to circle his neck, he let her heady scent filled his senses. He'd been waiting a long time for just this moment.

Unfortunately, like all good things, the hug came to an end.

He walked her to the door and then outside. They headed toward the horse barn. Tanner almost took her hand but refrained.

"See you soon," he said when the time came to part.

"You are planning on coming clean eventually?" she asked. "It's important to me that everyone knows you're innocent."

His soaring mood took a nosedive. As much as he understood that dishonesty had caused all of his and Jewel's woes, he wasn't ready to betray his brother. "I won't turn Daniel in."

"What if he turns himself in?"

"That would be entirely different, and I'll talk to him about it. After the holidays."

She compressed her lips as if she wanted to say more but decided against it.

"Give me time, Jewel. This isn't about just you and me and Ava. My entire family's future and financial security could be adversely affected if the arena owners decide to sue. Daniel's, especially. His medical bills are through the roof, and my parents have been helping him with some of the costs not covered by insurance."

"I don't want your family to suffer." She squared her shoulders. "It's just that I care about you, Tanner. And I hate seeing you blamed for something you didn't do."

"We're going to get through this. I promise."

"I want that, too." Her smile returned. "Very much."

They parted ways then, she returning to Sweetheart Ranch and he to work. No peck on the cheek or hug marked their separation, though Jewel did touch his arm, and he brushed a stray lock of hair from her face. After reporting in with Ethan and giving him a brief summary of his talk with Jewel, Tanner vowed to himself to move heaven and earth, if necessary, to convince Daniel to come clean.

CHAPTER NINE

JEWEL SAT IN the recliner, Ava on her lap. After a few seconds of back patting, the baby let out a very unladylike burp.

"Well. I take that to mean dinner is officially over."

Ava gurgled in response.

Cradling her in one arm, Jewel stood and went over to the quilt she'd spread on the floor. Laying Ava on her stomach—it was way too early for bed—Jewel watched as she batted a stuffed frog. Quickly bored, the baby tried rolling over onto her side.

It wouldn't be much longer before she succeeded. Once that happened, Jewel would have to watch Ava even more closely. And what about when she started crawling? Or walking?

The changes were happening practically daily. Changes Jewel would be sharing with Tanner.

A warm glow filled her as she remembered their last conversation. He was innocent! He hadn't tried to cheat.

Just as quickly, concern dampened her glow. If only everyone knew the truth. She understood his desire to wait. That didn't stop her from wanting to shout the news. He'd promised her they'd work things out. She had to believe him. Their future and Ava's depended on it.

As she watched, Ava stopped trying to roll over and grabbed for a bright yellow rattle. Fingers crossed, she'd stay occupied and awake until Tanner arrived, which should be soon.

The O'Malley-Foxworthy family portrait was scheduled for this evening at six thirty. Emily had decided the glittering Christmas lights would make a nice background, and Jewel agreed. She had her eye on the Christmas tree in the foyer with its angel topper, or possibly the gorgeously decorated veranda.

To fill the time until Tanner arrived at around six o'clock or so, Jewel tidied her quarters and checked on her refrigerated supply of expressed breast milk, satisfied there was plenty on hand for Ava's bedtime feeding should the photography session run late.

She was just finishing when her phone rang from its place on the counter. The "Grandma's on the line" ringtone let her know the caller's identity.

"Hi, Mom."

"You sound in a hurry."

"Just cleaning up before Tanner gets here to babysit."

"Tanner's babysitting!"

"Well, he is Ava's dad."

"Last you said, you weren't comfortable with him watching Ava."

"He's proving himself to be pretty reliable."

More reliable than her mother knew. She so wished she could tell her mom that she and Tanner were taking small steps forward. But then she'd have to reveal Tanner's innocence, and she'd agreed to say nothing for the time being.

"I'm glad, darling. I hated the idea of you two being at odds."

"Me, too."

Jewel's mood had been soaring all day, and not entirely because of Tanner's news. Their warm embrace continued to linger in her mind and on her lips. With very little encouragement, she might have kissed him. *Might* have.

Without meaning to, she let out a contented sigh.

"One of us is in a good mood," her mother commented.

"I am. Aren't you?"

"Very much. Your dad and I have picked ten homes to look at while we're there."

"Ten. Wow!"

"I'll probably pick out ten more before we

arrive next week. You know, you can research houses for sale online. Some even have virtual tours."

Jewel laughed. She supposed house hunting had changed in the thirty-something years her parents had resided in their current home.

"I can send you links if you want," her mom offered. She seemed to be having a grand time.

"Sure."

"Better yet, you could come with us to look. The real estate agent is very nice and quite knowledgeable. I can't imagine her minding you and Ava tagging along."

"Maybe. It'll depend on my work schedule. The weeks between now and New Year's are going to be hectic at the ranch. You won't believe how many weddings are scheduled. There are now three on Christmas Day alone."

She filled her mother in on the ranch's many nuptials. Granted, Jewel wasn't the photographer for all of them. Some couples had hired their own or recruited a family member in order to save money. But she was working a good many of the weddings and possibly even more if anyone changed their mind at the last minute.

"Any other reason for this good mood of yours?" Jewel's mom asked. "Is it the barrel racing?"

No, Jewel thought. *It's Tanner. He didn't cheat.*

"Partly. My times are right back up to where they were last year. Ronnie's convinced I'm ready to return to the circuit."

"Your hard work is really paying off."

"Ronnie deserves some of the credit. She's a good trainer."

"You're loving the photography, too. I can tell."

Jewel's smile widened. "More than I imagined. I have a portrait session tonight with the owners of Sweetheart Ranch. That's why Tanner's babysitting."

"I must admit," her mother said, "I had my doubts when you first announced you were going to Arizona. It does my heart good to hear how well things are going."

"I still haven't decided between rodeo and photography." If only there was a way for her to do both *and* be a full-time mother to Ava. "But I'm grateful I have a difficult choice to make. I could have bombed at both. Then where would I be?"

"Not to change the subject, but how's my beautiful granddaughter?"

"At the moment, she's growing restless."

Ava had begun to whimper. Jewel went over to the quilt, turned Ava onto her side, propped her up with a pillow, and gave her a teething ring. Though not yet getting teeth, she immediately stuffed the toy in her mouth and began gnawing on it.

"Have you and Tanner been discussing custody at all?"

"Some," Jewel admitted. "I heard from my attorney today. She's in talks with Tanner's attorney. For the moment, we're letting them handle all communication regarding custody."

"That's probably for the best. Less chance of arguing."

"According to his attorney," Jewel said, "he'd like to reside in the same state as me, either here or in Oklahoma."

"I'd think with his job and family being in Arizona and his brother's serious health issues, he wouldn't want to move away."

"Well, my attorney did suggest I stay in Arizona if at all possible. It would simplify whatever agreement we reach and give Tanner no reason to fight me for full custody."

"How do you feel about staying?"

"I'm open to the idea." After last night and Tanner's hug, Jewel was more open than ever. "Of course, I'll miss Justin and Cammie and little Erin," she said, referring to her brother, sister-in-law and niece. "But with you and Dad living here half the year, they'll be visiting."

She and her mom continued chatting, with Jewel's gaze divided between Ava and the clock. Tanner should have been arriving at any moment.

"I hope you're finding some personal time to enjoy the holidays," her mother said.

"Trust me. Mustang Valley takes the holidays pretty seriously. You'll be amazed when you get here. I swear, the whole town gets involved. Neighborhoods compete to out-decorate each other. Same with stores and businesses. On weekend nights, people in costumes sing carols outside the library. Homer's church is having a pageant. I may take Ava to that. Maybe we can all check out the sights one evening when you're here."

"Sounds wonderful! How can we refuse?"

"You'll love the ranch. It's gorgeous and the honeymoon cabins are adorable. Too bad you can't stay in one."

"That's an idea. Your dad and I have an anniversary coming up." Her mom changed the subject. "I've been looking at your online portfolio. I have to say, honey, your work keeps getting better and better."

"I think the subject matter helps. Photographing people on the best day of their life is, well, special." She chuckled to herself. "Don't laugh, but I feel like I'm contributing in some small way to their happiness."

"I'm not laughing. I can tell the work is satisfying for you and rewarding."

"It really is."

"If you ask me, you've made your decision. Obviously, photography is your passion. More than barrel racing."

Was it? Jewel had worked hard for years and invested a ton of money into her rodeo career. Did she want to return to it because it was her passion or simply because choosing photography felt like giving up?

No. If Emily didn't offer Jewel a permanent job, she'd be devastated. Part of her had been contemplating the possibility of doing both barrel racing and photography. But if she had to choose one...

"I do love photography."

A knock interrupted her before her mother could respond. Tanner was here! Jewel's heart gave a small tumble.

"Gotta go, Mom. Tanner's at the door."

"Tell him I said hello, would you?"

"Will do."

Was her mother ready to forgive Tanner for what she believed he'd done? If Jewel had to guess, she'd say yes. Wait until her mother learned the truth. She'd be overjoyed.

Disconnecting, she went to the door and opened it. Tanner stood on the landing holding a very large cardboard box with a smaller, flatter box on top of it.

"What's this?" she asked as he came in and set the boxes on the floor.

"Pizza." Grinning, he carried the smaller box to the table. "Have you eaten yet?"

"I was going to grab a quick sandwich." She lifted a corner of the pizza box, releasing the scent of garlic and pepperoni. Her stomach started to growl as her mouth watered. "This looks better and smells great. I haven't had pizza in ages."

"Help yourself."

She removed two paper plates from the kitchenette cupboard. "What's in the other box?"

Crossing the room, Tanner knelt down beside Ava. "Emily caught me on the way here. She had a few leftover Christmas decorations they weren't using and thought you might like to spruce up the place."

"How nice." Jewel dropped the paper plates on the table, the pizza momentarily forgotten, and investigated the box. "I've missed putting up decorations. Even after I moved out of my folks' house, I still decorated my apartment."

"I remember."

Yes, he would. He'd helped her often enough.

While she dug though the box, Tanner set Ava in her baby seat. "Hey, gorgeous. How's my best girl tonight?"

Ava wiggled her arms and legs, her grin matching the one he wore.

Jewel tried not to be enamored and, predictably, failed.

Lifting several strands of red and green garland from the box, she studied the room, debating where to hang them. "If she gets hungry while I'm gone, there are bottles in the fridge and a jar of strained pears on the counter. Her spoon's in the dish rack. Clean diapers, baby wipes and anything else you might need are on the changing table in the bathroom."

"We'll be fine, won't we, kiddo?"

"I'm sure you will."

Jewel gave them a few minutes to play, the most her demanding stomach would allow, and picked through the box's contents. She found an old but quaint nativity scene, a wreath for the door, a collection of whimsical nutcrackers, red and green candles, and a slightly misshapen two-foot-tall fake Christmas tree complete with miniature ornaments.

To Tanner's credit, his confidence with Ava was growing. He adored her, and the feeling was mutual. Not that Jewel blamed her daughter.

He could be incredibly charming. She, too, had fallen head over heels for him a long time ago.

Shaking herself out of her reverie, she said, "We should eat before the pizza gets cold."

He sat at the table across from her. Jewel served them both big slices, and they dug in. Small talk flowed easily. That the scene was very reminiscent of previous ones from their years together wasn't lost on her. She doubted it was lost on Tanner, either, if she read his expression correctly.

"Ethan offered me a job promotion," he announced as he finished his third slice.

Jewel had quit eating at two. "He did?"

"Head barn manager. It comes with a nice raise. He's having surgery on his bum leg and needs to take some time off."

She listened as he talked, carefully weighing each detail. "Are you taking the job?" she asked when he paused to wipe his hands on a napkin.

"I haven't decided. That will depend in large part on you. On us. And Ava's custody. I won't accept a job only to leave Ethan in a lurch by moving to Oklahoma after a few weeks."

"I hate to cause any problems for you and him, but I really want to hear from Emily before I make a decision."

"I understand. And so does Ethan. He's giving me until after the holidays."

"That's generous of him."

"He's a stand-up guy."

"But what about working for your dad?" she asked. "Would you take the barn manager job only to wind up leaving for Bridwell and Associates?"

"There's no way Dad'll let me join the company for at least another year. I could work as barn manager until then. I think Ethan would be agreeable with that. If all goes well, his leg will be better by then."

"You have a lot to think about," Jewel mused.

A steady job at Powell Ranch, one that came with a raise, made more sense than following Jewel home to Oklahoma where no job waited.

Which, in turn, gave her a lot to think about. Staying in Arizona would make Tanner's choices easier. It would also allow them to explore any potential relationship.

Was that what she wanted? Possibly. But not until everyone knew the truth about what really happened with the bull riding judge. It was important for all their sakes, including Ava's. She didn't deserve to live under the shadow of a father whose reputation was wrongly tainted. And no way could Jewel and Tanner have a loving relationship, rebuild their shattered trust, with this conflict always between them. He needed to clear his name. Unfortunately, based on Tanner's reluctance to make that fact public, she'd be waiting a while for that to happen.

Hearing her phone ping, she pulled it from her pocket, shook off her disappointment, and checked the display. Emily had sent a text saying they were ready earlier than planned for the photo session.

"I need to go." Jewel typed a quick reply. "Duty calls."

"Wait. Before you leave." Tanner closed the lid on the pizza box. "I was thinking we could take Ava to the Holly Daze Festival this weekend, if you're not working."

Jewel hesitated. How she answered would send a clear message to Tanner about the direction she saw them heading and her willingness to go there.

"I am working. On Saturday and Sunday." She reconsidered her reply for only a moment. "But I'm free on Friday."

"Is that a yes?"

"Can we get there when they open at five thirty? Ava usually starts fading by seven or seven thirty. That'll give us a couple of hours."

His eyes lit up. "It's a date."

A *date*. The word triggered mixed feelings of eagerness and trepidation.

Kissing Ava on the head and Tanner on the cheek, she hurried down the stairs and to the ranch house, her mind a whirl. She and Tanner's small steps forward had just turned into one big one.

JEWEL LET HERSELF into the main house through the back door. She'd been at Sweetheart Ranch long enough—almost two weeks now—that she no longer felt uncomfortable just walking in. Voices carried from the parlor to the kitchen, some she recognized and others she didn't. Had Emily invited more than immediate family members for the Christmas photo session?

Mild anxiety bloomed, and Jewel immediately chided herself. She had no reason to be nervous. She'd been doing well for the O'Malleys. They liked her and her work. This photo session would be no different.

Must be Tanner, their upcoming date and the whirlwind course her life had recently taken setting her on edge. Today alone, she'd learned he was innocent and he'd announced a potential job promotion. All good news. Still, she was left feeling flummoxed and conflicted.

If only she could get some kind of clarity about which career direction to take: rodeo or photography. She was more certain than when she'd first set foot in Mustang Valley. But if Emily didn't come through with a job offer, then Jewel would have an even bigger decision to make about whether to pursue photography entirely on her own and where. Oklahoma or Arizona?

She slowed her steps and willed herself to remain calm as she entered the parlor. She saw right away that the entire O'Malley-Foxworthy clan had assembled, including the children, and were wearing their matching holiday outfits. Also, there was a man and woman Jewel immediately recognized as the bride and groom from one of her first weddings at the ranch.

Emily spied Jewel and waved her over to where she and the couple stood by the buffet. "Jewel. You remember Amaia and Enrico."

"Of course." Jewel shook hands with the well-dressed middle-aged couple. "Nice to see you again."

Near the entrance to the foyer, the rest of the O'Malleys and Foxworthys scrambled to make last-minute wardrobe adjustments and smooth disarrayed hair. Except for Emily's husband, Homer. He didn't have enough hair to smooth.

"How's married life?" Jewel asked. She remembered that Amaia and Enrico had honeymooned in one of the ranch cabins.

"Wonderful," Amaia said.

Enrico put a loving arm around his wife. "If I had known how great it would be, I'd have accepted her proposal the first time she asked."

"Oh, you." She gave him a playful shove, then turned her attention to Jewel. "We love the photos you took of our wedding. They're just beautiful."

"Thank you."

"When I asked Emily if you did other kinds of photography, she recommended I talk to you directly. Since Enrico and I were going to be in the area this evening, we asked if we could drop by."

"Are you looking to have a portrait done?"

"Actually, no. I co-own an art shop in Fountain Hills. We sell one-of-a-kind original paintings and sculptures and some ceramics. All crafted by local artisans. My business partner has seen my wedding photos and raved about them. We'd love to hire you to photograph a selection of pieces for use in a new marketing campaign we're launching this spring."

"I've been raving about you, too," Emily added with a sly wink.

Jewel had to catch her breath. This wasn't at all what she'd been expecting. "I don't know what to say."

"Say yes." Amaia beamed.

"I won't mislead you. I've never photographed artwork. I tend to focus on live-action shots."

"I adore the picture you took of our rings. Your lighting was perfect. I've also seen the catering and wedding cake pictures you took for Bridget's catalogue."

"I showed them to her," Emily added.

Jewel only then noticed Bridget's catering binder lying open on the table.

"I can't imagine photographing artwork will be that much different," Amaia pressed.

For all Jewel knew, it could be vastly different. "Um…"

"You have a real knack for tiny details."

She should have been selling herself to a potential customer, but she was untested in this particular area of photography and reluctant. She'd hate to disappoint Amaia should her efforts fall short.

The art store owner was apparently unwilling to take no for an answer. "Look, why don't we set up a time for some sample shots? I'll pay you by the hour. If we're both unhappy with the end results, then we go our separate ways and no hard feelings."

"I have a better idea," Jewel said. "How about I take a series of sample shots free of charge? If you like my work and want to hire me, then we'll draw up a contract."

Amaia brightened. "We have a deal."

Emily excused herself in order to gather the children and supervise the arrangement of family members in front of the glittering Christmas tree.

Jewel and Amaia confirmed contact information and set a date and time during the third week in January for a store visit and to shoot the sample photos. Even if Jewel didn't have a permanent job at Sweetheart Ranch by then, she'd likely be staying in Mustang Valley to help her parents move into their winter home.

That would also allow her and Tanner to reach an agreement on Ava's custody without feeling rushed. And—her insides gave a little start—to see where things between them were leading.

She knew better than to factor any potential romance into her future plans. Not at this early stage. Taking her own good advice, however was proving difficult. His innocence was having a profound affect on their relationship, rekindling feelings she'd spent a year keeping at bay.

She, and not Emily, escorted the newlyweds to the front door where she thanked Amaia again. Jewel wasn't sure still lifes were the kind of photography work she wanted to pursue, if she ultimately chose photography over barrel racing. But it was an opportunity—a good one at that. And she could use all the credentials she could get.

Yet another reason to stay in Arizona? They were certainly mounting.

Not for the first time in recent days, Jewel began to doubt her initial reaction to Tanner's confession of cheating. Had she been wrong not to give him the chance he thought he'd deserved?

A stab of guilt struck her hard in the center of her chest. How different the outcome might have been had she not let her anger dictate her actions.

Utter chaos greeted her when she reached the foyer, completely distracting her from her mental musings. Emily reported that eating too many holidays cookies had resulted in a sugar high for the three children, who raced back and forth in a game of tag and refused to heed their dad's warnings to stop.

Eventually, with enough coaxing and the promise of a movie afterward, they settled, and the photo shoot went reasonably well. Jewel took several dozen shots from different angles and with various poses. She also convinced Emily and Homer to sit for an individual portrait, which was then followed by Bridget and Ryan and, lastly, Molly, her soon-to-be husband, Owen, and his children. Then, on impulse, Jewel took candid shots of only the children. She thought those might be the best ones of the night.

Committing to have the pictures ready the following morning, she gathered her camera bag and readied to leave. Molly stopped her just as she was zipping the bag closed.

"Do you have a second?"

"Sure." She assumed Molly wanted to discuss her upcoming nuptials to Owen on Christmas Eve. Were they really just over a week away?

"Let's talk over here where it's less noisy."

She led Jewel to the buffet where they helped themselves to some of the holiday cookies. Jewel chose an angel. It was absolutely delicious and melted in her mouth.

"First, I wanted to tell you about *Southwest Bride Magazine*," Molly said around a bite of a snowman's head. "Have you heard of them?"

"Oh, yes." Before Jewel and Tanner had opted for a simple Las Vegas wedding, she'd devoured every bride magazine available.

"We're fortunate to have appeared in two issues," Molly continued. "And we have a great relationship with the features reporter. I went ahead and emailed her photos from one of your weddings. The one on the veranda with the full moon rising behind the bride and groom."

The wedding of Ronnie's cousin. Jewel had been especially pleased with those photos.

"She's interested in using one of them in a future issue." Molly grinned.

"Really?"

"I gave her your phone number and email address. I hope you don't mind."

"Mind? Are you kidding!" Jewel couldn't wait to get back to her quarters and check out the magazine's latest online issue.

"*Southwest Bride* has a large circulation. If they publish your photo, you'd be seen by thousands of people. Hundreds of thousands, even."

"Wow." Jewel impulsively hugged Molly. "I can't thank you enough."

Here was yet another incredible career break just handed to her. How had she gotten this lucky?

"The features reporter said no promises," Molly warned her. "But I can tell she likes your work."

"I owe you."

"I know one way you can repay me." Molly's face lit with an impish smile.

"Name it."

"I have a few special requests for my wedding pictures."

"Absolutely."

It was difficult for Jewel to concentrate as Molly rambled on, but she did. Mostly, Molly wanted additional pictures of Owen's children taken before the ceremony as she feared they'd have trouble getting the youngsters to sit still afterward. Also, it would be late by then, and the youngest child was likely to be tired and cranky.

"No problem," Jewel assured her. "You're calling the shots."

They also discussed prewedding pictures in the dressing rooms and postwedding pictures at the reception.

"One last thing," Molly said, her demeanor turning suddenly reserved. "Yes, you're going to be the photographer, but Owen and I would also like you to be our guest at the reception. You don't have to be taking pictures every minute."

"I'd hate to miss a photo op."

"I'm serious, Jewel. We love having you at Sweetheart Ranch. You're becoming part of the family."

Warmth surrounded Jewel's heart like a hug. "That means a lot to me."

"Feel free to bring Tanner as your plus-one."

Molly's remark struck Jewel momentarily dumb. The O'Malleys were aware that Tanner was Ava's father. She didn't think they were aware of Jewel and Tanner recently growing closer or their planned date.

Unless... Could they be that obvious? He did give her lingering looks, which she returned.

"To be honest, he'll probably be babysitting Ava." She'd already checked with Tracee. The teenager was going to be busy with family doings on Christmas Eve.

"Bring her to the wedding. There'll be other children there."

Jewel shook her head. "She might cry."

"She won't be the only one." Molly squeezed Jewel's arm. "I guarantee my mom will be a basket case."

"I'll think about it. And talk to Tanner."

Jewel was inclined to say no and not because of Ava crying. Going as a family to the Holly Daze Festival was one thing. Stepping out as each other's wedding date—the wedding of her boss's daughter, no less—was quite another.

The more Jewel contemplated it, the more she wondered if she and Tanner were moving too fast. Her happiness in discovering his innocence might be affecting her normally good judgment and causing her to make wrong choices. As was their constant proximity.

Questions continued to nag at her all during the walk to her quarters. Would Tanner choose his family again over her if another situation arose? Did she trust him entirely? Was she willing to try again because she truly wanted that or because he was an old habit? An old habit who also happened to be her baby's father. Newfound guilt factoring in and the realization she might have acted hastily when she sent him away last year without first getting more of the story?

Confused and uncertain, she didn't mention the invitation to Molly's wedding once she returned. Neither did she mention the potential opportunity with *Southwest Bride Magazine*. And not because Ava was asleep and talking with Tanner might disturb her.

For now, she needed to hold back. If only to assure herself she remained in control. Jewel's heart wasn't the only one at risk of being broken—there was her daughter's, too.

"It's getting late," she said to him after checking on Ava.

While not really that late, Tanner didn't pressure her to let him stay. "I'll see you in the morning."

There was no repeat hug when she walked him to the door. Jewel slipped out of his grasp when he reached for her and mumbled, "Good night, Tanner."

Undeterred, he leaned down and nuzzled her cheek. "Night."

At least he was keeping his word and letting her set the pace. Although, a part of her almost wished his mouth had moved a few inches to the side and found hers.

CHAPTER TEN

TANNER STOOD OUTSIDE the designated rest area near the main entrance to the Holly Daze Festival. Despite several moments of unexplained tension between him and Jewel these past three days—something was bothering her but she'd yet to tell him what exactly—they'd stuck with their plan of taking Ava to the annual holiday event.

At the moment, she was in the mothers' lounge, changing and nursing Ava. They'd arrived only a few minutes ago, timing it so that Ava would be fed and hopefully content for the two or so hours they planned on attending the festival.

While he waited, he replayed the last few days in his mind, searching for what he might have said or done to cause the tension. Since his telling her the truth about Daniel, he'd assumed their differences were resolving. Especially in light of their growing intimacy. Evidently not.

Feeling his phone vibrate, Tanner withdrew

it from his jacket pocket and glanced at the display.

He answered with a cheery, "Hey, Mom."

"Sorry I missed your call earlier. I've been baking all day for the Bunko Goodies Galore exchange," she said.

Tanner imagined biting into one of his mother's white-chocolate-chip-and-macadamia-nut cookies. He wasn't sure whether he liked them best or her pumpkin bread. Both were favorites with the family and her Bunko pals.

"Hope you're making enough for me, too."

She chuckled merrily. "Of course. Come by this weekend, and I'll load you up."

"I just might do that."

"Where are you? Is that music I hear?"

"At the Holly Daze Festival. With Jewel and Ava."

"How fun! I'm glad you three are getting out together."

As they chatted, Tanner's gaze wandered. The park at the center of town had been completely transformed by the event. Food trucks and a tent-covered dining area occupied one entire corner of the festival grounds. A variety of vendor booths, including one from Sweetheart Ranch, were scattered throughout the many attractions. A few of the stops on Tanner and Jewel's list were the petting zoo, an interactive

Santa's workshop, a mini Christmas carousel, a life-size snowman family and a twelve-foot lighted Christmas tree in the center of the park.

The star of the festival was Santa himself, sitting on a mock throne in the center of his workshop. Beneath the costume and fake beard was Emily's husband, Homer. Santa's appearance at the festival was sponsored by his church. In exchange for a donation to their holiday meals for the homeless program, children could sit on Santa's lap and whisper to him what they wanted for Christmas.

From where Tanner stood, he could see each child leave with a candy cane. Most wore big smiles and skipped excitedly. A few cried.

"Listen," he told his mom during a break in the conversation. "I have something to tell you."

"What?" Worry instantly tinged her voice.

"Jewel and I talked the other night. She knows what happened."

There was no need to elaborate or ask how his mother felt. Her poignant, "Ah," spoke volumes. "You did."

He'd been debating all day whether to tell his parents or not and finally decided to test the waters with his mother. They'd find out eventually. Better coming from him than if Jewel let slip a remark.

"How'd she react?" his mom asked.

Tanner shrugged, though his mother couldn't see him. "She was relieved, of course. And happy."

She'd seemed happy, anyway. When she wasn't acting strange and distant.

"I imagine she is. Does this mean you two might reconcile?" Hope replaced the worry in his mother's voice. "She's a good match for you. And with the baby…"

"I don't know, Mom. Hard to say. There are feelings there, on both sides. But a lot has happened. It's not as if we can just pick up where we left off. Jewel's being cautious. She has Ava to think about now. We both do."

It occurred to Tanner he may have just stumbled on the reason behind her recent behavior. Their respective attorneys had been talking a lot this week.

"What do *you* want, honey?"

He recalled the two near kisses he and Jewel had shared. He swore she'd experienced the same thrill he had and would be lying to himself if he said he didn't still want to spend the rest of his life with her—as her husband, not just co-parenting their daughter. He wasn't ready to admit that to anyone, however. Even his mother.

"I want to be a good dad to Ava, whatever that takes. Remain here or move to Oklahoma. Though, given the choice, I'd rather stay put."

He told her about the promotion Ethan had offered him and that he'd yet to decide. "I'd like to accept the job, if I can. For the next year, anyway, until I can start at the company."

"Is Jewel willing to stay?"

"Possibly, now that her parents are planning on dividing their time between here and Oklahoma. But she hasn't committed either way. A lot depends on if she lands the position at Sweetheart Ranch."

"I'm crossing my fingers. You two deserve a second chance. My heart broke when she called off the wedding."

"She wants me to go public about the cheating," Tanner said. "Clear my name."

"Well, that only makes sense from her perspective. If she decides to return to the rodeo circuit, she won't want that black cloud following her."

"And there's Ava to consider. She'd hate for our daughter to grow up believing her dad was a cheater."

"Hmm… I suppose."

"What's wrong, Mom? I recognize that tone."

"Besides how your dad will take this news and how the truth coming out will affect your brother's marriage?"

"Jewel promised not to say anything."

"But she'd like *you* to say something."

"She hasn't issued any ultimatums."

"That could change," his mom said, "and we can't afford anymore controversy."

"Did something happen?"

"The arena owners have been making noise again."

Tanner didn't like the sound of that. "Noise as in bringing a lawsuit?"

"Apparently right before the NFR last week, the arena owners applied significant pressure to the PRCA, demanding they crack down on cheating."

"Was there another incident?"

"Not specifically. *American Rodeo Report* ran a segment on their show, a look back at last year's NFR. They mentioned the cheating and you. On top of that, your dad heard from some friends who attended this year's event. They said people were still talking, though not as much. Naturally, he's on edge."

"People talking is no big deal."

"*American Rodeo Report* has a lot of viewers. Any stirring of the pot could be bad for us."

Tanner considered that for a moment. "We probably shouldn't tell Dad that Jewel knows. No sense adding fuel to the fire."

"For now," his mom conceded. "But I don't like hiding things from him."

"I promise it won't be for long."

He appreciated her predicament. Like him, like all of them, she was caught between a rock and a hard place. She wanted to abide by her husband's wishes, protect her eldest son's reputation and his shaky marriage, and make his life easier by helping with his medical bills.

She was equally determined that Tanner not continue bearing an unfair burden. And she was committed to making a place in the family for her newest grandchild and that grandchild's mother. He couldn't ask more of her, not with a clear conscience.

"By the way, how are Daniel and Rosalyn doing?" he asked. "Any better? I haven't talked to him in a while."

"No, unfortunately. I'm more and more convinced they'll separate after Christmas. That's the last thing Daniel needs right now. He's barely holding it together."

Just then, Jewel emerged from the mothers' lounge, pushing Ava's stroller ahead of her.

"Hey. Sorry to cut you short, Mom. Jewel's here."

"You go. Have some fun, and don't fret about anything. There's no problem that won't wait until tomorrow."

"Tell Dad hi. I love you."

"Love you, too, son. Kiss Ava for me, and see you this weekend."

He flashed Jewel a huge grin as she neared. "There you are."

"Sorry we took so long. One of us was being fussy."

She must not have stopped in front of a mirror on her way out, for her pink stocking cap with its snowy white tassel sat askew on her head. Likely Ava's doing. Lately she'd been grabbing at any object within reach.

Tanner started to say something and then changed his mind. "Wait."

Without giving her the chance to object, he reached out and adjusted the cap, tugging it down over her ears. "Now you don't look like you've had one too many rum eggnogs."

Fortunately, she reacted with a laugh and didn't slap his hands away. "I appreciate you taking care of me."

He lowered his voice. "Always, Jewel. You and Ava."

Her laugh mellowed to a smile, and she stared at him with those large, luminous brown eyes. "Tanner…"

He figured she was about to warn him off again. Not tonight, he decided and drew her into his embrace.

"I know you're mad at me."

She tensed but didn't pull away. "I'm not mad at you."

"Confused? Cautious? Scared? Worried?"

"A little of each, to be honest. I'd rather not have my life implode two Christmases in a row. Neither do I want to give you false hope. I'm glad you didn't cheat. More than glad. I'm elated. But that doesn't make our problems disappear."

"I get it."

He wouldn't tell her what his mother had said about the arena owners and the *American Rodeo Report* news segment. She'd be that much more confused, cautious, scared and worried.

She met his gaze. "I have some news."

"Yeah?"

"I have a potential photography job. For an art store. They're launching a spring marketing campaign. One of the store owners was a recent bride at Sweetheart Ranch."

"Congratulations! That's great."

"It's not a done deal. I'm taking sample pictures first. If they like my work, we'll go from there."

"I have no doubt you'll wow them."

"We'll see."

At the odd note in her voice, he asked. "What's up?"

"The sample photo shoot is the third week of January."

Interesting. "You're staying on, then?"

"I'm staying longer. Not sure about the rest."

Longer was good enough for him. He tightened his hold on her. "Let's celebrate."

"No alcohol. I'm nursing."

He lowered his head. "I was thinking of something else."

"Why am I not surprised?"

"How about…" He nuzzled her cheek. Her skin was cold in contrast to her warm breath, which tickled his neck. "We…" He brushed his lips across hers and pressed his palm into the center of her back, bringing her closer. "Get… out of here."

Her brows shot up. "We just arrived."

"Get out of here and head to the concession stand for some hot chocolate."

She groaned with exaggerated frustration. "Quit teasing me."

Like that was possible. He loved getting a rise out of her. Plus, she made it easy.

Ava may have been fussy earlier. At the moment, however, she was satisfied with sitting in her stroller and looking about.

Tanner used the opportunity to its full potential and went in for the kiss, covering Jewel's mouth with his. He was determined there'd be no thwarted effort tonight. And, to his profound satisfaction, there wasn't.

Her lips moved in perfect harmony with

his, giving and then taking. Sweet yet sensual. When he would have ended the kiss—they were in public, after all—she grabbed the fabric of his jacket and crushed it between her fingers, keeping him anchored to her. Not that Tanner was going anywhere.

It had been far too long since he'd held her. Their connection, as always, was immediate and all consuming. Tanner kissed her like a man who'd lost the woman he loved and, thank God, found her again.

Eventually, common sense kicked in and, smiling shyly, they broke apart. As she moved away, Tanner vowed to himself he wouldn't wait so long to hold Jewel like that again.

"You ready for that hot chocolate?"

She inclined her head. "I think we should head over to see Santa first before the line gets too long. After that, can we stop by the table for Sweetheart Ranch? I promised Emily I'd take some pictures."

"No problem."

When she took hold of the stroller and turned it, he covered her hand with his. Together they pushed Ava. Tanner was convinced anyone observing them would see a family with two doting parents who were crazy about each other and their child. And they'd be right.

Three-foot-tall candy canes stuck in the

grassy ground formed a pathway to see Santa. Tanner, Jewel and Ava took their place behind the last people in line, a disinterested looking dad watching a basketball game on his phone and his two misbehaving youngsters. Tanner felt sorry for the man—he was missing out on a special time with his children, one he'd never get back.

That wouldn't be him. Whatever it took, he'd be an active, involved, devoted father.

The line moved slowly. They passed the time discussing Christmas plans—both Tanner and Jewel had yet to finish their Christmas shopping and agreed to check out the craft booths tonight if there was time. She didn't bring up his coming clean and instead stuck to neutral subjects like her photography work and a troublesome sore on Teddy Bear's side.

"The pictures from the barrel racing event came out really well," she said. "I might give some to the owner of the Poco Dinero." She bit her lower lip and looked chagrined. "Or would that be too pushy?"

"You hoping she'll hire you?"

"Or, that she'll put the pictures on display and give me credit."

"Free advertising? I say do it." Tanner touched her elbow and inched them ahead a few feet. "There's also that place up north that has bull riding events similar to the Poco Dinero. You might try them, too."

"Is that the Cave Creek Rough Stock Rental Company?"

"Yeah."

He didn't remind Jewel about that being the place the two high school barrel racers had mentioned—right before they'd started gossiping about her and Tanner. He didn't want to bring up any bad memories, not when the evening was going so well.

"Do they have a bar?" she asked.

"Only on the nights of events. They also give bull riding lessons on Saturday mornings."

"Hmm." Jewel's eyes sparked with interest. "Have you ever been?"

"No. Been thinking about it, though." Actually, he'd been wondering if they were in need of a bull riding instructor.

"You should."

"Compete?" He laughed. "I'm out of practice."

"Naw," she scoffed. "It's like riding a bike."

"Says the person who's never been on a bull."

She dragged him along with her as the line moved. "What did you tell me? Participating is practicing. Besides, I doubt you're that rusty."

"They do have an event tomorrow evening. At seven." He'd checked their web page this morning when the idea had come to him about an instructor position.

"You should go! I'm serious."

"Umm...no."

"Don't you miss bull riding?"

"Yeah, sure," he admitted.

"Are you afraid of being recognized? Is that what's holding you back?"

He would be recognized, and the other competitors might not be happy to see him. That wasn't the reason, however. His hide had grown pretty thick this last year. "I can handle a little trash talk."

"Come on, then. I competed in the barrel racing event. And look, I came in second."

"Ow!" He winced. "You swing pretty low."

"I'm not swinging, I'm motivating you."

That did it. Tanner wasn't about to be shown up by a barrel racer. "All right. But only if you come with me."

"I'm working."

"Chicken."

She gave an indignant snort. "I'll be done by three thirty. Pick us up at four thirty. That should leave us plenty of time to get to Cave Creek before the event starts."

Bull riding. For all his brave talk, was he really ready to try again?

Excitement coursed through him. Heck, yeah,

he was ready. And while he was there, he'd try and talk to the manager about an instructor job.

"How will your family feel?"

Jewel's question put a damper on his good mood. "They won't like it."

"You going to tell them?"

"Not right away." He grinned.

"I'm proud of you, Tanner."

He reached up and cupped her cheek. "Thanks. That means a lot to me."

Before long, it was their turn with Santa. Tanner had met Homer a few times. Even so, he wouldn't have recognized the man beneath the very convincing fake beard, red hat and added padding around his middle.

Ava didn't cry when she was placed in Santa's lap. Nor did she smile. She just stared. Jewel and Tanner took dozens of pictures with their phones. Jewel even recorded a short video, capturing Santa's hearty, "Ho, ho, ho," and Ava grabbing his beard. Good thing her grip wasn't strong enough to dislodge it.

Jewel pocketed the candy cane Santa's elf gave them when they departed. Tanner removed several bills from his wallet and left a donation in the decorated toy box. Outside the area, they stopped for a moment, laughing when they realized they were both sending pictures of Ava and Santa to their respective mothers.

They went from there to the table for Sweetheart Ranch where Jewel unpacked her camera from the stroller and quickly took several shots from different angles.

"How about that hot chocolate?" Tanner asked when she was done.

It was getting cold and he could use something to warm his insides. Since cuddling with Jewel was out of the question, for the meantime, anyway, he'd have to settle for a hot drink.

Hopefully, that would change. Bull riding tomorrow in Cave Creek could wind up being a disaster. It could also be exactly the step he needed to take to fix his broken life. He was willing to take the chance. With Jewel, he thought, and reached for her hand.

THE REASON TANNER stored his bull riding equipment at his parents' home wasn't because he lacked room at Powell Ranch. He simply preferred as few reminders of his glory days as possible. Neither of his parents had remarked much when he'd carted the various canvas bags and cases containing his protective gear, bull ropes, boots, chaps, spurs, gloves and even his favorite shirt to the tack room in the barn behind their house last January.

What could they have said? "You're doing the right thing," from his dad and, "I'm so sorry, honey," from his mom wouldn't have healed his wounds.

No doubt they'd have something to say today when he retrieved those items. He could already hear his dad's, "What the heck are you thinking?" and his mom's, "Is this wise, honey?"

Tanner was dropping by their house with the excuse of picking up the holiday cookies and pumpkin bread his mom had offered him yesterday. Depending on how the visit went, he might tell them of his plans to compete tonight at the bull riding event in Cave Creek. More likely he'd sneak out back when no one was looking.

As he turned onto their street and neared the house, he spied his sister-in-law's minivan and muttered under his breath. He'd have enough of a fight on his hands if his parents discovered him retrieving his equipment. Daniel and Rosalyn being there would make it far worse.

He briefly considered driving past the house and calling his mom to tell her an emergency had arisen at work. But then he wouldn't have his equipment for tonight, and competing was important to him. He needed to prove to himself and Jewel that he was serious about taking his life back and committed to their future.

Parking in the driveway next to Rosalyn's minivan, he got out and headed up the walkway to the front door. After knocking loudly, he entered. His parents had a come-on-in rule where close family was concerned, particularly when the visit was expected like this one.

"Anybody home?" he called out to the empty living room.

"In here." His mother's voice carried from the large great room.

Rounding the corner, he found his parents, brother and sister-in-law sitting at the dining table. Tanner's four-year-old niece and two-year-old nephew were sprawled out on the nearby sectional couch, watching cartoons on the TV.

"Morning, son." His mom pushed away from the table and gave him a hug. "Perfect timing. Daniel, Rosalyn and the children just got here."

The rest greeted him with big smiles and warm hellos. Kisses on cheeks and claps on backs were exchanged. Tanner's niece Lisa-Anne popped up from her place on the sectional and scrambled over.

"Hi, Uncle Tanner."

"Hi to you, kiddo." Sitting in the nearest empty chair, he ruffled her hair affectionately.

"Did you bring my baby cousin?"

"Sorry. Not this time."

"When?" she pleaded. She'd been eager to meet Ava from the moment she'd learned about her.

"On Christmas when we all go to brunch."

"That's sooooo long." She twisted sideways and threw herself dramatically onto his knee.

"Five days. Not that long."

"I wanna play with her."

"She's too little for playing. But you can hold her."

"Yay!" Lisa-Anne hauled herself upright and clapped.

Little Montgomery—Monty for short—didn't have much interest in conversing with Tanner. He made straight for his grandmother who lifted him onto her lap where he snuggled close and stuck his thumb in his mouth.

With no baby cousin to see, Lisa-Anne lost interest in Tanner and pestered her mother for more juice. Balancing a full cup, she returned to her place in front of the TV.

Tanner helped himself to some coffee from the pot on the table. "Didn't expect to see you here," he said to his brother as he poured.

"Mom and Dad are babysitting for us while we run errands." Daniel stressed the last two words.

"Ah." Tanner nodded. Santa's helpers must be needing some alone time for shopping.

He grabbed a piece of the coffee cake his mom had set out on a platter. Taking a bite, he mentally formulated a plan to get to the barn for his equipment without raising suspicion.

"I told Rosalyn she could go alone and that I'd watch the kids, rather than inconvenience the folks." Daniel patted his wife's hand. "She insisted I come with her."

"It's nice you're shopping together," Tanner's mom said. "And we don't mind babysitting. Nothing I love more."

"I don't think she trusts me alone with the kids."

"Quit making jokes like that." Rosalyn slid her hand away. "They're not funny."

"But they're true."

Her mouth flattened in annoyance.

Tanner wondered if he was the only one who noticed she didn't contradict Daniel. Taking another bite of coffee cake, he studied her discreetly.

Her features were more strained than usual, and he was fairly certain she'd lost even more weight. Her hair, normally styled attractively, had been knotted and stuffed into one of those cheap plastic clips. The red lipstick she'd applied stood out against the pallor of her cheeks.

Given her appearance and Daniel's biting remark, Tanner assumed the situation at home wasn't any better. Likely worse.

Truthfully, and sadly, Rosalyn didn't trust Daniel alone with the kids and dreaded leaving him in charge. In her defense, his mobility limitations made chasing after a trouble-seeking toddler and lively preschooler hard. His meds slowed his responses even further. And there were his unpredictable mood swings and temper outbursts. Without Rosalyn to act as a buffer, the kids would receive the brunt of his anger and impatience should something set him off.

Tanner wasn't especially close to Rosalyn, and they'd had their differences in the past. But he wouldn't have wished this on her for the world.

They chatted about nothing much for the next ten minutes. Tanner's mom had received a number of cards from family members and old friends, including a holiday letter, and she recounted the noteworthy news.

When the topic turned to politics—Tanner's dad and brother didn't see eye to eye—Tanner offered an excuse and headed out back. He quickly located the equipment bags in the tack room and carried them to his truck. If a moment presented itself, he'd tell his parents. If not, he'd call them tomorrow. After he'd competed tonight.

He'd no sooner secured the equipment in the bed of his truck than he turned to find Rosalyn standing there, wearing only a light cardigan and clutching her middle. She looked thinner than she had inside and as fragile as a dried leaf.

Surprised, Tanner said, "Hey, Rosalyn. What's up?"

"Do you have a minute? I need to ask you something."

His gut warned him this was a conversation he'd rather avoid. She hadn't tracked him down to inquire about gift suggestions for Daniel. Leaning an elbow on the truck bed, he attempted a casualness he didn't feel.

"Ask away."

"Have you talked to Daniel lately?"

"The other day." He didn't mention they'd been shopping for emerald earrings.

"What about?"

He had no intention of revealing they'd argued. Instead, he deflected. "Is something going on I should know about?"

"I think Daniel's lying to me," she blurted out.

Tanner fought to control his reaction. "You do?"

"Several times recently I've walked in while he's on the phone with your dad. The second he sees me, he yells at me to get out or hangs up. When I ask him about the calls, he says it's work or nothing important. If I press, we end up fighting. Funny thing is, I don't think he's mad at me. I think he's trying to distract me from the calls."

She was more astute than Daniel gave her credit for. "Maybe it is just work or nothing important."

"No." She shook her head and hugged herself tighter. "I've caught enough of the conversations to tell they're about what happened last year."

"We all talk about that," Tanner answered carefully. "Mom and I just had a conversation the other day."

"My point exactly. Why would Daniel feel the need for secret calls with your dad and then lie to me about them?" She continued without giving him a chance to respond. "Then there's the remark our marriage counselor made."

"What remark is that?"

"We've each had several private sessions with her. I don't know what Daniel's discussed with her, but last week she brought up the scandal and him having regrets."

"Daniel does regret what happened. To me," Tanner added.

"Yeah, except that's not how she phrased it. She specifically used the word *guilt*." Rosalyn brought her folded hands to her mouth and blew on them.

"Why don't you go inside? It's cold out here."

She ignored him. "He got really upset with her and almost walked out of the session. I had to twist his arm to return with me this week."

"I have no idea what's going on," Tanner lied. He wouldn't be the one to tell Rosalyn that Daniel, and not he, had tried to cheat. "Sorry."

"We have so many problems." Tears clogged her voice. "We don't need another one."

This wasn't another one. Not really. The problems she and Daniel faced were all tied together. Daniel's brain cancer, his surgery and resulting aftereffects, the cheating, the potential risk to Bridwell and Associates, his marital problems. Though the family wanted only to support Daniel and help however possible, they'd been sucked down into a dark mire of his creation.

"He's trying his best." Tanner felt the need to defend his brother. "Much of this isn't his fault."

That didn't absolve him in Tanner's opinion. He could make changes moving forward, including leveling with his wife.

"I know." Rosalyn seemed to grow smaller. "I was just hoping he'd confided in you."

"'fraid not." Tanner tried another approach. "What about the marriage counselor? Maybe she can convince Daniel to open up to you."

Rosalyn crumpled in on herself. "I'm just so tired of complaining to her."

"You aren't complaining. You're unloading. It's her job to listen."

She wiped at her damp eyes.

252 THE COWBOY'S CHRISTMAS BABY

He put an arm around her shoulders and squeezed. "Don't give up on Daniel yet. In another year, this will all be over."

"If I can wait that long."

Having no clue how to respond, he said, "Let's go in the house before you freeze to death."

"Leaving so soon?" his mom asked when they returned to the dining area. Monty had abandoned her lap and rejoined his sister in front of the TV.

"Have to." Tanner bent and kissed his mom on top of the head. "I'll call you later."

"Wait a minute. I'll walk you out." His dad rose and came around the table. "There's something I need to ask you."

Tanner's radar went on high alert. "I don't have much time, Dad."

"This won't take long."

He said goodbye to everyone and left with a big tin of cookies and two loaves of pumpkin bread tucked under his arm.

"I didn't want your mother to hear," his dad said the moment they were outside.

Tanner braced himself. "Hear what?"

His dad motioned to the bed of the truck as they neared. "I saw you through the window when I went to the kitchen. What are you planning on doing with those?"

"Last time I checked, they're mine to do with what I want. But I appreciate you storing them for me."

"Come on, son. What are you hiding?"

"I'm competing tonight at the Cave Creek Rough Stock Rental Company."

"Why, in God's name?"

Obviously, his mom hadn't mentioned their talk yesterday. Left with no other choice, Tanner did. "I told Jewel what really happened last year."

"Have you lost your mind? The arena owners are—"

"I was tired of her believing I'd cheated. If we have any chance of getting back together, she had to know the truth."

"So, now you're going to announce your whereabouts to everyone by competing tonight. Good grief, son, are you single-handedly trying to ruin the company?"

"I'll sign over my shares in the company to you." Even as Tanner spoke, he wondered why he hadn't thought of this before. His having no financial interest in Bridwell and Associates might solve all their problems. "Or to Daniel. Whatever you want."

His dad thrust his fingers through his thinning gray hair. It was only then that Tanner realized how much his dad had aged this past year. His mom, too.

Tanner gentled his voice. "Dad, don't take this the wrong way, please. But I'm tired of you holding the company and its demise over me like a hammer. If signing over my shares to you stops that, then hand me a pen."

His remark appeared to take his father aback, and his features fell. "That'll shatter your mom. Me, too. We've worked hard for almost thirty years. We want nothing more than to pass Bridwell and Associates down to you and Daniel."

The admission, delivered with surprising sincerity, weakened Tanner's resolve.

"I want that, too, Dad."

"One more year. That's all you have to wait. Don't throw away everything we've worked so hard for."

"I'm just competing in an amateur event. Not taking an ad out on the front page of the newspaper. Nothing's going to happen."

"You can't be sure."

"I need to move forward, make a life with my daughter and hopefully Jewel." A conviction Tanner hadn't felt before filled him and purpose. "If I can't do that here, I'll move to Oklahoma with them."

"What about your mother? And your brother?

You'd leave them when they both need you the most?"

"I don't want to. And I hope you don't put me in a position where I'm forced to choose. But I've sacrificed enough for Daniel."

His dad lost even more of his bluster. "All I've ever wanted was what's best for this family."

"I understand." Tanner put an arm around his dad's shoulders, feeling a closeness he hadn't for a long time. He couldn't ignore the pronounced creases in his dad's face or chronic worry in his eyes, also new this past year. They each wore the stress differently. "I really do. Becoming a father has changed my perspective on a lot of things."

His dad's voice broke when he spoke. "Be careful tonight."

"I will."

"And good luck."

"Thanks. That means a lot."

Tanner was both lighter and heavier of heart when he left his parents' house. On the one hand, he and his dad had made progress. On the other hand, he was even more worried about Daniel and Rosalyn's rocky marriage.

Maybe he'd call his brother tomorrow and urge him to be honest with Rosalyn. Tanner had learned a very hard lesson this past year:

deception will destroy even the most loving of relationships. Having finally told Jewel the truth, he'd never hide anything from her again.

CHAPTER ELEVEN

"Thanks for agreeing to babysit on such short notice." Jewel opened the door of her quarters to admit Tracee.

"No problem." The teenager entered and removed her hoodie. "I'm finished with school finals. And I could use the extra cash for Christmas presents."

"There are bottles ready to go in the fridge." Jewel pointed as she walked to the center of the room where Ava sat on the floor in her foam baby seat. "And a jar of strained pears on the counter."

"Yummy!"

"Ugh, not really. I've tasted them."

Kneeling down beside Ava, Jewel lavished her daughter with hugs and kisses. She hated leaving. When the reason was personal and not work-related, she hated it that much more. But Tanner was competing in the bull riding tonight, and she wanted to be there for him.

She'd considered taking Ava with them but decided against it. Between the cold weather, long drive, late night and typically raucous crowd that attended bull riding events, Ava was better off at home.

One more kiss, one more word of instruction for Tracee, and Jewel was off, coat and camera bag in hand. At the bottom of the stairs, her phone pinged with a text. Tanner, it seemed, was running a few minutes late. Rather than return to her quarters and endure another wrenching goodbye with Ava, she plopped down on the bench in front of the stables to wait.

She'd no sooner buttoned her coat than her phone started playing "Joy to the World," her mother's favorite Christmas song. Jewel had changed the ringtone yesterday.

Swiping the screen, she answered, "Hi, Mom."

"Hi to you, too. Is this a good time?"

"I have a few minutes. Tanner's on his way here." She explained about the bull riding.

"Wait. Hold on a second. Your dad wants to talk to you."

Jewel suppressed a groan as her mother put her on speakerphone.

"Frankly, honey, we're stunned. We had no idea Tanner was returning to rodeoing."

"He's not. Not yet, anyway. Possibly, eventually, he will." When the mess with Daniel was resolved once and for all.

"Is he allowed?" her dad asked. "I thought he was banned."

"Temporarily. And, anyway, this is a non-professional event. It's not governed by the same rules."

"Of course, it's none of our business, but do you really want to go?" Her mother's concern came across loud and clear. "After everything you went through last year, I'd think you'd avoid places where you might be recognized and… taunted."

Taunted. Such a gentle word for what Jewel had endured. Attacked, bullied, tormented were more like it. Was she ready for a repeat?

"Most of the competitors are amateurs. They may not have heard about the scandal."

"You don't really believe that, do you?"

She didn't. She was grasping at straws. "We're going, Mom. We can't keep hiding forever. I competed at the Poco Dinero a couple weeks ago and nothing bad happened."

There had been one or two dirty looks cast her way, and she was sure a few of the competitors had been gossiping about her. Nothing overt or unkind had been said to her face, however. Or Tanner's.

Her father harrumphed. "If he cared about you at all, he'd insist you stay home."

"I'm the one insisting on going."

"Tell me you're not taking Ava," her mother cut in.

"No. Tracee's babysitting."

"Thank God."

"It's bull riding, Mom." Jewel's voice rose and her booted foot tapped in frustration. Her parents would feel differently if they knew the truth. "We're not facing a violent mob."

"You could be. You've been treated horribly in the past. All that name-calling and insults and threats. I hate to see you suffer again and for no reason."

"Tanner has a reason to compete. A good one."

"I can't imagine what that is." Her mother sniffed, whether with sorrow or indignation Jewel wasn't certain.

"I've always tried to think the best of him," her dad said. "After today, I'm wondering if I was wrong. No decent man worth his salt would put you through this."

"He's not putting me through anything." Clearly, they weren't listening to her.

"You're confused, honey. Having him back in your life has—"

"He's innocent, Mom," Jewel blurted and then gasped when she realized she'd spoken out loud.

"How can you say that after what he did?"

Jewel realized she could fix this, tell her mother that she'd misunderstood or heard incorrectly.

Except, she couldn't. She desperately wanted her parents to know they'd been right to think the best of Tanner. Even when she'd cut the last thread of her belief in him, they'd clung to one.

"It's true. He is innocent. He didn't try to bribe that judge."

"He confessed," her dad insisted.

"Daniel's the one who tried to cheat. Tanner took the blame for him."

The pause that followed lasted several seconds. "He told you that?"

"Yes. He did."

"And you're *sure* he wasn't lying?"

"Dad!"

"I just find it hard to believe he'd give up his shot at a championship title, throw away his entire career *and* leave behind the woman he was about to marry in a few days for his brother."

"Daniel was having dangerous brain surgery the next week." Jewel's voice rose. "Tanner wasn't sure he'd see Daniel alive again. Helping him out makes Tanner a pretty decent guy in my book."

Another long pause ensued before her dad said, "He could be trying to manipulate you,

Jewel. Get you on his side so that you won't move back home and take Ava."

"That's not what he's doing." She recounted the story, including how Tanner's dad was behind the cover up. She ended with Tanner's intention of coming clean.

"When?" her dad asked.

"Soon. After the holidays." Hopefully, though, that was more her wish and less Tanner's.

Her mom released a long pitiful sigh. "What a mess."

"It is that."

"Tanner must love his brother very much."

"He really does."

"Assuming I buy all this," her dad interrupted, "and I'm not saying I do. That doesn't change the fact that tonight could be very difficult for the two of you."

"It could also be a good test for us."

"Are you two back together?"

"We're taking things slow," Jewel hedged, convinced her parents saw right through her. "Very slow."

At that moment, Tanner's truck bumped onto the long driveway leading to the ranch. From her higher vantage point, she tracked its progress, the late afternoon sun glinting off the chrome fender and bumper.

"I need to go. Tanner's here."

Her dad wasn't finished speaking his piece. "We'll talk more about this when we see you in a few days."

"You can't say anything to Tanner. To anyone. Especially his parents. I'm serious."

"We won't."

Jewel imagined her dad and mom exchanging looks. "It's important."

"You have our word."

She prayed it would be stronger than her word to Tanner, which she'd just broken.

Dropping her phone into her coat pocket, she plastered a smile on her face. Guilt ate a hole in her stomach. She'd been wrong to tell her parents about Tanner's innocence, even if her intentions were good.

The second his truck came to a stop, she climbed in the passenger side. She'd no sooner buckled her seat belt than he leaned across the center console and gave her a quick hard kiss. The gesture was so much like when they'd been together, for a brief moment she forgot about her huge mistake and the potential repercussions.

"There," he said as if he'd been waiting hours to kiss her.

Had he?

"There's something I need to tell you."

He sent her a curious stare. "Should I be worried?"

"I accidentally told my parents that it was Daniel and not you who tried to bribe the judge."

"Accidentally?"

"It slipped out." She couldn't bring herself to look at him. This was hardly the first time she'd reacted emotionally and failed to think first. For instance, in Vegas when she'd sent Tanner packing. "We were talking about the bull riding tonight, and they were...were..."

"Giving you grief?"

"Something like that."

He turned onto the main road. "And you felt the need to defend me."

"I'm really sorry."

He said nothing for the next couple of miles, silently mulling over her admission.

"Tanner?"

"It's okay."

"What? No! Are you sure?" He couldn't be letting her off this easy. "I promised you I'd stay quiet, and I didn't last more than a few days."

"As long as they don't bring it up in front of my parents, we'll be fine. You did warn them not to?"

"Of course!"

"Okay," he repeated.

She studied his face with its rigid, bristled

jaw. Was that the start of a new beard? With him coming clean soon, no reason he couldn't go back to his former look.

"You're mad at me," she said.

"I'm not mad."

"You should be. I screwed up."

"Getting mad won't solve anything."

How could he be so darn understanding? If the situation were reversed and he'd been the one to break a promise, she'd be furious with him.

He startled her by reaching for her hand. "We'll get through this, Jewel."

"Will we?"

"All right. I'd rather your folks didn't know yet. But I'm kind of glad, too. I never liked them thinking poorly of me."

"Me, neither." She dared to smile a little.

"They'll be here in, what, three days? You must be excited to see them."

"I am."

Glad for a change in subject, she babbled on about her parents' house hunting plans and Christmas Day brunch. Tanner made the appropriate responses at the appropriate places, being far nicer to her than she deserved.

"I had something interesting happen today," he said when she was done. "Rosalyn cornered me while I was loading my equipment in the truck. She suspects Daniel's lying to her."

"Oh, dear. What did you say?"

"Nothing." Tanner slowed as he merged onto the freeway. "It's Daniel's place to tell her, not mine."

"Or, I could tell her, seeing as I have a big mouth."

"Very funny." The genuine grin he sent her eased her residual concerns. "It gets crazier. Dad spotted me sneaking off to the barn and confronted me. I admitted I was competing tonight."

"I bet he wasn't happy."

"Not at first. I told him I was sick and tired of him always holding the lawsuit over my head and I'd sign my shares in the company over to him or Daniel if that would stop him."

"How'd he take that?"

"Better than I thought he would. He actually backed down a little."

Jewel couldn't contain her happiness. Tanner standing up to his dad and entering the bull riding tonight were big steps toward a life free of the chains around his neck. Unfortunately, the good feeling didn't last.

"I'm going to talk to the livestock manager tonight," he said. "About a bull riding instructor position."

She thought he must have lost his mind. What she said was, "Is that a good idea? He's probably heard about the cheating scandal."

"We'll see."

We'll see? What kind of answer was that? "You can bet some of the students have heard. They may not like you or respect you or want a confessed cheater for an instructor."

"It's just an idea. No big deal."

She could see he'd been counting on her sharing his excitement and that she'd disappointed him.

"Maybe you should wait until you've come clean."

"You made your point," he snapped. "I won't talk to the manager."

Great. She'd screwed up again. "I'm just looking out for you."

"Are you?"

"I'm sorry?"

"I don't like thinking you're manipulating me."

She nearly came off the seat. "I'm doing no such thing."

"No? Telling your parents feels a little like your way of applying pressure, getting me to come clean faster."

Had she? "I swear, that's not what happened."

"You haven't believed in me for a long time, Jewel. It can't be easy changing."

"I do believe in you." *I do. Really. I want to...*

He switched the radio to a different station. "How's Ava today?"

For the rest of the drive, they stuck to small talk. Tanner was about to climb on the back of an eighteen-hundred-pound bull. He didn't need to be distracted by an argument with her. Maybe she should have waited until later tonight to tell him about her blunder. Too late now.

They reached Cave Creek a short time later. Jewel had never been before and was struck by the similarities to Mustang Valley. Along with the Old West atmosphere, there were modern-day watering holes, cowboy-themed tourist attractions and people on horseback riding through the center of town.

The Cave Creek Rough Stock Rental Company was located a few miles outside of town to the east. Judging by the crammed visitor parking lot, the distance wasn't a deterrent for attendees.

Tanner had explained that the company's main business was renting bucking stock to rodeos. Nearly two decades ago, the owner had started a bull and bronc riding school. With the success of that, he'd later added amateur events.

"Supposedly, this is where the owner of the

Poco Dinero got her idea to have bull riding and barrel racing events," Tanner said.

Jewel studied the rustic building, which resembled those from old TV Westerns she'd watched as a child. Behind it, the top rows of the arena stands were visible above the roofline. "I bet the owner doesn't like having competition."

"Given the size of this crowd, I don't think it's a problem."

A large banner strung across the front of the main building advertised the Holiday Extravaganza Jackpot. Arrows pointed out where to park, where to eat, where the restrooms were located and where to sign in. Jewel noted there were only two horse trailers in the parking lot. Unlike barrel racing, bull and bronc riders didn't require their own mounts to compete.

Tanner went to the back of his truck and removed the canvas cases containing his gear and safety equipment. Together they started toward the main building, Jewel slinging her camera bag over her shoulder. Her goal was to get some pictures of Tanner but, as always, she'd keep her eyes peeled for any interesting photo opportunities.

Before they parted, she gave him a hug. It turned into a lingering kiss that erased most of her earlier concerns about the state of their relationship.

"Stay safe."

He sifted his hands through her hair. "I'll look for you in the stands."

At the entrance, she paid for her admission while Tanner headed around the side to where the participants registered. Making her way up the steps to the only available seats in the top rows, she searched for any unfriendly glances aimed in her direction and noticed none. That was a good sign.

Once seated, she removed her camera from the case and began taking pictures—mostly to keep herself occupied and her nerves under control.

She jerked and let out a small gasp when the PA system crackled to life and the first bulls made their noisy entrance into the bucking chutes, angrily kicking and snorting.

The crowd cheered when cowboys on horseback rode into the arena. It was their job to pull the rider off the bull if necessary, release the bucking strap and then herd the bull to the gate at the far end of the arena. The cowboys were followed by the bullfighters, always a crowd favorite in their colorful jerseys and face paint. Their highly dangerous job was to distract the bull from the rider with often humorous antics, allowing him to scramble to safety.

She suddenly didn't care about rude remarks

or mean glances. All she wanted was for Tanner to be safe and come through his ride in one piece. It was all she'd ever wanted.

"YOU HAVE A lot of nerve, Bridwell, showing your face here. Or within a mile of any rodeo arena." The man stared down Tanner, hands braced on his chaps-clad hips, a menacing scowl darkening his features.

"You'd better watch your back," the man's buddy warned, a clenched fist raised.

The angry pair weren't the only competitors unhappy to see Tanner. Three more stood outside the bucking chutes at the Cave Creek Rough Stock Rental Company looking ready to join in at the least provocation.

He wasn't intimidated—he'd expected this kind of welcome. He was, however, on guard. He avoided fights, which were a not an uncommon occurrence at rodeos where emotions ran high. They rarely solved anything, and he'd walk away if necessary, taking the hit to his pride.

"I'm just here to practice like the rest of you." He mustered what he hoped was a friendly I-don't-want-any-trouble smile.

"You ain't thinking of getting back in the game?" the first guy said, his tone threatening. He was about Tanner's height, though a bit wirier, something he compensated for by puffing out his chest.

"I'd be a fool to be thinking that, wouldn't I?"

Truthfully, he'd thought about it a lot lately. But until the PRCA lifted his ban and Daniel came clean, events like the one tonight were all he could participate in.

"Nobody wants you here," the second guy said.

"Hey, man. I paid my entry fee. The cashier didn't have a problem taking my money."

Tanner had opted not to talk to the manager about the instructor position—a smart decision based on the treatment he was getting. Jewel had been right. He had enough problems on his plate and had no business courting more.

"I'm up soon. Keep an eye on him." The first man elbowed his buddy. "Make sure he doesn't get alone with the judge."

The second man, a shorter, burlier version of the first one, barked an ugly laugh. "Ain't happening."

At this rate, Tanner would be on his own. No one to help him with his bull rope or keep an eye on the bull during the dangerous mounting or, most importantly, lend moral support.

He told himself it didn't matter. He was here to prove his commitment to Jewel and their future, not to win or even get a high score.

Darn it, but he missed Daniel and the relationship they'd once had. Even when vying for the same win, they'd always been there for each other.

Walking toward the arena fence, he scanned the stands. He spotted Jewel sitting near the top, no one occupying the seats on either side of her. Was she purposely avoiding people? God, he hoped not. The temptation to call her hit him hard, but he resisted. He needed to focus.

Hooking a boot on the lower rung of the fence, he hauled himself up in order to watch. From the corner of his eye, he noticed Jewel taking pictures. Good. All must be well.

While waiting for his number to be called, he studied the performance of the bulls and their riders. Several of the men, like the ones who'd confronted him earlier, were semiprofessional locals. For them, rodeo was a hobby rather than a full-time passion. He recognized a handful of retired champs who were recapturing the addictive jolt of adrenaline from their younger days or perhaps practicing for one of the senior-pro rodeos.

He had no idea how well he'd do tonight. He prayed muscle memory would kick in. Then again, it had been a full year, and he was sorely out of practice. In hindsight, he should have practiced on a mechanical bull a few times before attempting the real thing.

The jolt to his system when his number was finally called had him hopping off the fence, his boots hitting the hard ground with a thud. Ignoring the laser glares from the two men—both had gone already and done passably well—he made his way to the chutes. A few minutes remained to ready himself, and he'd need every one of them.

While watching the stockmen guide the bull he'd drawn—a pure-black burly brute named Haboob—into the chute, he felt a hand on his shoulder. Tanner cranked his head around to meet the gap-toothed grin of a young cowboy he'd watched compete earlier.

"Need a hand?" he asked. "Name's Cory."

"You sure about this?" Tanner eyed his new friend skeptically. "I'm not very popular around these parts."

"I ain't looking to make any friends."

"Are you looking to make a few enemies? Because you might."

"Got me an ulterior motive," Cory admitted sheepishly. "I was hoping you'd give me some pointers when you're done. Ain't nobody can hang on like you, 'ceptin' maybe your brother."

"If you're sure."

Tanner was grateful for the assistance and

the conversation. Both took his mind off his lack of practice and boosted his confidence. He climbed onto the chute containing Haboob and rechecked the fasteners on his protective vest. Satisfied, he swung his right leg to the other side of the chute and balanced himself directly above Haboob's back. The animal instantly tensed, nervous energy pulsating through him.

He wasn't the only one. Tanner's muscles were hard as concrete.

"I probably should have tried this at least once before tonight."

Cory straddled the chute alongside Tanner. "Like riding a bike."

"Yeah, says who?"

Tanner carefully lowered himself onto Haboob's back. Instantly, the bull jerked and shimmied, bashing his horns into the metal sides and creating an enormous clamor.

Tugging on the end of his glove, Tanner slipped his palm under the bull rope's braided handle and wrapped the loose end once around his hand.

He then directed his entire attention onto the top of Haboob's head and cleared every thought except those of him and the bull and their cannon launch from the chute. In the distance, as if through a tunnel, he heard someone holler his name. They weren't cheering him on.

Cory slapped him on the back. "You got this."

Did he? Tanner wasn't sure.

He uttered a silent prayer, raised his left arm over his head and nodded to the cowboy manning the chute door, signaling he was ready.

The chute door flew open with a sharp clang. At the exact same instant, Haboob launched his entire eighteen hundred pounds into the arena. His back legs shot straight up like a rocket, and his head dipped so low his nose nearly touched the ground.

Tanner instinctively adjusted his weight and centered himself on Haboob's back, his fingers gripping the braided handle tighter and his heels digging into the bull's shoulders. Leaning back, he encouraged the bull to buck higher and harder. Haboob obliged. He jerked sideways and spun in a tight circle, knocking Tanner about and jarring his insides until he was convinced his lungs were where his stomach should be. By some small miracle, he held on, but he never achieved the exact right rhythm.

Dimly, he heard the buzzer sound. He'd made it! He'd lasted eight seconds. Releasing the bull rope, he threw himself off Haboob and scrambled away through the deep dirt on shaky legs. The bullfighters flashed across his line of vision as they attempted to distract Haboob. By the time Tanner slipped through the side gate, the cowboys on horseback were herding the bull toward the opposite end of the arena.

Catching his breath, his hand automatically went to his head, and he discovered he still wore his hat. Fancy that. He'd stayed on *and* kept his hat.

There'd been only a smattering of applause and cheers from the stands at the end of his ride, along with a few boos.

Brushing off his jeans, he again sought out Jewel. She was on her feet, her camera dangling from her neck. He could tell from her posture and stance that she'd been worried. He considered waving but refrained, preferring not to draw attention to her. He instead looked at the scoreboard. After a few seconds, a seventy-three appeared. Not great. Not embarrassing. Tanner could tell the ride had been far from his best.

He'd get better, if he continued to practice and attend events like this one. And, he knew with sudden certainty, he would. Whether professionally or not, Tanner would continue bull riding. He hadn't been ready when he'd been forced to retire. He still wasn't.

With only a few competitors left, he decided not to stick around.

"Good ride, cowboy," Cory called and hopped down from his perch on the arena fence.

They met up and chatted briefly about what Tanner had done right during his ride and what he'd done wrong. He liked the young cowboy, and they agreed to stay in touch.

Shaking his hand, Tanner said, "See you around."

"Count on it."

He didn't get far before he was approached by the two cowboys from earlier. One had finished with a score close to Tanner's. The other had done better.

"Guess you didn't cheat this time, Bridwell," the first one said. "Not with those numbers."

Tanner refused to engage them. Instead, he tugged on the brim of his hat and started off. "Have a nice Christmas."

"If you've got a lick of sense, you won't come 'round here again."

What he'd give to tell the jerk where to shove it. Words fought for escape, but Tanner bit down hard.

He started ahead a second time, only to draw up short. Not because of the cowboys. Jewel was hurrying straight for him, a radiant smile on her lovely face.

"You did great."

His arms went around her, and he drew her close. This exact same scene may have played out hundreds of times before, but today, for Tanner, it felt brand-new.

They still fit together perfectly, his chin the exact right height to rest on the top of her head. Her cheek found his chest and lay against it as her arms squeezed.

They stood like that for indeterminable moments, reveling in the sweet comfort of holding each other—until they were interrupted.

"Fancy that, his partner in crime is with him."

Apparently, the pair of cowboys weren't done harassing him.

The taller one shouldered his buddy. "The way I heard it, she helped him cheat by cozying up to the judge."

Nothing could have been further from the truth, and Tanner's blood boiled. He could take whatever mud they chose to sling at him. But he wouldn't allow them to mistreat or malign Jewel.

In a low lethal voice, he growled, "Leave her out of this."

The first man reddened with fury. "There ain't no place for the likes of you two in rodeo. Get out!"

Tanner immediately hustled Jewel away, ignoring her protests. Her safety was his main concern.

"Weren't those the same men talking to you

earlier?" she asked when they entered the parking area.

"They're nobody."

"What did they say to you, Tanner?"

They couldn't get to his truck fast enough. "I don't remember."

"You're lying."

"It doesn't matter." His grip on her arm tightened. "Did anyone else talk to you?"

"No. If they recognized me, they didn't let on." She watched him return his equipment to the canvas bags. "I'm sorry. This was all my fault."

"Don't be ridiculous."

"I was the one who encouraged you to enter."

"I wanted to see what would happen if I tried. Now I know."

"Bad idea."

"No, it wasn't." He opened the passenger door.

Rather than climb in, Jewel continued to stand there. "What if you come on the road with me, and this kind of thing keeps happening?"

"Let's not make any decisions tonight. I still need to talk to my dad and Daniel."

"Will you? Soon?"

"I'll try."

He wished they didn't always circle back to the same old subject. He was still grappling with residual excitement from the bull ride and anger from his confrontations with the cowboys.

"Tanner, if you would tell—"

"Not now, Jewel."

She stiffened at his curt response before climbing into the passenger seat. "All right."

He shut the door and walked around the front of the truck to the driver's side, hopping in behind the steering wheel.

"I'm sorry," he said, starting the truck.

"I realize I can be pushy. It's just that I feel we can't move forward with any kind of relationship and we can't be a real family until this is resolved. Your dad has forced you into an untenable situation. Me and Ava, too."

"No, he didn't. I agreed."

"Without knowing how bad the repercussions would be."

"Doesn't change anything." Tanner drove toward the exit. "I don't regret helping Daniel. I do regret not telling you the truth sooner."

"You've given up so much. You shouldn't have to keep paying for Daniel's mistake."

"Enough, Jewel. Give it a rest," he snapped. He was sick and tired of being pushed and pulled in a dozen different directions.

"I just want what's best for us."

"I want that, too. But constantly using Ava

and her custody as a bargaining chip isn't help-ing."

She gasped.

He hit the gas only to remind himself to slow down.

"I'm not doing that," she insisted.

"Aren't you?"

She was quiet after that. Stonily quiet.

So much for taking small steps forward. The evening he'd hoped would end on a positive note and a heated kiss instead resulted in a mostly silent ride home and a terse goodbye.

CHAPTER TWELVE

ALL RIGHT, JEWEL had been wrong to argue with Tanner. But she wasn't wrong in wanting them to be able to move forward and for him to clear his name. And no way did she use Ava's custody as a bargaining chip. Or, did she?

She replayed tonight's disagreement in her head while trudging up the stairs to her quarters, her camera bag slung over her shoulder and her hands shoved into her coat pockets. Her timing hadn't been the best. He'd just been confronted by those two cowboys and his defenses were up. She should have waited.

Tomorrow, she'd apologize. For her timing. Not for wanting his brother to come clean or for using Ava.

Okay, maybe for that part about Ava, too. She did mention their daughter often, but only to motivate Tanner, not to manipulate him.

At the top of the stairs, she dug in her coat pocket for her key. Before she could retrieve it, Tracee swung open the door, a finger pressed to her lips.

"Shh."

"Ava asleep?" Jewel whispered.

Tracee nodded. "Since about eight. She had her bottle and went right off."

"Good."

Jewel set her purse and camera bag on the table, her glance cutting to the travel crib. Ava lay on her side, only her down-covered head showing from beneath the baby blanket, a peaceful expression on her face.

At least one of them was getting a decent night's rest. Jewel was too wound up from the bull riding and her argument with Tanner to nod off anytime soon.

"You okay?" Tracee whispered. "You seem upset."

"Not at all. Just distracted." She smiled at the teenager. "I have a big day tomorrow, what with work and getting ready for my parents' visit. They arrive on Monday."

"You picking them up at the airport?"

"They're driving from Oklahoma. They're looking at winter homes while they're here and need a car. That, and my mom's not a fan of flying."

Tracee quietly gathered her hoodie, mittens, phone, earbuds and various other belongings she'd brought with her to keep herself entertained while Ava slept.

Jewel tried to listen and respond accordingly as she hung up her coat and went over to the crib. A quick brush of her fingertips across Ava's cheek didn't wake the baby, but it did melt Jewel's heart. She would never grow tired of gazing upon her daughter.

"See you tomorrow," Tracee said softly when Jewel walked her to the door.

"Thanks again. I couldn't have taken this job without your help. I realize it's only for baby-sitting, but if you ever need a job reference, let me know."

"Cool. I will."

Jewel made a mental note to give Tracee a Christmas bonus. She'd earned it, especially for her wonderful attitude. Maybe a gift card to one of those clothing stores at the mall.

After a ten-minute session with the breast pump, Jewel changed into pajamas and a warm fuzzy robe. Hoping a cup of lemon tea might relax her, she fixed herself one and settled in the recliner with her tablet, opening an ebook. Thirty minutes later, she was still reading and still wide-awake. So much for tea and a book.

Not that she'd gotten far. Twice, she'd come to a stop, realizing she'd scanned several pages without remembering a single word and then gone back. Three times she checked her phone on the table beside her to see if she'd missed a text from Tanner. She hadn't. Apparently, he wasn't having a restless night like her or feeling bad about earlier.

Could be he was giving her some space or planning what he was going to say to her tomorrow. No, Jewel was the one giving *him* space and planning what *she'd* say.

She released a low, miserable groan as tears filled her eyes. Why had everything changed for her and Tanner? In the beginning, their lives together had been perfect. They'd had a fun-filled courtship starting with their first meeting at the Parada Del Sol Rodeo almost three years ago and ending with a dream-like engagement. Tanner had even asked for her dad's permission before proposing and then hidden her engagement ring in a piece of cake at her birthday party. She must have watched the video her friend took of that moment a hundred times.

They got along well with each other's families. Both sets of parents had supported the marriage and couldn't have been more enthusiastic. They'd shared a love of rodeo, a desire for a family of their own and had had compatible career aspirations.

Before the cheating scandal, Tanner had been everything she'd wanted in a husband and life partner. Reliable, dependable, trustworthy, loyal, kind, compassionate, generous. All traits that she admired and respected. Also, the same traits that had compelled him to take the blame for his brother.

She was furious at him for his actions and for destroying their future. At the same time, deep down, she admired him for what he'd done and, dare she say it, loved him. Tanner was a good man. And she was possibly too hard on him.

Ava stirred. Jewel popped up from the recliner as if the baby had screamed, simultaneously wiping at her eyes. By the time she reached the crib, Ava was already drifting back to sleep. Were Jewel in a better mood, she'd have laughed at herself.

Noticing the clock, she sighed. It was almost eleven o'clock. She hadn't lied to Tracee, she did have a big day tomorrow, and Ava would wake in an hour or two, hungry and needing a diaper change. Jewel really should try and sleep.

But rather than pull down the bed cover, she went over to the table and removed her camera from the bag. Turning it over, she reviewed the pictures she'd taken that evening. Many were of Tanner.

"Hmm…not too shabby."

Quite excellent, in fact. Jewel liked taking action shots, which was possibly why she received the most compliments on her candid wedding photos rather than the staged ones.

She stopped scrolling when she came to a

picture of the bull riding chutes that included the two men who'd confronted her and Tanner. They didn't look angry or rough there, just two regular cowboys intently watching the competition.

Funny how pictures could be deceiving. They could also, just as often, show a person's true side. Were these men really as mean as they had seemed? They could have been simply defending what they believed was an age-old, honorable profession, one whose members held themselves to a high moral code. In their eyes, Tanner had violated that code.

Did Tanner believe his brother had done the same? He'd told her he took the blame for Daniel in order that, should he not survive his surgery, he wouldn't be remembered as a cheater. Yet Tanner had been willing to let people see him as one.

She rubbed a dull ache in her temple. It was all so confusing.

A minute later, she came to the pictures of him during his ride—from straddling the chute to dusting himself off and jogging out of the arena. Sweet heaven, he was handsome in his element like that. A natural. The camera loved him.

She returned to her favorite shot, zooming in to study his face. Timing was everything, and she'd been able to capture his expression at just the right moment, when it had conveyed a multitude of emotions. Determination, excitement, the tiniest trace of fear.

"Not bad," she murmured to herself. "Not bad at all." She'd seen plenty like these in rodeo magazines and websites dedicated to the sport.

An idea sprang to mind. Could she? Dare she?

Why not? No harm in trying. She'd done it before, more than once.

Wait, would Tanner object? Ooh, he might and then be very annoyed with her. The last thing they needed right now was another fight.

But positive exposure for him could go a long way in repairing his reputation. Especially when Daniel came clean. Which he would. Soon. Long before these pictures appeared, if the magazine even accepted them. Should Tanner object, and she didn't think he would, she'd contact the magazine and withdraw the photos from consideration.

With growing excitement—there'd be no sleeping for a while yet—Jewel transferred seven of the best photos to her tablet. After that, she pulled up the website for *Oklahoma Rodeo News*. They'd both appeared in the magazine previously. Jewel had once been the subject of a feature article when she'd won the state championship.

She completed the brief submission form, including a description of the event, and then uploaded that and the pictures to the magazine. By the time she finished, she was humming with excitement.

She may have just committed a giant mistake, one she'd come to regret. She didn't think so, however. She had to believe in Tanner. In them. And take chances.

Something she hadn't done a year ago and now wished she had.

"YOU HAVEN'T TOLD me yet, how do you like the Airbnb?" Jewel asked her parents.

"It's nice enough."

They were heading down the stairs from her quarters, her dad right behind her and her mom behind him, carrying Ava in the baby wrap. Her parents had arrived last evening ahead of schedule. Tired and road-weary, they'd settled into their vacation rental on the west side of Mustang Valley rather than visit. After a full morning of sleeping in, unpacking and stocking up on groceries at the market, they'd appeared at Jewel's door with lunch.

She was grateful for the extra time to herself. Her attorney had phoned during her morning coffee with upsetting news. Jewel had yet to recover and pretending nothing was amiss had begun to wear on her. She could discuss the matter with her parents, but she wasn't ready. Neither did she want to ruin their good moods and plans for the day.

By one thirty, Ava had pretty much reached her fill of doting grandparents and began fussing. Jewel suggested they take a tour of Sweetheart Ranch before nap time, and her parents enthusiastically agreed.

"It's a little on the small side," her mom said, referring to the Airbnb. She had her arms wrapped tightly around Ava as if not trusting the wrap. "But it has all the necessary creature comforts."

"We'd better get used to small," her father added, taking his wife's arm to steady her down the last few steps. "Any place we buy won't be big."

Jewel gestured toward the road leading to the ranch house. As they passed the honeymoon cabins and clubhouse, she gave them a rundown on the various amenities offered and a short history of the ranch.

"Maybe I can arrange a carriage ride for you while you're here."

"We'd love that, wouldn't we, Gary?"

"A carriage ride at Sweetheart Ranch with my sweetheart. What could be better?"

"What places are you looking at today?"

Jewel asked, only half paying attention, her thoughts continually returning to earlier.

"We're meeting the real estate agent at three." Her dad described the five condos and townhomes they were planning on viewing. "We have six more lined up for tomorrow."

She tried to imagine her parents occupying a place one-third the size of their home in Oklahoma, which sat on two acres and boasted a sprawling yard. The redwood deck her parents had constructed after all their children moved out was a popular neighborhood gathering spot for cookouts and parties.

"Are you sure you'll be happy with only twelve hundred square feet?"

"Don't you worry." Her mom patted Ava as they walked. "Anything we buy will have a guest room and a place for this one. I intend to be available whenever you need a babysitter."

Jewel didn't respond, the reminder of her conversation with her attorney sending her into an emotional tailspin.

The woman had phoned to let Jewel know about Tanner's attorney forwarding the preliminary custody agreement. Before emailing a copy, she'd warned Jewel not to get upset and assured her this was nothing more than a starting point. They'd take the entire two weeks allowed to consider before responding and per-haps longer.

"Let them cool their heels," her attorney had said.

The warning hadn't worked, and Jewel was a wreck after reading the agreement on her tab-let. Most of the terms were reasonable except Tanner wanted Ava to stay in Arizona! She'd immediately called the attorney back.

"Can he do that?" she'd asked in an anxious voice.

"Relax. It's like any negotiation," her attorney had assured her. "One party starts out asking for way more than they're willing to settle for. Think of this as a chess game. They make a move, and then we make a move."

Jewel hadn't been relieved. Once her initial fear had subsided, she'd gotten angry and called Tanner, demanding to know why he hadn't brought up the custody agreement yesterday when he came over. He'd instantly bristled and echoed what her attorney told her: this was just a starting point and not to be upset.

As if that was remotely possible. Not for the first time, Jewel wondered if she'd brought this on herself with their latest disagreement. Tan-ner, at least the Tanner she knew, wasn't the kind of person to strike back out of spite. But then, he'd never been fighting for shared custody of his child.

If only she'd apologized like she'd planned, she might have read very different terms in the custody agreement. She'd wanted to apologize, except when he'd shown up yesterday, he'd been distant, and that had annoyed her. Behaving childishly clearly wasn't the right response. That hadn't stopped her.

Reaching the ranch house a few minutes later, Jewel took her parents in the front way so they could see the veranda running the entire length of the house, and the charming porch swing.

"What a fabulous place. I can't wait until tonight when the decorations are lit." Her mom released a long, wistful breath. "Makes me wish I'd gotten married here."

Jewel's dad captured his wife's free hand. "I'll marry you again, darling. Right here if you'll have me."

"Oh, Gary." She blushed prettily, and for a moment, Jewel saw the young woman her mom had been on that first date when the man she would eventually marry had swept her off her feet. And obviously still did.

Her parents were equally impressed with the inside of the ranch house. Standing in the foyer, her mom craned her neck to peer at the gaily decorated Christmas tree next to the antique rolltop desk that served as a registration counter.

"Is that a cowgirl angel on top? How adorable."

"Look up there." Her dad pointed to the light fixture directly above them, from which hung a small green sprig with a red ribbon tied around it. "Mistletoe." He stole a quick kiss from his wife, and they both laughed.

Jewel had always wanted a loving relationship like the one her parents shared. She'd believed she'd found that with Tanner. Maybe she had, she thought, recalling their heated kisses and mutual attraction.

But that was before this latest stumbling block. What she'd give to relive the other night. Or yesterday when she'd missed her apology opportunity.

Another piece of her heart broke off. It seemed to Jewel that she and Tanner were doomed to failure.

With great effort, she shoved thoughts of Tanner aside and took her parents into the parlor where her mom couldn't stop exclaiming over the antique buffet. Next stop was the former library—what was left of it, anyway. The room had been stripped bare. Drop cloths covered the floor and a stepladder sat between a pair of worn wooden sawhorses.

"The O'Malleys are renovating this into a wedding boutique," Jewel explained. "When they're done, these two walls will have floor-to-ceiling shelves for displaying products."

"I'm impressed," her mom said while attempting to distract a fussy Ava. Jewel debated taking the baby but resisted. She got to spend plenty of time with her daughter whereas her mother hadn't seen Ava for weeks.

After seeing the soon-to-be wedding boutique, Jewel and her parents crossed to the other side of the house where the chapel was located.

"It's absolutely stunning." Her mother stared openmouthed, taking in the poinsettias placed throughout, the gold and silver bells suspended from the ceiling, the matching bows adorning the pews and the holly-covered arch at the altar. "A Christmas wedding wonderland."

"There you are, Jewel!" Emily hailed as she and Homer entered the chapel.

"Just giving my parents a tour. Hope you don't mind."

"Not in the least." She and Homer strode forward. "It's such a pleasure to meet you. We've heard so many good things."

"Same here," Jewel's mom said.

Introductions and handshakes were made all around. Emily, Homer and Jewel's dad immediately hit it off, the three of them being avid golfers. It was one of the reasons her parents wanted to spend five months of the year in this part of Arizona. A dozen golf courses were within an easy twenty-minute drive.

While the best courses and favorite putters were being debated, Jewel and her mom snuck off to see the bride and groom dressing rooms with their exquisite antique accessories. Fortunately, Ava had fallen asleep again, looking adorable with her head nestled in her grandmother's neck.

Her mom must have been waiting until she and Jewel were alone, for she wasted no time asking, "How are you and Tanner doing? I don't mean to pry, but you seem stressed."

"His attorney sent over a preliminary custody agreement this morning."

"And?"

"My attorney assures me this is just a starting point. We'll respond after the holidays."

"Is it fair?"

"Mostly. Other than he wants Ava to stay in Arizona."

"Aren't you already leaning that way?" her mom asked.

"Kind of."

"What's wrong, then?"

"Nothing."

"Jewel…"

"I wished he'd spoken to me about it first," she admitted.

"And how would you have responded if he did? By your own admission, you two haven't been seeing eye to eye recently."

"I'm not wrong, Mom. He needs to clear his name." This, Jewel realized, bothered her more than his requiring Ava to stay in Arizona.

"He will, sweetie. When he's ready. You have to be patient. What difference does it make if it happens now or a few weeks from now or another year?"

Jewel didn't respond for fear of sounding petulant.

"Ah." Her mom chuckled knowingly.

"What does that mean?"

"You want to reconcile with him."

Jewel drew up short. "I didn't say that."

"You didn't have to. You're my daughter. I know what you're thinking. I also know how in love you were with him. You'd stay here in a heartbeat if you were convinced the two of you had a chance."

She really hated it when her mother was right.

"I'd stay in a heartbeat if I had a permanent job. As it is, I don't."

"You're making excuses."

"Hmm."

"Give him a little more time," her mom insisted. "Don't ruin Ava's first Christmas, and our families' first Christmas together in two years, because Tanner isn't adhering to your schedule."

When her mom put it like that…

They were just leaving the dressing rooms when Jewel's phone pinged, signaling an email. She checked it while her mom hummed a lullaby to Ava, praying it wasn't more bad news.

Seeing *Oklahoma Rodeo News* on the sender's line, her stomach lurched even as her feet came to an abrupt halt. She hadn't expected a reply so soon. It must be a rejection, she told herself. Otherwise, they'd have taken longer to respond.

Holding her breath and mentally crossing her fingers, she opened the email and skimmed the words. When she reached the middle of the first paragraph and the words, We would like to purchase your photograph marked #CCRS-17, she gave an involuntary squeak.

Her mom turned, her expression one of concern. "Is something the matter?"

"*Oklahoma Rodeo News* wants to buy one of my pictures!"

"That's wonderful!"

"Oh, my God. There's more." Jewel kept reading. "They also want to talk to me about becoming a regular freelance photographer and will call after the first of the year to discuss it."

"What? Really?" Her mom backtracked to read over Jewel's shoulder. "Does this mean you'll be moving back to Oklahoma?"

"I don't know. I don't think so. I imagine I can freelance from anywhere."

Her mind scrambled to absorb the information. If she returned to barrel racing, she'd have plenty of photography opportunities for all rodeo events. Though the money might not be enough to support her, even with child support. She'd have to be consistently winning.

"Congratulations, sweetie."

"I don't have the job yet."

With slightly shaking fingers, Jewel replied to the email, having to start over several times because of pressing the wrong keys. She thanked them for their interest in her photograph and assured them she'd complete and return the necessary forms soon. She then expressed her interest in doing freelance work for them and ended with her eagerly looking forward to the phone call in January.

"Come on." Her mom pulled her along. "Let's tell your dad."

"Okay, but we have to hurry. The wedding party will be arriving shortly, and we need to make ourselves scarce."

Jewel was photographing the wedding this

afternoon and, because her parents were house hunting, Tracee had agreed to watch Ava.

In the foyer, Jewel's dad, Emily and Homer waited beside the Christmas tree. Emily was showing off the framed O'Malley holiday portrait Jewel had taken so she held off sharing the email from *Oklahoma Rodeo News*.

"Did you see this, Margie?" Emily asked Jewel's mom as they approached and held out the picture.

Jewel's mom leaned forward to admire it. "You have a handsome family, Emily. You must be very proud of them."

"You, too. Your daughter's quite talented."

"You'll get no argument from me."

Emily returned the picture to its place on the reception desk, then faced Jewel. "I have an early Christmas surprise for you. I was going to wait until tomorrow to tell you, but seeing as your parents are here…" She clasped her hands in excitement.

Jewel suppressed a start. Could this be the news she'd been hoping for? Surely, Emily wouldn't use *Christmas* and *surprise* in the same sentence if she intended to let Jewel go with a thanks but no thanks.

"You're doing an excellent job here," Emily said. "Better than we expected. Our clients have nothing but praise for you, and your personality fits perfectly with Sweetheart Ranch." She paused, building the suspense. "Please say you'll agree to come on board permanently. We'll give you an increase in pay and you can continue living above the carriage house until you find something suitable for you and little Ava." She gazed adoringly at the baby.

Jewel's mom whooped, startling Ava awake. Her father kissed her cheek. Homer chuckled merrily.

"Well?" Emily gazed at Jewel expectantly. "Don't keep me in suspense."

Could Jewel manage everything? Freelance for the *Oklahoma Rodeo News*, work at Sweetheart Ranch and take on the occasional side job like the marketing launch for the art store and the anniversary portrait of Ronnie's parents? And what about barrel racing?

It seemed to Jewel as if a path were appearing before her, one that, should she follow it, required she give up rodeo and stay in Mustang Valley.

Was that what she wanted? And how would Tanner feel? Should she talk to him first? Wait, he hadn't talked to her about the preliminary custody agreement.

She admonished herself for once again being childish. That kind of attitude would hurt, not help, their relationship—whatever that turned out to be.

"We're waiting," Emily said.

Jewel's reply was to give the older woman a warm hug. "I accept. And thank you so much!"

"You almost gave me a heart attack there when you were so quiet."

The next moment a car pulled into the ranch and parked in front of the house. The wedding party had arrived. Everyone but Emily skedaddled.

"What do you think Tanner will say?" Jewel's mom asked on their walk back to her quarters.

Before she could answer, her phone pinged. Speak of the devil. It was a text from Tanner asking her when was a good time to come and visit Ava.

"Guess we'll find out soon."

Jewel was suddenly no longer distressed about the custody agreement. And should the right moment present itself, she'd give him that apology he deserved.

CHAPTER THIRTEEN

TANNER STOOD ON the landing outside of Jewel's door. He didn't usually hesitate before knocking. Tonight, however, her parents were inside along with her and Ava. He knew this because their car was parked in front of the carriage house.

Secretly, he'd hoped to avoid them tonight. Not that he didn't like Gary and Margie. They were nice people and had always treated him and his family well. And with Jewel having told them he was innocent, he didn't worry about seeing that harsh look of disappointment in their eyes.

But his attorney had relayed through Jewel's attorney that she was distressed about the proposed custody agreement. Which, now that he thought about it, could explain her parents' presence. She might be using them as a means to postpone any discussion of the agreement. That, or she'd recruited them as her allies in an attempt to change his mind regarding the terms.

Unable to delay any longer, he raised his hand and knocked. Jewel must have been standing nearby, for the door immediately swung open and she stood in front of him.

He swallowed, momentarily dazzled by the sight of her. Always attractive, tonight she looked downright gorgeous. She'd donned a Christmas sweater that fit snugly over a pair of trim black slacks. The dark green and red colors emphasized her lovely rosy complexion and the twinkle sparking in her amber-brown eyes.

She didn't look like someone distressed about the terms of the custody agreement.

"Hi! Come on in."

"Thanks."

He squeezed past her, detecting a hint of vanilla and cinnamon. Were her parents not sitting a few feet away at the table—and were he not convinced he'd be rebuked—he'd have taken her in his arms and seen if she tasted as good as she smelled.

"Hello, Margie. Gary." Tanner smiled. Whatever their reaction, he wouldn't turn tail and run.

Jewel parents immediately stood. Gary walked toward him, his hand extended. "Great to see you again, son. It's been too long."

Margie wouldn't settle for anything less than

a hug. "How are you? And your family? Jewel told us your brother's surgery was a success and that he's doing better."

"They're well. Thanks for asking."

Tanner gave Jewel's parents a brief rundown of his family's doings before excusing himself and retrieving Ava from where she lay on the quilt. Her silly grin and giggle when he picked her up was like a reprise after a long, grueling ordeal. It filled every inch of him with contentment.

She'd been bathed and dressed in holiday pajamas that matched her mother's sweater. He cupped her perfectly round head in his palm and tucked it under his chin.

"I was just getting her cereal ready," Jewel said. "Have a seat and you can feed her."

He did. Margie immediately dropped into the seat opposite him while Gary chose the recliner. They chatted nonstop, nothing about their animated demeanors or tones resembling the last time the four of them were together.

Tanner was uncertain how to respond and remained mostly quiet.

"It's a big day," Jewel said from the tiny kitchen unit. "We're having applesauce mixed in with our rice cereal."

All of a sudden, Margie sprang up from the chair. "Where's my phone? I want some pictures of Tanner feeding Ava." She laughed and sent Jewel a wink. "Not that I'm any good. Jewel's the expert. If we didn't think that before today, we do now."

Margie's remark and wink were baffling, like everything else.

Balancing Ava in his arms, he stood and carried her over to where Jewel scraped the last dollop of the applesauce from the jar.

She turned and smiled up at him. Smiled? Yesterday, she'd been scowling. Something was definitely amiss. Or, possibly right. What had changed?

Now may not be the best time to bring up the custody agreement. He did, anyway.

"I figured you'd be angry with me about the not being able to take Ava out of state."

"I was at first," she whispered. "I didn't like hearing about it from my attorney and thought you should have talked to me. But, now I'm not."

"Any reason?"

"I'll tell you after Mom and Dad leave."

He disliked being put off. It felt too much like a game, something Jewel didn't normally do.

"Ready!" Margie called out.

Tanner sent Jewel a we'll-talk-later look. She sent him a yes-we-will look in return and they both crossed the room to rejoin her parents.

Once he was seated with Ava on his lap, Jewel set the bowl of cereal down in front of him and handed him the baby spoon. Ava ate hungrily, her eyes growing wide and her arms waving happily each time the spoon neared her mouth. In between bites, Tanner wiped her face.

"Isn't that the most precious thing you've ever seen?" Margie cooed and took one picture after another until Gary cautioned her not to overdo it. "She has your chin, Tanner."

That was about all she'd inherited from him. Thankfully, Ava was a miniature version of her mother with her button nose and cherub smile.

"We'd better get going." Gary came up behind Margie and squeezed her shoulders. "We have an early appointment tomorrow."

"Mom and Dad are meeting the real estate agent," Jewel said.

"Our second outing," Margie said. "We also went yesterday. Have to fit in as many home viewings as we can. We won't be able to go out again until the twenty-seventh. Our agent says no one wants to show their home over the holidays, and I guess I understand."

"We'll be busy, anyway." Gary helped Margie on with her coat.

Tanner rose from the table, still holding Ava. "Nice seeing you again."

"Indeed." Margie gave him a peck on the cheek. "Christmas Day, if not before."

"Good luck tomorrow."

She couldn't part from Ava without pinching her chin and telling her to be a good girl. Gary shook Tanner's free hand.

"You and my little girl have yourself some fun tonight."

Fun? Tanner shook his head. What the heck was going on?

Jewel escorted her parents to the door. Tanner carried Ava to the crib and laid her on her back. She whimpered a little until he gave her a plush toy. When he returned to the table, Jewel was already seated.

"Care to tell me what's going on?" he asked. "Your folks were acting kind of weird."

"I, um, have some news."

Tanner sat down, preparing himself for the worst.

"I sent some pictures to *Oklahoma Rodeo News*, and they want to use one of them."

"Pictures of what?"

"The bull riding event from Saturday night."

He didn't like where this was going. "Any with me in them?"

"I did send two of you."

"I wish you hadn't."

"I wouldn't have let them print the pictures without your consent, Tanner. I promise."

That made him feel better.

"Turns out," Jewel continued, "they chose a different picture. Not sure you know the guy. He has red hair and a very impressive mustache." She hurried on before Tanner could respond. "The magazine requires a release, but that won't be a problem. I had the guy's entry number and called Cave Creek Rough Stock Rental Company. They were nice enough to pass my name and number on to him, and he called me right before you got here."

"Congratulations, Jewel."

"It gets better. The magazine wants to talk to me about a freelance photographer job."

"Full-time?"

"Hardly. One or two pictures an issue at most." She smiled with pride. "I'll get a photo credit and my name in print."

She was making her dream come true. Tanner was pleased for her—she certainly deserved it. He was also a little jealous. Even if—no, when—Daniel came clean, Tanner still may not be able to return to bull riding. He had a daughter to support; she was his priority, and making a good living at rodeoing wasn't guaranteed.

A part of him did wish, like Jewel, he could

do both. Pursue his dream and earn a decent wage. It likely wasn't possible.

"I'll have to attend some rodeos," she said.

"You're returning to the circuit, then?"

"No. Here's the best part. Emily offered me a permanent job. I said yes!"

This explained her parents' weird behavior. And why she wasn't angry at him about preferring Ava stay in Arizona.

"Good." His chest grew tight with an unexpected surge of emotion. Jewel was staying, and he wouldn't have to battle her for Ava's shared custody.

Apparently, she'd read his mind. "You won't need that clause about me moving out of state."

The remark was meant to be funny, but Tanner couldn't quite return her banter. She may be working in Arizona for the present. That could change, and with their relationship constantly on the up and down, he wasn't taking any chances.

Rather than mentioning that, he asked, "Will you be looking for a different place to live?"

"Soon. Ava will be crawling in the next few months, and we'll need more space. Plus, the stairs worry me."

"What about barrel racing?"

"I don't see how I can. I'll be working weddings most weekends, though I am going to have to attend some rodeos if I want to freelance for *Oklahoma Rodeo News*. I'll know more in a week or two when I talk to them."

"Are you okay giving up barrel racing?"

"I am," she said with conviction. "I love photography. I'll still do it for fun, of course, and to keep Teddy Bear in shape."

Ava eventually stopped playing with the toy and drifted off to sleep. Jewel continued her stream of chatter, wondering if she could obtain a press pass for rodeos and how she'd rearrange her schedule to accommodate Ava's child care.

"It'll be easier with my parents nearby for five months of the year. They can babysit."

Her parents? What about him? "I'll watch Ava."

Jewel blinked and straightened as if she'd just remembered they'd be sharing custody. "Ah… yeah. Sure."

"Is that a problem?"

"No. Not per se."

"How is your parents watching Ava different than me? I'm getting pretty good at feeding and diaper changing."

"It's not that," she insisted.

"Still not ready to relinquish control?"

"No, it's not that!"

Really? Tanner thought so. It was that or,

despite her objections to the contrary, she was continuing to use Ava as a bargaining chip.

"But you're working, too," she added. "And might not always be available to babysit."

"In that case, we decide together."

"I'm Ava's primary caregiver. You agreed to that in the custody agreement. You can't expect me to consult you on every little decision."

"I can when it comes to who's watching her. Especially when we live in the same town, minutes away from each other."

Her brows shot up, and she stiffened. Apparently, she hadn't anticipated any resistance.

"I've been fair and reasonable, Jewel, and generous with child support. And I'll keep being fair and reasonable as long as you are, too."

He was right, and Jewel knew it. His attorney had gone so far as to suggest, should Jewel balk, they bring up the point that she'd failed to inform his parents of her pregnancy when she'd had the chance. Tanner didn't like the idea of fighting dirty and refused. Both he and Jewel were at fault for what happened between them. They were also both right about certain things.

"I don't want to turn the custody settlement into a circus." She gazed at him imploringly. "This was supposed to be a night of celebration. Emily offered me a job, and I'm staying in Mustang Valley."

He instantly regretted bristling. "I'm sorry. I've been on edge since the bull riding event."

"That's my fault. I was wrong to start an argument with you." She reached for his hand. "Truce?"

"Yeah." He linked their fingers. "Truce."

"I really want this to be a wonderful Christmas for us."

"Me, too."

To Tanner's disappointment, she extracted her hand. He took that as his cue to leave and, pushing away from the table, went over to the crib. Reaching in, he rubbed his knuckles along Ava's satiny cheek.

"Sleep tight, honey pie."

Jewel was waiting for him when he returned to the table, soft and pretty and inviting.

"I don't want to go," he said. "Problems aside, there's no one else I'd rather be with than you."

She met his gaze. "I'd rather you stayed, too. But I'm not sure it's wise."

He mustered the last of his willpower and reached for his jacket. "See you tomorrow?"

"Count on it."

She moved closer to him, her lips parted and her head tilted at an appealing angle.

He caught another whiff of that vanilla-and-cinnamon scent she wore. "Tell me you're willing to try and make this work with us."

"I'm more than willing, Tanner. I'm determined."

She initiated the kiss this time, placing her hands on his bristled cheeks and drawing him down to meet her full mouth. The world receded, and he didn't dare move for fear of breaking the spell she cast.

"Goodnight, Tanner," she breathed against his lips.

"What if we wait until it's morning?" He wasn't ready for this to end.

She laughed and pushed him toward the door. He went out and down the stairs, but he left his heart behind him.

Jewel had a job and was remaining here. She was also determined to make things work with them.

Tanner didn't need any more incentive. He'd talk to Daniel, convince him to come clean and take back his life. It was past time.

JEWEL STOOD NEAR the kitchen unit, watching the gathering of people in her minuscule quarters. Lack of space aside, she was reminded of previous Christmases with the Bridwells and the Saunderses. Or, more accurately, what she'd imagined family Christmas mornings would be like once she and Tanner were married and had a baby.

She'd had to collapse the travel crib and stow it in the back of her truck in order to make enough room—along with some of the boxes and bins she'd been using for storage. Tanner had carried everything down earlier. He'd arrived ahead of time to help her with last-minute preparations and to give them a few romantic moments alone during their first Christmas with Ava.

They'd spent more of those moments locked in romantic embraces than readying her quarters, finishing mere seconds before Jewel's parents arrived, bearing gifts and wearing what Jewel was sure were amused smiles. Tanner's parents showed up not long after them.

Currently, Ava occupied her baby seat in the middle of the floor and was the center of both grandmothers' attention. Jewel's mom and Shirley Bridwell, chummy before the events of a year ago, were bonding even more over their shared granddaughter. They'd taken turns opening all of Ava's many presents from parents and grandparents, showing each one to her and describing it as if Ava could understand.

A sizable stack of goodies now sat on the bed. Jewel had no idea where she was going to put everything. Tanner had done well in choosing his gifts for Ava. The purple-and-pink pajamas were adorable. Jewel would think of him and this lovely holiday morning every time Ava wore them.

Unfortunately, Tanner's dad and Jewel's dad were less chummy than the grandmothers. They'd greeted each other politely enough and chatted amiably for a few minutes before retreating to their respective corners.

Tanner had tried without success to engage his dad in conversations about sports and the stock market. But even he, with all his charm and good cheer, couldn't force his stubborn dad to participate. As a result, Tanner and his dad occupied the chairs at the table and Jewel's dad sat in the recliner, periodically bending forward to pat Ava's head or return a toy she'd dropped.

That left Jewel with nowhere to sit. She didn't mind. Standing beside the kitchen unit gave her the ideal spot to observe the goings-on and refill empty coffee mugs.

Despite Huck Bridwell's mulishness, the morning was progressing well. Expecting everyone to act like the past year hadn't happened wasn't realistic, though the grandmothers were doing a fairly decent job.

What mattered most was her and Tanner and how well *they* were doing. After last night, Jewel couldn't be happier.

They'd attended Molly and Owen's Christmas Eve wedding, which had been a dream from start to finish. Tanner had kept Ava busy while Jewel photographed the before, during and after shots. They'd taken Ava to the reception for a short while. Dressed like a little doll in a pink dress and with bows in her hair, she'd received almost as much attention as the bride. Jewel and Tanner had also received their share of doting looks from Emily.

When all was done, they'd bundled Ava up and gone for a drive around town to view the lights. Ava had fallen asleep almost immediately, leaving her parents free to make future plans and steal the occasional kiss. They'd stopped by Homer's church for the holiday service but left partway through when Ava awoke and started crying. At home, they'd put Ava to bed and shared a hot chocolate.

Considering how late Tanner had stayed, they should have both been exhausted today. Instead, they were filled with energy and excitement.

All at once, Ava burst into a loud wail reminiscent of last night at church, disrupting Jewel's ruminations. She knew that cry—her daughter was hungry. Making her way past the table, her gaze connected briefly with Tanner's, and she saw the question in his eyes: *is everything okay?* She nodded.

"What's the matter, darling?" Shirley cooed and tried to distract Ava with one of her new toys.

The baby would have none of it, and screwed her little face into a beet-red mask of fury and frustration.

"Does she need her diaper changed?" Jewel's mom asked.

"She's hungry." Jewel reached down and lifted Ava from the seat.

There wasn't anywhere in the small quarters to nurse discreetly, other than the bathroom. That didn't appeal to Jewel. Grabbing a shawl off the chair, she returned to the kitchen unit. There, she draped the shawl over her and Ava, turned her back to the room and began to nurse.

Behind her, she heard Tanner telling everyone about his bull ride the other night. She had to smile. He was doing his best to divert attention from her, and she appreciated it.

When Ava finished, Jewel rearranged her clothes. Without thinking, she began rocking Ava and humming softly. Tanner wandered over, having given up his chair to his mom.

"Hey," she said softly.

"How's it going?"

"One of us is tuckered out."

"So I see." He withdrew a small wrapped

package from behind his back and held it out. "I meant to give this to you earlier."

"Oh, Tanner. Thank you." Using her one available hand, she opened the gift. Beneath the tissue paper lay a beautiful leather wallet. "I love it."

"I wasn't sure…"

She ran a fingertip over the intricate tooling. "Just what I needed." Still using one hand, she opened the wallet. "There's a dollar in it!"

"My grandmother always said if you give a wallet as a gift, you should put money in it for good luck. I figured we could use a little. More than a little."

Jewel examined his face, seeing her feelings for him reflected back at her. "Thank you." She inclined her head toward the tiny counter and the gift sitting there. "I have something for you, too."

"Yeah?" Grinning, he picked up the gift, held it to his ear and shook. "Hmm, nothing rattling."

"Quit it," she admonished with a soft chuckle.

He reached into the gift bag and removed a small photo album. "What's this?"

"You'll have to look."

He opened the album, taking so long staring at each picture she was afraid he didn't like it.

"Your mom helped me a little," she admitted.

"It's great."

She thought she might have detected a trace of emotion in his voice. The good kind. "Really?"

He nodded. "Yeah."

Between the pictures of Tanner that Jewel had taken of him over the years, and those his mother provided, Jewel had put together a photo history of Tanner's bull riding, from the time he was a kid and had his first go-round on a mechanical bull to the other day at the Cave Creek Rough Stock Rental Company.

"That last picture," she inclined her head, "is the one I sent to *Oklahoma Rodeo News* and that they didn't want. It's what gave me the idea. I made extra copies of the album for your mom and—" she hesitated "—one for Ava. I thought one day she might like seeing how her dad started and how he got to where he was."

Tanner nodded solemnly. "Thank you."

"There's room for more pictures, in case you return to bull riding."

"I see that."

A thought occurred to her, one she hadn't considered before. "I'm not making another attempt at pressuring you, Tanner. I swear."

"I know. I'm going to talk to Dad and Daniel. Tomorrow or the day after. I don't want to ruin Christmas."

"Okay." She wasn't entirely convinced but

said nothing as Tanner's mom had risen from the table and was bearing down on them.

"We should probably leave for the restaurant soon. Our reservation is at eleven thirty."

They'd opted for an early meal in order for Tanner's parents to have ample time to spend with Daniel and his wife and their other grandchildren. Jewel's parents had mentioned driving by an adult retirement community in Rio Verde, just to have a quick peek before Saturday's home touring marathon with the real estate agent.

"No problem." Jewel shifted Ava. She'd dressed the baby in a cute holiday outfit with socks that resembled elf shoes, right down to the bells on the toes. She need only wrap Ava in a warm blanket. "Hopefully, she'll stay asleep during the drive to the restaurant, then wake up in a good mood."

There was no dashing downstairs to the car and zooming away when a baby and two families were involved. They took three separate vehicles since they would all be leaving in different directions after the meal. Jewel made sure to pack a jar of applesauce for Ava in the diaper bag, just in case finding a place to nurse in seclusion presented a problem.

She and Tanner went together in her truck as she had the car seat for Ava. Jewel's crossed fingers worked—Ava didn't wake while being carried downstairs or during the drive, giving Jewel and Tanner another chance to converse and hold hands across the console.

Like the old days. Back then, they'd touched whenever they were within a few feet of each other. They hadn't been able to help themselves. They still couldn't.

The three vehicles made a caravan for the twenty-minute ride. Ava woke up the second they pulled into a parking space and Jewel shut off the engine.

"Well, hello, sleepy pie." Tanner gazed over his shoulder at Ava who blinked, owl-eyed. "Have a good nap?"

She gurgled and peered around as if realizing she'd woken up in a different place from her mother's arms, where she'd fallen asleep.

The group gathered and walked together across the parking lot to the restaurant entrance, Jewel pushing Ava in the stroller.

"I'm always amazed at how many people eat out on Christmas Day," Shirley commented.

Inside the well-appointed restaurant, they were greeted by a hostess. Daniel and his family hadn't yet arrived, and it was mutually decided they'd wait at their table in the dining area. When they were seated, a chair was removed between Jewel and Tanner's mom to make room for the stroller, which Jewel adjusted so that Ava was sitting up rather than reclined. She waved her hands and smiled whenever someone spoke to her or played with her. Tanner, sitting on Jewel's other side, gave her knee an affectionate squeeze.

Finally, Daniel and his family entered the dining room. The adults at the table stood to greet them. Daniel's daughter, an adorable imp of four, skipped over to Ava's side.

"Can I hold the baby?" she asked excitedly.

"Oh, I think you're too young for that," Shirley told her granddaughter.

"Maybe when we've finished eating," Jewel said, "if you promise to sit quietly."

The little girl jumped up and down. "I will, I will."

Ava made a happy sound, seeming to take an instant liking to her older cousin.

A booster chair was brought for Daniel's toddler son. He wasn't the least bit interested in Ava, and when Jewel spoke to him, he clung shyly to his mother's side.

She hadn't seen Daniel since before his surgery, and made a conscious effort to hide her shock at his altered appearance. He'd grown thinner, a combination of muscle and weight loss, and looked ten years older than his actual age. Behind his right ear, the tail of a long scar extended from beneath his hairline. It made Jewel want to wince, as did his severe limp.

She found herself hugging him warmly despite her anger at what he'd done to her and Tanner. Here was someone who'd been through a grueling hardship and obviously continued to struggle.

"Merry Christmas," she told Rosalyn, hugging her, too. "It's great to see you again."

"Same here." She bent over to peer at Ava. "My, my. Aren't you adorable? Congratulations, Jewel."

Once everyone was seated, casual conversation ensued, menus were studied and beverages ordered. No one broached any subject more controversial than the weather and Jewel being hired permanently at Sweetheart Ranch. There would be no disagreement or tension today if it could be helped.

The drinks arrived along with baskets of fresh-from-the-oven rolls. Jewel and Tanner both opted for the traditional Christmas special of roasted turkey with all the fixings.

Every once in a while, Tanner would reach beneath the table for Jewel's hand. She was sure the others noticed. Her mom, certainly, who sat on his other side. Jewel was also sure no one was surprised, their approving smiles giving them away. The idea pleased her. Was it possible? Could things be going to work out for her and Tanner at last?

At the end of their main course, their waiter came by and asked who wanted dessert. All the complaints about eating too much and being full were forgotten as orders were placed for pumpkin pie and coffee.

"While we're waiting," Daniel said, an enormous smile splitting his face, "I have an announcement."

Rosalyn stared at him curiously. "An announcement?"

"Tell us," Shirley said.

Jewel's glance traveled to Tanner's dad, who wore a pleased expression. Whatever Daniel was about to say, Huck already knew.

All at once, her hopes soared. Could Daniel be about to reveal he'd been the one who attempted to cheat? Beaming, she turned toward Tanner. He shrugged, indicating he was out of the loop.

"I was contacted by the Southern Arizona Professional Rodeo Association," Daniel said, still smiling. "They're going to honor me during a special presentation at the Double Eights Rodeo in January."

"Honor you?" Shirley straightened in surprise and possibly mild alarm.

She wasn't the only one. Jewel's smile dimmed, and she felt herself grow cold. Her parents became unusually quiet.

"I'm to receive their Cowboy of the Year award." Daniel reached over and ruffled his son's hair. "Hear that, partner? Your old man's going to get an award for being a good cowboy."

"Oh, Daniel." Rosalyn glowed, impulsively kissing him. "That's wonderful."

"Can we come?" his daughter asked.

"You betcha." Daniel gestured broadly. "Everyone's invited."

"I'm proud of you, son," Tanner's dad said. "We both are." He looked at Tanner's mom, almost daring her to disagree. "Right?"

"Um…" She laughed awkwardly. "Yes. Very proud."

"He doesn't deserve an award," Jewel heard her dad whisper to her mom, and her insides constricted. She couldn't agree more.

Beside her, Tanner had gone rigid. She placed her hand on his arm in an attempt to comfort him.

He ignored her. He ignored everyone at the table. She tried to imagine what he was thinking but couldn't. His expression revealed little.

How could his parents just sit there and do

nothing? Well, not her. She opened her mouth to protest. Tanner stopped her with a low, "No."

Who, she wondered, was he talking to? Her or Daniel?

CHAPTER FOURTEEN

THE CONVERSATION SURROUNDING Tanner buzzed in his ear like a swarm of locusts. Try as he might, he couldn't make sense of the words above the deafening din.

Daniel was receiving an award from the Southern Arizona Professional Rodeo Association for—what had he told his son?—being a good cowboy. The thought burned a giant hole in Tanner's gut. Or was it his heart?

Without making the conscious decision, he pushed back from the table and rose, his knees barely able to support his weight. "Excuse me," he murmured and stumbled away, bumping into a neighboring chair.

Above the buzzing in his ears, he heard Jewel ask someone, probably her mother, to watch Ava. He sensed her following him, although he didn't stop. He wasn't in the mood for another lecture.

Reaching the lobby, he stormed past the host podium and pushed through the main doors. Frigid air hit him in the face, stunning him. He ground to a halt and glanced around, getting his bearings. Straight ahead in the parking lot sat Jewel's truck. Tanner went to the right, his boot heels hitting the concrete like sledgehammers.

At the corner of the building, he paused again. To the north stretched the golf course's meticulously tended greens and water features. He halfway considered breaking course rules and forging ahead, the heck with appropriate footwear. Then, he heard Jewel's voice.

"Tanner. Wait! Please."

He swallowed a sharp retort. She wasn't the cause of his anger and shouldn't have to endure the brunt of it.

"Are you okay?" she asked, breathless from her exertion.

He noticed she'd forgotten her coat. She'd be cold once her heart rate returned to normal.

"I'm fine." Who was he kidding? He was far from fine.

"Seriously?" She reached for him.

He retreated a step. "I just need a few minutes." By himself. To punch a wall. Kick a post. Yell. "I'll catch up with you later."

She remained put. "What are you going to do about Daniel and the award?"

"I don't know yet."

"Tanner, you have to confront him."

If he clenched his teeth any harder, he'd break

a molar. "I'm not making a scene. Not today, and not in there."

"Okay. But soon." She shivered and wiped at her nose. The cold was starting to get to her. "The Double Eights Rodeo is in two weeks."

"I'm well aware of that."

"This can't drag on."

"You've made your point, Jewel. Repeatedly."

Disbelief at his biting tone registered on her face. "I'm on your side, Tanner."

He almost said she hadn't been on his side a year ago. Instead, he held his tongue, though not without tremendous effort. "I appreciate that. But what I really need right now is to be left alone for a while."

She ignored his remark. "Let's go back inside."

"I'm going home."

"Without talking to Daniel? You might as well clap him on the back and congratulate him."

"I told you, I'm not making a scene."

"If the nominating committee discovered he was the one who tried to bribe that judge, they'd rescind the award."

"Don't you dare tell them, Jewel. It's not your place."

"I won't. I promise. But, Tanner, you're every bit as deserving as Daniel. More so."

"I didn't win a world championship."

"And Daniel wouldn't have, either, if not for you. He'd have been disqualified."

Tanner lashed out, unable to stop himself. "I'm sick and tired of constantly rehashing this. Can we give it a rest for one day?"

"You're procrastinating. Again. Why don't you just admit it? You have no intention of confronting your brother. Now or ever."

Tanner whirled on her. "For the first time in a long time, Rosalyn is happy. Did you see her face at the table? My whole family is happy. I won't, I can't, deprive them of that."

"Even if that happiness is based on a sham? Even when the cost is your happiness, your rodeo career and our future together?"

By now, she was hugging her middle, and her teeth chattered. If Tanner had brought his jacket with him, he'd have offered it to her.

"You're cold. You should go inside."

"Not until we've finished talking."

He put an arm around her shoulder and drew her to him. "Let Daniel and Rosalyn have this moment. Please. They've endured a difficult year. And, really, when you think about it, what difference does it make?"

"It makes a huge difference to me."

"You're overreacting."

She pulled away from him. "Daniel is a liar.

And now he's defrauding the rodeo association. If your family attends the ceremony and cheers him on, they'll be hypocrites. And if you allow it, you'll be an enabler."

Tanner shoved his fingers through his hair, trying to maintain the tenuous hold he had on his temper. "You've made punishing Daniel your personal crusade."

She glared at him, her tone challenging. "My personal crusade is seeing you get what you deserve and that you're treated fairly by your family. That doesn't make me a bad person. If anything, it makes me a loving and supportive life partner."

"A supportive life partner doesn't force the other person to choose between them and their family."

Her eyes widened and then narrowed. "Ava's your daughter, and I'm supposed to be the woman you want to be with. Aren't we your family?"

"Yes. Of course."

"Then we should be your priority. Always."

"Daniel receiving some award isn't hurting Ava or you. I might agree if you were returning to barrel racing. But you aren't."

"It's hurting *you*, and I refuse to stand idly by while that happens."

"It's what I want, Jewel."

"Daniel has stolen everything important from you."

"Really? I'm not sure about that. I have you. I have Ava. I have a decent job with a brand-new promotion I need only accept. A position with Bridwell and Associates in another year. I'm not seeing where he's taken everything."

"Your reputation is damaged, and you lost any chance of becoming a bull riding champion. Who knows where your career might have gone if not for Daniel."

"That doesn't matter to me."

"I find that hard to believe. I saw your face this morning when you looked at the photo album I made you. You miss bull riding."

"I do. You're not wrong. But I'm more than willing to give it up for a future with you and Ava."

"You shouldn't have to."

"Are you ashamed of me?" He'd asked her that question once before and had accepted her denial. Maybe he shouldn't have. What other reason could there be for her insistence? "Be honest for once. Is that the real reason you're pushing me to confront Daniel?"

"Absolutely not!"

"Then why can't you let this go?"

"I hate that Daniel acts like he's done nothing wrong. It sticks in my craw. Instead of being remorseful or guilty, he's bragging to his son about being a *good cowboy*." She emphasized the last part. "How can it not stick in your craw, too?"

"It does. The difference is I refuse to draw a line in the sand, not when it'll result in dividing my family."

"You were okay with confronting him the other day. What changed?"

"Seeing Rosalyn's face when Daniel announced he was receiving the award," he said. "It may save their marriage."

"You care more about him than us. You always have."

"Now wait a minute." Tanner's hackles rose all over again. "All I'm asking for, all I've ever asked for, is time. You've been back in my life three weeks. I've already made a lot of changes, and I'll continue to. But tearing my family apart isn't one of them. Not after everything they've been through. There has to be another way."

"We're all living under a dark cloud, Tanner, one that won't just go away. It'll keep following us and negatively impacting us if we don't do something."

"Only if we let it."

Tears sprang to her eyes. "I love you. I want to be together. Free from this god-awful mess."

"Jewel, honey, I want that, too." He moved toward her.

She stopped him with a raised hand. "I can't keep coming in second with you. I refuse."

Her remark hit him wrong. Tanner had spent the last twelve months putting everyone else's welfare before his own, including Jewel's. Daniel wasn't the only reason he'd hidden out at Powell Ranch. He'd also wanted to protect Jewel by giving people less fuel for the fire. Yet, she refused see that.

"Well, you've made it pretty clear I come in second with you."

"What!" Her head snapped up, and her eyes flashed. "That's untrue."

"You didn't tell my parents you were pregnant when you had the chance. You went through the motions of trying to find me but, by your own admission, gave up after—"

"I had some serious pregnancy issues."

"What about later when you were further along? You never resumed the search, and you easily could have."

The miserable look on her face spoke volumes.

"And then last year you sent me packing without giving me a chance or trusting me to make things right," he continued. "Have you any idea how much that hurt?"

He knew in that instant he'd never truly gotten over her abruptly breaking off their engagement.

Her cheeks went bright red with indignation. "Ava. That's who we should both put first."

It was as if she hadn't heard a thing he said. "Yeah? That's funny coming from someone willing to let her grow up without a father."

Their stares met and clashed. No one looked away for several moments. Tanner was vaguely aware he might have gone too far. He didn't back down, however.

She squared her shoulders before saying, "I think, under the circumstances, it's a good thing your attorney sent over a preliminary custody agreement. It appears we're going to need one."

A bitter laugh erupted from his throat. He hadn't been willing to draw a line in the sand with his family. She, apparently, had no trouble doing the same with him.

"Isn't that just like you," he said. "Whenever I don't give you what you want, your solution is to get rid of me."

"I'm not getting rid of you. You're walking away from me and Ava. By choice." Tears reappeared in her eyes. "I'm suddenly realizing you're not the man I thought you were."

"I guess that goes both ways," he answered coldly. "I'm realizing you aren't the woman I thought you were, either."

She gasped and then her features hardened. For a brief second, Tanner wished he could retract what he'd said. His pride wouldn't let him.

"I'll find my own ride home," he told her. "Merry Christmas, Jewel."

He strode off across the parking lot, already reaching for his phone. Unlocking the screen, he opened the app for the on-demand ride service he'd used before. With luck, their drivers worked on holidays.

TANNER DROVE THE tractor around the arena in ever widening circles, grading the soft dirt and erasing thousands of horse and human prints. They'd had a big day at Powell Ranch. Twice a year the ranch hosted a stud auction the second Saturday after the New Year. In addition to the many fine quarter horse and thoroughbred stallions, whose "services" were sold to the highest bidders, there was also the occasional Arabian, jack donkey and mustang—the latter from the nearby mustang sanctuary.

The auction had started promptly at seven this morning and ended when the last stallion was led through the arena at ten past three. All usual activities—including lessons, horse rentals, trail and pleasure riding—had been canceled for the day, allowing the ranch to dedicate all available resources and personnel to the auction.

Tanner, in his new official position as head barn manager, had been insanely busy from the moment he'd risen this morning. That was okay with him—less opportunity to dwell on Jewel and his many regrets.

But now the mundane job of grading the arena allowed his mind to wander. As if guided by GPS, it went straight to Jewel.

His glance cut to the horse barn. She wasn't there, not that he'd expected to see her. Even if she wasn't working a Saturday wedding, she'd have received the notice about the stud auction.

Their respective schedules were pretty much all she and Tanner had discussed since their big blowup on Christmas Day. With the assistance of their attorneys, they'd mutually agreed on a visitation schedule. Tanner had Ava two evenings during the week, one weekend day and one full weekend each month from Friday when he got off work to Sunday evening.

Jewel's lack of resistance had been unexpected. He supposed he should be glad. Instead, he questioned the about-face. Had her attorney advised her not to fight him and work at getting along? Was she attempting to make amends for pressuring him about Daniel? Resigned to accepting what she couldn't change? Simply in need of a babysitter? He didn't know, and, given that their personal exchanges were limited, he'd likely remain guessing.

With the grading complete, he drove the tractor to the south side, climbed down and opened the gate. Before driving through, he evaluated the results of his handiwork. Nice even rows, level ground. The arena was in perfect shape for Monday when morning barrel racing practice resumed.

He'd stopped looking for Jewel a week ago. With her accepting the permanent job at Sweetheart and choosing photography as a career over barrel racing, her lessons with Ronnie had come to an end.

She still rode Teddy Bear most weekdays, though not at any set time. Usually, she took him for a jaunt on one of the many trails in the nearby foothills or to the equestrian park at the center of town. Her diligently avoiding Tanner caused him to think about her that much more. Her *and* Ava.

His little daughter was amazing, growing and changing every day. She'd recently learned to roll over on her own, requiring a more attentive eye. Twice, she'd propped herself up with her hands to a near sitting position. Her personality was emerging, too. She laughed when amused, pouted when unhappy and cried when ignored.

Though not yet talking, she'd begun babbling. Tanner's mom swore Ava had said, "Hi," twice.

Tanner's parents had come over on New Year's Eve. They'd celebrated quietly in his bunkhouse—Jewel had been photographing a New Year's Eve wedding. Tanner had offered to watch Ava overnight, but Jewel had declined and fetched the sleeping baby shortly after midnight. There'd been no New Year's Eve kiss, not even a hug.

He'd have his first full weekend alone with Ava a week from today when Jewel attended a rodeo in Tucson. She was planning to drive down Saturday morning and return the next day. He knew she was nervous about leaving Ava with him, even though she'd said nothing. He'd casually on purpose mentioned that his mother would be dropping by to help. That had appeared to eliminate some of her anxiety.

Her parents had purchased a townhouse in Rio Verde, the closest community to Mustang Valley, that was ideal for their needs. The escrow was closing next month. They'd delayed their departure and in a few days were driving home to Oklahoma in order to pack and purchase the items and furnishings they'd need for the townhouse. They would then rent a moving truck and return to Arizona a day or two before the closing.

Had Jewel and Tanner not argued, the Saunderses and Bridwells might have spent New Year's Eve as one large happy family. His sadness and remorse over their split hadn't changed his mind, however, despite the unbearable loneliness he felt whenever no one was around. At least Daniel and Rosalyn were doing better. He had that to console him.

Most days, it wasn't enough. He resented Daniel for the award he was receiving tonight at the Double Eights Rodeo and had chosen to boycott the event. His mom had tried repeatedly to change his mind, encountering a brick wall when she did.

His dad had thrown Tanner for a loop when he'd expressed regret that it wasn't Tanner receiving the award. But his dad hadn't tried to talk Daniel out of going to the rodeo. To everyone but Tanner, his dad was supportive and proud of his oldest son.

In fact, all talk of Daniel clearing Tanner's name had ceased. He refused to even consider it, and Tanner didn't press him. Why bother? Since he and Jewel were no longer together, he'd lost interest in proving himself right, fighting for what he deserved and correcting past wrongs.

Other than Ava, and a promotion, he was right back where he'd been before Jewel had arrived in Mustang Valley. Alone, keeping to himself and miserable.

Parking the tractor behind the horse barn, he hopped down from the seat. At that same moment, Ethan appeared from around the corner. He walked with less of a limp than a few weeks ago, having had his surgery to repair the nerve damage to his leg right after Christmas.

"We had a good turnout today," he commented when they met up beside the hay shed. "Better than last summer."

"That's what the guys were saying."

Every ranch hand, along with Ethan's wife and their part-time bookkeeper, had been recruited to work the stud sale. Most had gone home after the last truck and trailer had exited the parking area. Tanner had volunteered to remain and grade the arena, as much to distract himself as because he felt that it was his responsibility as the new head barn manager.

"We made a decent profit." Ethan wore a big smile.

"Can't knock that."

Tanner didn't know the full details, only that the ranch received a small percentage on each stud service sale. The higher the price, the more money the ranch made.

Together, they ambled toward the ranch office located in the horse barn. "You mind if I sign out now?" Tanner asked.

"Hardly. You've worked your tail off today." Ethan entered the office first. "You decide to attend Daniel's award ceremony, after all?"

"Naw."

"You must be seeing Jewel, then."

Tanner grabbed a pen and filled in his hours on his time sheet, then replaced it in the slot with his name. "Nope. Just getting ready for having Ava tomorrow. Mom brought over a secondhand playpen the other day and a high chair and a bunch of other baby stuff I have no idea how to use."

"You'll get the hang of it." Ethan chuckled. He was the father of two youngsters himself. "Jewel working tonight?"

Why did his boss care? "She had a wedding this afternoon."

"Maybe you should call her. See if she's free later."

"Ha. I doubt she has any interest in seeing me."

Ethan gave his head a disgusted shake. "How long has it been? A week? Two?"

Tanner didn't have to ask what his boss was referring to. He knew. The fight with Jewel on Christmas Day. "Two. Why?"

"I just figured you'd have come to your senses by now."

"I'm not wrong. She backed me into a corner and then gave up on us the first chance she got."

"She did do that."

"Then why am I the one who needs to come to their senses?"

"You aren't wrong, Tanner. Jewel let you down. But that doesn't mean you aren't making a mistake."

"About what?"

"You should go tonight to watch your brother."

"Uh-uh. Not happening."

He'd told Ethan the entire story and Ethan had agreed that Tanner was in a tough spot with no good option. That his boss would now take a different stand irritated Tanner.

"Daniel knows why I'm staying home," he answered flatly.

"He's not the reason you should go. Jewel and Ava are."

"What does me seeing Daniel receive his award have to do with them?"

Ethan thumped the side of Tanner's cowboy hat. "Man, if you don't recognize the connection, you're not as smart as I thought you were."

Tanner wasn't one for riddles. "Speak plainly, pal."

"First off." Ethan perched on the corner of an old battered desk. "Daniel needs to see you there. You ignoring him makes it easy for him to pretend he did nothing wrong."

Jewel had previously said something similar. At the time, Tanner hadn't been ready to listen. He was now.

"You need to make this hard on him," his boss continued. "Rub his face in it. Dare him to look you in the eyes."

Could Tanner do that? He wanted to. Every waking moment.

"And second," Ethan went on, "for the life of me, I can't understand why you're not fighting for Jewel. You love her, don't you? And your kid?"

Tanner nodded, his throat closing.

"Then let her know by telling Daniel to his face, at the rodeo tonight if possible, he has no right to that award."

"I wouldn't confront him at the restaurant. I sure won't do it in front of a crowd. Enough people enjoyed seeing my dirty laundry the last time. I'm not ready for a repeat."

"There's always beforehand or afterward. But you need to confront Daniel and your dad. They've taken everything from you. Twice."

"Not their fault. I'm the one who went along."

"Because you're a good, decent man, Tanner.

But there's a limit to how much you're required to sacrifice for Daniel's sake."

"He wasn't responsible for what he did."

"Neither are you. Yet you're the one paying the price." Ethan shifted. "As I see it, the problem is that you can't separate Daniel's illness from the cheating incident. And you need to. It's the only way you can fix this mess."

"Easy for you to say."

Ethan squeezed his shoulder. "You did everything you could for him when he needed you the most. Now, it's his turn to do right by you."

"I can't force him to come clean."

"You can try. And that's all Jewel wants from you. An honest effort."

Tanner hesitated. Why did fighting for Jewel have to pit him against his sick brother?

"The Tanner I've known all these years isn't a quitter."

Ethan's dig had the desired effect. Something snapped inside Tanner. He wasn't a quitter and didn't like being called one. Quitters didn't outperform the competition and become contenders for a world championship. They didn't leave the women they loved even when they were shown the door.

The good news was that Jewel hadn't left Mustang Valley. They still had a chance. One he shouldn't throw away.

A glance at the office clock confirmed he had plenty of time to change clothes and drive to the Double Eights Rodeo in Apache Junction.

"What are you waiting for?" Ethan asked.

Tanner blew through the office door, tossing a, "See you tomorrow," over his shoulder to Ethan.

Once in his truck, Tanner drove straight for the freeway. If traffic cooperated, he'd reach the rodeo arena before the ceremony. He didn't call Daniel or his dad to let them know he was coming—he preferred the element of surprise.

The rodeo was in full swing when he arrived. Finding a space in the crammed parking lot, he jogged to the sales windows. There were only a few stragglers like him in line. He purchased a general admission ticket and hurried toward the entrance gate. Handing the attendant his ticket, he entered the bustling front area and fished out his phone.

"Where are you?" he asked in response to Daniel's hello.

"We're in the VIP section down front."

Tanner wouldn't be allowed there, not without a similar pass.

"When's the award ceremony?" Over the tops of heads, he spotted a sign pointing to the VIP section and started walking that way. He bumped shoulders with and navigated between people coming and going to the concession stands and restrooms.

"In about an hour," Daniel said. "Right after the calf roping and before the bull riding."

"Can you meet me outside of…" He peered around. "Section one-sixteen?" That was the closest he could get to the VIP section without going in.

"You're here?"

"I am."

"You're kidding! That's great."

Tanner heard the smile in his brother's voice. He must think all was forgiven. Too bad he was in for a rude awakening.

"Come meet me," Tanner said.

"We'll be right there."

"No. Alone."

"What's going on?" Daniel had obviously become suspicious.

"Just meet me, okay? It's important."

"Fine. Be there in a few."

By the time Daniel emerged from the throng of people, Tanner was jittery with anticipation.

"What's going on, bro?"

"Let's find somewhere to talk."

Not wanting a repeat of their public argument at the mall, he led Daniel to a relatively empty corner next to a vendor booth. While not private, they were removed from the path of rodeo patrons.

He didn't beat around the bush. "You can't accept this award, Daniel."

"The heck I can't."

"You're my brother, and I love you. But you didn't earn it, and you have no right to it."

"I did earn it. I've had a great career, and I won a world championship."

"If I'd told the truth about the judge, you'd have been disqualified. Not me."

"This is the first good thing to happen to me since my diagnosis." His anger faded and desperation took its place.

"I'm not asking you to confess. Just to turn down the award. You owe me that much."

"I know you sacrificed a lot for me, and I'm grateful. Someday, somehow, I promise I'll repay you. But I need this one award. My marriage depends on it."

When was it going to stop? Tanner wondered. "I lost Jewel. She's done with me. And I only get to see my daughter a few times a week. You see your kids every day."

Daniel's anger reappeared as quickly as it had vanished. "Yeah, well you get to hold down a job. My paycheck comes in the form of a disability payment from the government."

"For once, put me ahead of you."

"You're just jealous."

"What I am, brother, is good and angry. I've also had my fill of letting you take advantage of me."

"Right. What are you going to do?"

"For starters," Tanner said, "tell the truth about what really happened that night in the bar with the judge."

Daniel's expression darkened. "Dad won't like this."

"You're thirty-four years old. Time you stopped running to Dad every time you don't get your way."

"I have cancer."

"And that just sucks. It doesn't, however, give you a free pass to take advantage of others. You made a mistake. Granted, you weren't thinking clearly. There's no one who won't understand that, including Rosalyn and, probably, the arena owners."

"You wasted your time coming here tonight." Daniel squeezed the handle on his cane and turned on shaky legs. "What's done is done. We need to move on, and you need to stop living in the past."

Tanner grabbed his brother's arm before he could escape. "I'd have traded places with you in a heartbeat if I could. Been the one with cancer. I love you that much."

"Then why won't you let this go?" Daniel's eyes glistened.

"Because I finally realized being the kind of man Jewel wants for a husband, the kind of father Ava deserves, is more important to me than covering for you. And in order for you to be the kind of man Rosalyn and your kids deserve, you need to come clean."

Daniel stared at Tanner, and for a brief moment, he thought his brother might relent. He was wrong.

"Sorry you came all this way for nothing." Daniel ripped his arm away and progressed unsteadily toward the VIP section.

Tanner stood there, watching until his brother disappeared into the crowd. Had he done enough? Would Jewel take him back?

He removed the general admission ticket from his jacket pocket and studied it, the printed words and numbers swimming before his eyes. Staying for the awards ceremony would serve no purpose. If he had any sense, he'd leave.

For reasons beyond his comprehension, he spun on his heel and went in the opposite direction to the closest general admission seating section.

CHAPTER FIFTEEN

JEWEL CLEARED THE tiny kitchen unit counter, washing and drying the few remaining dirty dishes. Her parents had arrived a short while ago, their faces bright and their moods elated. They'd met with a contractor at the townhouse. Before moving in, they were having the entire inside repainted, new carpeting laid, custom interior doors hung and shelving installed in the closets and garage.

"Who's hungry?" her dad asked. He sat in the recliner, bouncing Ava on his knee. "We could go to the café for dinner. The food's good."

"And it's a family place," her mom added. She sat across from him on one of the dining chairs, participating in playtime with a very active Ava. "No one will mind a baby."

Her dad had to repeat the question. "Jewel? You listening?"

"Yeah. The café sounds good. Let me finish with the dishes."

"You okay, honey?" her mom asked.

"Fine."

A bald-faced lie. She was far from fine. Tonight, Tanner's brother was being honored at the Double Eights Rodeo—in roughly one hour, according to the schedule posted online. She'd looked. Several times.

Anger at Daniel and Huck Bridwell, at what they'd put Tanner and her through, gnawed at her relentlessly. She failed to understand how Tanner could let his brother get away with it. Yes, he was boycotting the event, but big deal. Thousands of people were going to watch Daniel and believe him worthy of all the accolades.

Poor Tanner. At the thought of him, her anger, vivid and consuming a moment ago, diminished. How she wished she was with him, wherever he might be. Except they were hardly talking. Which, to be honest, was her fault.

"I have to say, that's the longest dishwashing in history."

Hearing her mom's voice, Jewel turned, embarrassed at being caught daydreaming. "I'm almost done. Give me another second."

"We don't have to go to the café. We can send your dad out for pizza."

The mention of pizza reminded Jewel of that night not long ago when she and Tanner had shared a pizza and kissed.

"Or," her mom continued, "we can leave and eat by ourselves if you're not feeling up to it."

"No. I'll go."

She did need to eat. She'd skipped lunch today, her breakfast sitting like a lead ball in her stomach. Emily had noticed her preoccupation during the wedding and become concerned. After that, Jewel had forced herself to concentrate.

"Is it the rodeo tonight that has you distracted?" her mom asked.

"Among other things."

"Feel like talking?"

Jewel released a heavy sigh. "I had a conversation with my attorney yesterday. I'm thinking of renegotiating the custody agreement."

Her mom blinked and then frowned. "Really?"

"With Tanner and I being at such odds, I'm not sure I'm ready for him to have Ava two whole days."

"What brought this on?"

"I hate the idea of being separated from her overnight. I'd hate it less if you and Dad were babysitting, but you won't be here."

"Attending the Tucson rodeo was your idea."

"I know." She placed the last two spoons in the dish rack. "I can't imagine what I was thinking when I accepted the assignment."

She'd been given two choices, Tucson or the Double Eights Rodeo. Apache Junction was an hour away, no staying overnight. But no way could she bear watching Daniel receive this award.

"Take Ava with you," her mom suggested.

"It's Tanner's weekend with her. I doubt he'll let me."

"What about switching with him?" her mom suggested. "Or he could go with you. Wasn't traveling together an option when you were still considering returning to rodeo?"

"Mmm...no. Not a good idea."

Her mom pursed her mouth. "Can I say something without you getting mad?"

"When you put it like that, no promises."

"Don't punish Tanner because you two broke up."

It was Jewel's turn to blink and frown. "I'm not punishing him!"

"Then what's the real reason for this sudden need to renegotiate the custody agreement?"

"I'm not the vindictive type, Mom."

"Not intentionally." Her mom lifted one shoulder. "But you're angry and hurt."

"With good reason. Tanner should have stood up to his dad and brother." Jewel vented her frustration on the dish towel, snapping it into shape and ruthlessly stuffing it onto the holder.

"You're far too hard on him, sweetie. All he's done is try to help his sick brother and protect his dad's company. Very admirable of him if you ask me."

"I never said he wasn't a great guy."

"Then why be so unreasonable?"

Jewel was aghast. "How is wanting him to be exonerated being unreasonable?"

"It's not. But your timetable is. *Very* unreasonable. And unrealistic."

She chewed on that for a moment. "I admit I can be a little impatient."

"A little?" Her mom chuckled.

"Tanner said that if I loved him, I'd have stood by him and not ended our engagement without giving him a chance."

"Why didn't you?"

"Hello! He told me he'd cheated."

"Did he? I thought you *heard* he cheated from some other barrel racers."

"He admitted it when I confronted him," Jewel insisted.

"There's a difference between admitting to something and not denying an accusation."

Jewel searched her memory, trying to recall the exact conversation she and Tanner had had in the hotel room.

"My God," she whispered. "He didn't tell me. I immediately laid into him the second he walked through the door."

No wonder he'd left without putting up a

fight. He must have been as disappointed in her as she was in him. Except she'd been wrong and he hadn't been.

Her mom placed a hand on her arm. "If Tanner's that unselfish and generous with his brother and family, just think how unselfish and generous he'll be with you and Ava."

Tears flooded Jewel's eyes. "What should I do?"

"Tell him how you feel. Relationships are give-and-take. Even if you and Tanner don't work things out, you still have to co-parent Ava."

"You're right."

"There's something I learned back when your father and I were first married." She waited until Jewel met her gaze. "Nothing repairs a burned bridge like an apology. If you and Tanner truly love each other, if you're meant to be together, he'll accept your apology and the two of you will work through this."

"And if he doesn't accept my apology?"

"Come on. You can't honestly believe he won't."

"I said some pretty terrible things to him."

"Well, the best you can do is try. If he rejects you, then you'll have your answer. But he may be glad one of you finally had the guts to take the first step."

Her mom was right. Again.

"I need to call him."

Before she lost her courage, Jewel grabbed her phone and dialed Tanner. After several rings, his voice mail picked up. Had he shut off his phone or was the battery dead? At this time of day, he should be getting ready for the evening feeding at the horse barn, if it wasn't already underway.

She tried again, with the same results. "He's not answering."

"Go to the ranch. Find him."

She could. And if she did, she might change everything. "Will you and Dad watch Ava?"

"Of course!" Her mom pulled her into a warm embrace. "Good luck, sweetie. I'm praying for you."

"Where're you off to?" her dad asked when, coat in hand, she kissed him and Ava goodbye.

"Mom will explain."

Ten minutes later, she was knocking for a third time on Tanner's darkened bunkhouse door. Why, she didn't know. He clearly wasn't home, as evidenced by his missing truck.

"You looking for Tanner?"

She whirled to see his boss approaching. "Hi, Ethan. Yeah, I am."

"He went to the rodeo."

"Oh. He did?" She slumped against the bunkhouse door. He must have changed his mind and decided to support Daniel, after all.

"He's hoping to pound some sense into that brother of his. Convince him to refuse the award."

"He is?" Like that, hope bloomed.

"Don't know if he'll succeed. But he needed to try."

For her. And Ava. Love filled Jewel, starting inside her heart and radiating outward to the tips of her fingers and toes.

"Gotta go." She pushed off the door and nearly ran to her truck.

"I'll tell him you stopped by," Ethan said.

"That won't be necessary. I'll see him at the rodeo."

"Thatta girl." He broke into a wide grin and waved as she jumped into her truck.

With the help of her phone, she found the quickest route to the rodeo, pushing the speed limit the entire time. Twice more she tried calling Tanner and twice more she got his voice mail greeting.

The attendant at the rodeo sales window gave her a quizzical look when she asked to purchase a ticket. The rodeo would be over soon. Was she sure she wanted to pay?

"Yes." Jewel repeated her request. "One general admission."

The only available seats were up in the nose-bleed section. Jewel sat just as a man entered the arena holding a wireless microphone. He was accompanied by several other individuals, one of them carrying what appeared to be a large plaque. They proceeded to the center of the arena, a spotlight tracking their journey.

She surveyed the crowd for Tanner and his family, eventually spotting them down below in the front row. No, wait. His parents and Rosalyn were there, along with Tanner's niece and nephew. He wasn't with them!

That made no sense. Ethan had said Tanner was coming here tonight. Maybe he was with Daniel, trying to talk him out of accepting the award. But then why were the award committee members readying to make the presentation?

With a sinking heart, Jewel realized Tanner must have failed. Daniel was going through with it. Her fears were confirmed when, a moment later, a man's voice announced the award and Daniel limped into the arena. The crowd cheered as he proceeded slowly and unsteadily across the uneven dirt to the smiling individuals waiting for him.

Jewel wanted to cry. She'd give anything to be with Tanner right now.

After a touching introduction that included Daniel's illustrious bull riding career and his

battle with cancer, the crowd broke into uproarious applause. Daniel stared at the plaque in the
other man's hands, head lowered, the epitome
of humbleness. When the noise died down, the
man in charge handed the microphone to Daniel, encouraging him to say a few words.

He didn't speak for several moments, perhaps
overcome with emotion. Finally, he held the microphone to his mouth and cleared his throat.

"Thank you all very much. But…but…" He
faltered. Cleared his throat again. "I…can't accept this honor. I don't deserve it. I… I'm not
the person everyone thinks I am."

Jewel stared, heart drumming and hands
gripping the armrests on her chair. What in the
world was going on, and where was Tanner?

TANNER WAS ON his feet the instant his brother
started to tell the story. *Their* story.

"Hey, sit down," someone behind him yelled.

Was he seeing things? No, he wasn't. Daniel
stood in the center of the arena before thousands of people, admitting he was the one
who'd attempted to bribe the bull riding judge.
Murmurings gave way to dead silence, and the
crowd watched, completely mesmerized.

Except for that one angry man behind Tanner. "I said, sit down!"

Ignoring him, Tanner propelled himself forward, stumbling past his seat neighbors to the aisle. Curious and annoyed stares burned into the back of his head as he jogged down the stairs toward the first row. The arena's high fence blocked him from going any farther.

Unless he jumped it. For a moment, he considered doing just that.

"Hey!" A woman's high-pitched voice rang out. "Isn't that Tanner Bridwell?"

Several shocked gasps followed. "My God," someone said. "You're right. It is him!"

Fingers were pointed. He paid no attention, his gaze riveted on Daniel. His brother had reached the part of their story where, against the odds, he'd survived his surgery, though not without permanent damage to his motor skills and serious memory issues. He talked on about the difficulties he'd faced after the surgery, the hardships he and his family had endured and would continue to endure. His inability to work. His depression. His anger issues. And through it all, his wife and family had stood by his side, their devotion unwavering and undeserved.

Tanner gripped the top rail of the arena fence, felt the cold metal dig into his palms. Could this really be happening? Daniel had refused Tanner's every plea to come clean. Why the sudden change?

"Believe me when I say, nothing I've been through compares to what my brother Tanner has suffered," Daniel said. "By taking the blame for me, he sacrificed everything. His rodeo career. A potential championship. His fiancée, Jewel. Being there for the birth of his daughter and the first four months of her life. A job with our dad's firm. During this past year, he's lived every day with the threat of a lawsuit hanging over him."

Daniel paused. Removing a handkerchief from his pocket, he wiped his brow before continuing. "He, along with Jewel, were harassed for months. Called names to their faces and online, bullied, ostracized and had their reputations destroyed. All because of me."

"We love you, Daniel," someone hollered. It was followed by a round of applause, whoops and whistles.

He pressed the handkerchief to his face, and his shoulders shook. Tanner thought he might be holding in a sob.

When Daniel could speak again, he raised his head and put the microphone to his mouth. "What I did was unforgivable. I was sick and I was scared, but that's no excuse for the misery I caused."

The man beside Daniel, the one holding the plaque, put a sympathetic arm around his shoulder and leaned in. Whatever he said to Daniel couldn't be heard.

"I owe my brother everything. I should've been disqualified last year and banned from the sport of rodeo. Because of him, I had the best ride of my life. It was a gift I can never repay." Daniel wiped his eyes, and his voice broke. "I don't know if you're out there, bro. If you are, if you can hear me, you gotta know how sorry I am and how much I regret what happened. I'm going to make this right, count on it."

"He's standing right here," the woman from earlier hollered and jumped out of her seat.

As if on cue, every head in the arena swiveled to find Tanner. Only then did he realize that people had their phones out and were taking pictures and videos of Daniel's speech. How had he missed that or the dozens of phones now trained on him?

Would the pictures and videos wind up online? Be passed from person to person? And then what? Tanner and Jewel had been found guilty and punished by the sometimes nameless and faceless masses on social media. Would they now be vindicated?

To Tanner's amazement, he found he didn't care like he had before. The only person who mattered was Jewel.

"Tanner? Are you out there?"

Daniel's voice penetrated the fog surrounding him. He tried to answer but couldn't.

"Section one-twenty," another person yelled.

More cheers went up, the sound deafening. Suddenly, a dozen hands grabbed Tanner's arms and legs, and the ground disappeared from beneath his feet.

"Go on," a man yelled into his ear. "What are you waiting for?"

Tanner was half lifted, half pushed over the arena fence. Blood racing, gut tightening, he dropped down on the other side, almost falling to his knees before righting himself.

The distance between section one-twenty and where Daniel stood stretched endlessly ahead, as if at the end of a long tunnel. His name was shouted, and the cheers increased in volume with each step he took.

What waited for him at the end of this short yet crucial journey? Daniel had admitted he was to blame and not Tanner. What if the arena owners came after Daniel instead? Would Rosalyn take the kids and leave him like he feared? Did Tanner and Jewel have any chance of reconciling once she heard about this?

He wasn't sure. There were more issues between them than just the cheating scandal.

The rodeo association representatives smiled and beckoned Tanner to hurry. Daniel stood motionless, dread, remorse and hope reflected in his features.

Tanner turned to search the VIP section. Where was his family? A glance in the other direction located them near the arena gate. His mom and Rosalyn clung to each other and were crying. His dad… Tanner did a double take. His dad was smiling.

"Hi, bro," Daniel said when Tanner neared. "You gonna shake my hand or punch me in the face?"

"Neither." Tanner stopped in front of him.

"What, then?" When Tanner didn't answer right away, Daniel chuckled nervously. "Give me a warning either way, will you?"

Tanner reached out and pulled his brother into a bear hug.

The entire arena went wild. Tanner was vaguely aware of his name being chanted and the rodeo association representatives slapping him on the back.

"I love you, Tanner," his brother said into his ear. "I'm sorry for everything."

"I love you, too."

They separated and, after two full minutes of clapping and foot stomping, the noise eventually died down. Tanner shook hands all around, accepting the genuine congratulations offered. Though he still had no clue what lay ahead after tonight, this moment was enough for now.

Jewel was the one exception, and he wished she was here with him.

Tanner, Daniel and the others made their way toward the gate as the start of the bull riding was announced. They went slow to accommodate Daniel, the end of his cane sinking a good six inches into the dirt.

At the gate, they were welcomed by their family and escorted by security personnel to an area behind the announcer's booth where they could catch their breaths, well out of the path of cowboys and bulls.

"Tanner."

Hearing his father, he turned, and was pulled into a hug as fierce as the one he'd given Daniel.

"I've been a selfish son of a gun and the worst dad possible. I promise you that'll change. I only hope you can forgive me. Forgive all of us."

Tanner faced a life-altering decision: he either rejected his dad's apology or accepted it and moved forward.

"I understand, Dad. I always did. You were worried. For Daniel. For the company. For the family. I was, too."

His dad swallowed. "You're a better man than me. If I had to do it over again, I would have never asked you to take the blame."

"Me, neither," Daniel echoed.

"What I'd really like," Tanner said, "is for both of you to apologize to Jewel."

His dad nodded. "Consider it done."

It would happen. Tanner had no doubt. "Thanks, Dad."

His mom pushed past his dad and threw herself at Tanner, blubbering inconsolably.

"It's okay, Mom." He patted her back.

"I'm so glad this is finally over."

Tanner, too, despite having lost Jewel for a second time. But at least, after tonight, the world would know he hadn't tried to cheat, and his life could return to a semblance of normal that included his beautiful daughter, Ava.

As he held his mom, he watched his brother and sister-in-law. Rosalyn gazed up at Daniel, her teary face aglow. "I'm proud of you. What you did took incredible courage."

He attempted a weak smile. "I know you must hate me for lying to you."

She looped her arms around his neck and drew him close. "You did the right thing in the end. That's what counts."

"Will you let me visit you and the kids at your folks?"

"We're not going anywhere." She planted a tender kiss on his lips. "Not anymore."

"I don't deserve you."

She laughed gaily for the first time in Tanner

couldn't remember how long. "No, you don't. But you're stuck with me, anyway."

Tanner's mom released her hold on him and drew in a shaky breath. "It's been a long night," she said. "Let's go home."

Home. She was referring to the house she and Tanner's dad owned. The one he and Daniel had grown up in. And yet, it didn't feel like home to Tanner. Not anymore and not after everything he'd been through. What he really wanted was to return to Powell Ranch.

No, to Sweetheart Ranch. To Jewel and Ava. It might not make a difference, but he wanted to, needed to, see them. Maybe find one of those videos that were hopefully posted online already and show her Daniel's speech.

"If it's all right with you, I'd—"

"Tanner." A familiar figure slowly emerged from around a podium.

Jewel? He rubbed his eyes. When he looked again, she was still standing there, her face radiating joy.

This night had been filled with all kinds of miracles. Here was one more, the best yet.

He muttered, "Excuse me, Mom," before hurrying forward to meet Jewel. "You came."

"I tried calling. I think your phone's off."

He clumsily patted his jacket pocket containing his phone. "Must be."

"I heard Daniel's speech."

"You did?" She'd been here the whole time. He was too stunned to ask how that had come about.

"I'm happy for you." She nodded in Daniel and Rosalyn's direction. "For them, too. I think they're going to be fine."

"You were right about that." Tanner took a tentative step forward. It was now or never. He either laid his heart bare to her or went home, giving up completely. "What about us, Jewel? Are we going to be fine? Because there's nothing in the world I want more. I'm willing to wait. You don't have to decide right this second."

The corners of her mouth lifted. "I am going to need a little time. Two seconds, at least." She tapped an index finger against her cheek, pretending to think.

He didn't give it to her. Wrapping her in his arms, he lifted her off her feet and crushed his mouth to hers.

Yet another miracle occurred when all the open wounds inside Tanner magically healed.

Eventually, he ended the kiss. "Don't ever leave me," he said into her hair. "I love you, Jewel. You and Ava. More than anything in the world."

"Oh, Tanner. I was wrong. About so many things. I should have—"

He cut her off. "None of that matters now."

"We need to talk. There's so much I have to say to you."

"We will. Later. For now, this." He pressed her head to his chest.

"Sounds good to me."

"First thing we need to discuss is the custody agreement. There's some changes I want to make."

She pulled back to gape at him. "Changes?"

"Maybe *changes* isn't the right word. I want to get rid of the agreement altogether. And replace it with a new document."

"What kind of document?"

"Instead of a custody agreement, I want a marriage license."

Her eyes widened. "Are you proposing?"

"Darn straight I am. And this time, let's do it right. Have a big wedding at Sweetheart Ranch with a couple hundred people. A reception. Cake. Honeymoon. No elopement."

She kissed him again, lovingly, passionately, giving him an answer that couldn't possibly be misinterpreted. "I like that idea. Though, we'll have to hire someone else to be the photographer."

Grinning, he swung her up into his arms and twirled her around.

"What's going on?" his mom asked, although the twinkle in her eyes said she already knew.

"Jewel's agreed to make an honest man of me," Tanner said.

His mom shrieked with delight, and everyone came over to wish them well.

"We have to celebrate," his dad said. "I'll stop for champagne on the way back to the house."

"Tomorrow." Tanner drew Jewel to his side. "Tonight, we're going back to Jewel's place and telling Ava the good news."

"She's a little too young to understand, don't you think?" Jewel asked. "And will probably be sleeping."

"Maybe. But one day, when she's older, she'll hear how we couldn't wait to include her."

"I like that," Jewel said and slipped her hand into Tanner's, where it stayed for the next several hours.

EPILOGUE

Eleven months later

"OKAY, EVERYONE SQUEEZE in just a little closer."
Jewel motioned with her hands. Once the group
of ten individuals had done as she requested,
she bent and checked the viewfinder on her
camera. "Looking good."

Behind them, the Christmas tree twinkled
merrily, the lights blinking and the gold star on
top shimmering. Red and green strands of garland hung from the fireplace next to the tree,
along with brightly colored stockings—one
with her name on it, one with Tanner's, one
with Ava's and the last one with no name and
just a bow.

Jewel had started decorating their new home the
Saturday after Thanksgiving in order to be ready
for this combined Bridwell–Saunders portrait session. That way, they'd all have copies in plenty of
time to include with their Christmas cards.

"Mama!" Ava called from Tanner's arms and
wriggled her fingers at Jewel. "Mama!"

"Be right there, baby girl." She fiddled with the camera settings.

Jewel was nothing if not a perfectionist. She had a reputation to uphold. Her photos regularly appeared in other publications besides *Oklahoma Rodeo News*. And in addition to her job at Sweetheart Ranch, she'd developed a growing side business that included portraits.

"You might want to hurry," Tanner said. "The kids are getting restless."

He was referring to not just Ava but Daniel and Rosalyn's two. Their daughter had started kindergarten this past fall, and their son was a rambunctious three-year-old who, according to his mother, terrorized his preschool classmates.

As anticipated, Daniel's world championship title had been rescinded. He didn't seem to mind much. As of his last checkup a month ago, his cancer remained in remission. He'd started taking online college classes and, with no lawsuit filed, was spending two days a week at Bridwell and Associates learning the ropes. His mood swings and anger issues were under control. The improvement to his and Rosalyn's marriage could be seen in their tender exchanges whenever they were together.

"I am hurrying." Jewel set the camera's timer,

marveling at the amazing changes she and Tanner had experienced this past year. The complete opposite of the previous two Christmases.

News of Tanner's innocence had spread almost as quickly as the cheating scandal had originally. With his name cleared, he'd returned to bull riding. He'd had a rough start, being sorely out of practice, but as of late November, he'd qualified for the National Finals Rodeo in Vegas. He wasn't betting on himself to win, claiming he'd be happy just to make it to the final round. Maybe next year, if he didn't hang up his spurs. Tanner swore he liked being a husband and dad too much to keep leaving home most weekends.

Jewel and Ava would continue going with him when her schedule allowed and if the rodeo wasn't too far away. There'd always be a few pictures she could later submit with the prospect of selling. Most of her days were spent at Sweetheart Ranch, capturing the happiest day of people's lives.

The place had become even more special to her since her and Tanner's marriage last June. She couldn't help recalling that incredible day with each wedding she photographed. Ava, in her adorable frilly white dress and flowered headband, had been the center of attention, possibly outshining Jewel. Which had been just fine with her.

Eventually, Tanner would join his dad's company alongside his brother. Or teach bull riding. He hadn't dismissed that idea entirely and, when he wasn't rodeoing, spent a lot of weekends at the Cave Creek Rough Stock Rental Company.

They were both planning on taking six weeks off this coming March and April. Before they returned to work, Jewel would need to hire an assistant. Or a full-time nanny. She hadn't decided yet.

"Okay!" She scurried out from behind the camera and tripod. "We're ready. Everyone say cheese."

She rushed to join the others, which included her parents and Tanner's, and settled in beside Tanner.

His arm came around to circle her expanding tummy, his hand resting directly above where their baby nestled. Another little girl. Tanner was elated, and Jewel couldn't have asked for a better Christmas gift.

Just as the camera flashed, Tanner lowered his head and whispered in her ear, "I love you, Jewel."

"Oh, you," she teased. "The picture's ruined." She didn't need to look to know they were in for a retake.

Returning to the camera, she reviewed the display and smiled to herself. She'd be keeping this picture and looking at it whenever she wanted to remember just how lucky she and Tanner were to have found each other again.

* * * * *

Get 4 FREE REWARDS!

We'll send you 2 FREE Books
plus 2 FREE Mystery Gifts.

Love Inspired® books feature contemporary inspirational romances with Christian characters facing the challenges of life and love.

FREE Value Over **$20**

Get 4 FREE REWARDS!

We'll send you 2 FREE Books plus <u>2 FREE Mystery Gifts.</u>

Love Inspired® Suspense books feature Christian characters facing challenges to their faith... and lives.

FREE
Value Over
$20

YES! Please send me 2 FREE Love Inspired® Suspense novels and my 2 FREE mystery gifts (gifts are worth about $10 retail). After receiving them, if I don't wish to receive any more books, I can return the shipping statement marked "cancel." If I don't cancel, I will receive 6 brand-new novels every month and be billed just $5.24 each for the regular-print edition or $5.99 each for the larger-print edition in the U.S., or $5.74 each for the regular-print edition or $6.24 each for the larger-print edition in Canada. That's a savings of at least 13% off the cover price. It's quite a bargain! Shipping and handling is just 50¢ per book in the U.S. and $1.25 per book in Canada.* I understand that accepting the 2 free books and gifts places me under no obligation to buy anything. I can always return a shipment and cancel at any time. The free books and gifts are mine to keep no matter what I decide.

Choose one: ☐ **Love Inspired® Suspense Regular-Print** (153/353 IDN GNWN) ☐ **Love Inspired® Suspense Larger-Print** (107/307 IDN GNWN)

Name (please print)

Address   Apt. #

City   State/Province   Zip/Postal Code

Mail to the **Reader Service:**
IN U.S.A.: P.O. Box 1341, Buffalo, NY 14240-8531
IN CANADA: P.O. Box 603, Fort Erie, Ontario L2A 5X3

Want to try 2 free books from another series! Call 1-800-873-8635 or visit www.ReaderService.com.

*Terms and prices subject to change without notice. Prices do not include sales taxes, which will be charged (if applicable) based on your state or country of residence. Canadian residents will be charged applicable taxes. Offer not valid in Quebec. This offer is limited to one order per household. Books received may not be as shown. Not valid for current subscribers to Love Inspired Suspense books. All orders subject to approval. Credit or debit balances in a customer's account(s) may be offset by any other outstanding balance owed by or to the customer. Please allow 4 to 6 weeks for delivery. Offer available while quantities last.

Your Privacy—The Reader Service is committed to protecting your privacy. Our Privacy Policy is available online at www.ReaderService.com or upon request from the Reader Service. We make a portion of our mailing list available to reputable third parties that offer products we believe may interest you. If you prefer that we not exchange your name with third parties, or if you wish to clarify or modify your communication preferences, please visit us at www.ReaderService.com/consumerschoice or write to us at Reader Service Preference Service, P.O. Box 9062, Buffalo, NY 14240-9062. Include your complete name and address.

LIS20

THE CHRISTMAS ROMANCE COLLECTION!

10 FREE BOOKS IN ALL!

'Tis the season for romance!
You're sure to fall in love with these tenderhearted love stories from some of your favorite bestselling authors!

YES! Please send me the first shipment of three books from the **Christmas Romance Collection** which includes a **FREE** Christmas potholder and one **FREE** Christmas spatula (approx. retail value of $5.99 each). If I do not cancel, I will continue to receive three books a month for four additional months, and I will be billed at the same discount price of $16.99 U.S./$22.99 CAN., plus $1.99 U.S./$3.99 CAN. for shipping and handling*. And, I'll complete my set of 4 FREE Christmas Spatulas!

☐ 279 HCN 4981   ☐ 479 HCN 4985

Name (please print)

Address   Apt. #

City   State/Province   Zip/Postal Code

Mail to the **Reader Service:**
IN U.S.A.: P.O. Box 1341, Buffalo, NY 14240-8531
IN CANADA: P.O. Box 603, Fort Erie, Ontario L2A 5X3

ReaderService.com has a new look!

We have refreshed our website and we want to share our new look with you. Head over to ReaderService.com and check it out!

On ReaderService.com, you can:

- Try 2 free books from any series
- Access risk-free special offers
- View your account history & manage payments
- Browse the latest Bonus Bucks catalog

Don't miss out!

If you want to stay up-to-date on the latest at the Reader Service and enjoy more Harlequin content, make sure you've signed up for our monthly News & Notes email newsletter. Sign up online at ReaderService.com.